ENTANGLED WITH YOU

DIANA KNIGHTLEY

For Kevin, I have a diagram in my backpack, I'll show you someday…

A MISSING ENTANGLEMENT

PROLOGUE

Originally published as book 4.5

~

If Magnus and Kaitlyn's life is a tapestry, then these first seven chapters, dear reader, would be an unraveling thread.

This happened. Tis the truth of it, as our beloved Magnus would say, except no one in the world knows or remembers.

The fifth part of their story can be told without this thread. We could snip it off and drop it to the floor, except...

We ought to know of it to carry on. We can remember.

Because this strand, that once weaved their life is gone now — replaced by another, stronger, more exquisite weaving — but it existed. And it changed their whole story.

~

PROLOGUE - KAITLYN

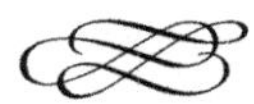

SUNDAY, NOVEMBER 25, 2:05 PM.

Amelia Island, Florida

Magnus tugged my bodice down to my waist. We tucked in all the layers of long underwear. Then I gathered my hair to the side while Magnus tightened the laces one by one and tied them secure. Then he rested his hands on my waist and pressed his lips to the back of my neck. "How come as soon as I finish with your lacings I want tae take them off again?"

I wrapped my arm around his head and held him embracing me from behind. His arms around. I loved this position. Wrapped, pressed. His strength was a shield around me, enveloped and protected. His voice near my ear, his breaths, now sure and healthy, warm and deep, filling the air around me. The scent of him on me. I pressed back and nestled into his chest. He kissed my ear and ran his hands up and down my tight bodice. This position was protection and desire, both, wrapped.

"Can we stay here, like this?"

His arms wrapped tighter around, a hug that warmed me. His cheek pressed to my forehead. We held it for a long time. It was very much like a parting embrace, though we weren't, but what we were doing was so full of uncertainty that we held each other like a goodbye anyway.

His voice rumbled up from his heart. "I want ye tae ken, mo reul-iuil, that I love ye beyond what I have the words tae say. I canna describe the depths of it, but I want ye tae ken that I will live my life tryin' tae speak tae ye on it."

I pressed against him. "Then I will spend my whole life listening."

"Aye, mo ghradh, I thank ye for it."

Finally we pulled away.

Magnus strapped a knife to my leg.

And then he finished dressing, quietly, methodically, it was how I knew he was scared.

We drove through McDonald's for three combo meals, one for me, two for Magnus, and we, with ac blasting, were headed south to a few acres of unused land outside of Gainesville, where we had hidden our vessels.

PROLOGUE - KAITLYN

SUNDAY, NOVEMBER 25, 4:45 PM.

en route to Gainesville

Zach called, "Wanted to let you know that Emma, Ben, and I are headed home, our honeymoon was great."

"We won't be there to greet you, we're on our way to Gainesville right now, we're going to get Quentin."

"Good. Tell Magnus I said I'll have dinner ready when you all get back."

"His eyes are closed. I think he's sleeping."

Magnus said, "I am nae sleepin', but ye are hurtlin' the car down the highway and tis too fast."

"It's not too fast, Magnus, I'm only going 65." To Zach I said, "He's grumbling about my speed."

"Tell him we're teaching him to drive when he gets back."

"Perfect, we'll try and get back within the week. With Quentin."

"It would be great if you guys were here for Christmas."

"That's my plan."

Zach hung up.

I looked over at Magnus. "You're going to love Christmas: the tree, the presents, the feast."

~

An hour into the ride, Magnus asleep, a Sean Mendez song came on the radio. I cranked it up because I was bored and sang, loudly. Magnus opened one eye. I turned and sang dramatically, directly to him, emoting, wailing. He smiled and watched me for a moment.

"What is this then?"

"This is the song of our moment, sing with me. Listen to the words. It's talking about us." I tapped on the dashboard during the music, then pointed at him when the chorus started. "Follow me..." I sang and Magnus sang some of the words, a beat behind, watching me for cues. The song wound down. I tapped Spotify on my phone to play it again. "Once more!"

I was belting out. I said, "Okay, chorus again, now sing it to me." He sang in a deep baritone voice and it vibrated all my insides, so sexy and oh so yummy.

"Awesome. Thank you."

"Twas quite a good song once I kent the words."

I jokingly fanned my lap. "Twas quite hot once ye sang the words. I don't think I've ever heard you sing before."

He laughed and joked, "Twas almost as good as the songs back home." He began to sing. "I heard the liltin', at the yowe-milking, the lassies a-lilting afore the dawn o' day; but now they are moaning on ilka green loanin', the Flowers of the Forest are a' wede away."

"What is that one about?"

"The battle of Flodden, a verra long time ago, and the men haena returned from the war."

"A tragedy, we have to be dramatic for it. Sing more."

Magnus sang, "We'll hae nae mair liltin' at the ewe-milkin', the women and bairns are dowie and wae. Sighin' and moaning, on ilka green loanin', the Flowers of the forest are all wede away."

"That's beautiful."

"Aye. But do yours once again, m'fair lassie, I have a need for the loud music of the time tae keep my mind off the comin' storms."

I picked up my phone to push play again. And we sang.

PROLOGUE - KAITLYN

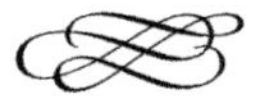

SUNDAY, NOVEMBER 25, 5:45 PM.

Near Gainesville, Florida

I pulled the Mustang down the dirt road that wasn't marked except for a rusted mailbox and a broken down gate leaned across the entrance. The gate didn't do anything but pretend to be a gate, sort of, just by looking like one. Magnus jumped out of the car and swung it open. I drove through and he swung the gate closed across the road behind me.

We followed the dirt road winding through the woods. It was now rutted with thick mud because of the storms yesterday. I drove around the deeper puddles hoping that the Mustang wouldn't get stuck. Mud sprayed up behind my wheels. Our car would need a really good washing when we got back. The tires slid a bit on a wet patch. "Come on come on come on." I did not want to deal with a car stuck in mud while wearing all of these layers of woolen clothes. Plus it was growing dark out here.

We finally made it to the grassy slope near the small dock at the edge of the freshwater spring. We parked our car to the side under the pine trees.

I popped the trunk. Magnus and I made a trip carrying our supplies from the trunk to the dock. I had a new leather backpack. We had a small stack of wool blankets, some clean towels. Some protein bars wrapped in wax paper. I had a kit for medical—

My attention moved up the slope to the trees. "Do you hear horses?"

PROLOGUE - MAGNUS

SUNDAY, NOVEMBER 25, 6:10 PM.

Near Gainesville, Florida

Horses, at least three, were coming through the trees. I yelled, "Get down!" I bolted for the Mustang. I had left my sword there, the box of guns, I had nae prepared for an attack.

Over my right arm I saw them leap from the woods: three soldiers, armored, swords drawn, their horses chargin'. At the sight of me, two turned and followed.

I yanked the car door open, grasped my sword, and spun as they were on me. I fought the first, swinging up, my back to the car so I couldna retreat. I had tae fight forward. I sliced up and forced his horse careening back. I carved my sword down through the reins. The horse bucked and the man slipped sideways. Then I sheared down, gashin' the top of his thigh.

The second soldier was behind me. I spun and arced up toward him, piercin' his lower arm. I charged forward swingin' wildly. Then from down at the docks — Kaitlyn screamed.

I yelled over m'shoulder, "Kaitlyn!" and fought forward tryin' tae reach the dock, tae get tae her.

My heart fell as the third soldier joined the others against me — I bellowed, knocking a man from his horse and stabbin' him clean through. I yanked my sword free. The second soldier dropped from his horse and we fought blade tae blade, his injured arm makin' him fight poorly, until finally I struck him down: a cut deep in the shoulder, blood sprayin'. The third soldier I pierced through the thigh, then as he hung off the side of his horse, I pulled him down by his belt, and shoved my sword into his side. He tumbled tae the ground.

I kicked him free of my blade and raced to the dock.

Kaitlyn lay there lifeless.

I slid to my knees and pulled her head to my lap, "Kaitlyn? Och, Kaitlyn, nae." Blood flowed around her, covering the dock and dripping down between the wood slats. "Mo reul-iuil, speak tae me." She was growin' cold and without a breath in her lungs. "Nae Kaitlyn. Nae. Daena go without me, please."

I stroked the back of her hair. "Please, mo reul-iuil, I am so sorry, I — please daena go." I cried and we sat like this for a long time. Me and my dyin' Kaitlyn — *nae, daena, ye canna leave me* — until I kent I had tae stand up and do what came next.

I lay her gently on the dock, wiped my eyes, and hand over hand I pulled the chain from the water until the case emerged from the deep spring. I pulled it drippin' wet tae the boards. I opened the lock and pulled from inside it one of the vessels in a waterproof bag. I opened the seal and twisted the ends of the vessel bringin' it tae life. I recited the numbers, changin' only one, the date, tae yesterday.

PROLOGUE - MAGNUS

SUNDAY, NOVEMBER 24, 5:30 PM.

Near Gainesville, Florida
Second Try

I woke on the grassy slope near the dock. Twas evenin'.

There were nae bodies and I was all alone. I kent the nearby house was empty, but I dinna want tae go inside away from the clearin'. I went tae the tree line and leaned against a tree and watched the road, listenin' for the horses. I focused on my mission, nae the purpose. Whenever I thought of Kaitlyn the pain was enough tae bring me tae my knees.

The night was long. There was nae a sound except for the woods comin' alive with night animals and spirits. If it were a Scottish forest I would be used tae the beasts I was hearin', but twas foreign, desolate, and verra lonely.

In the morning I walked the perimeter searchin' for signs of the horses. Nae body was here. I pulled the case up from the water —

it had only one vessel inside. The other was in my sporran. I left the case open on the dock, a sign tae myself: be on guard, someone else is here.

I waited all day. In the afternoon there was a storm, loud — the wind ravaged the trees. I tried tae go tae the center of it, tae find the soldiers, but twas impossible tae walk against the gale. Then I heard from the east the Mustang drivin' down the road.

I followed it tae the clearing and remained hidden in the shade of the forest's edge. The storm was abatin'. I wasna sure what I would need tae do but I had a gun and a sword tae do it with.

Kaitlyn climbed from the car. Another Magnus stepped from the other side. They walked their supplies toward the dock. As soon as the other Magnus noticed the case had been pulled from the water, he raced tae the Mustang for his sword.

He carried the guns with him tae the dock. I was relieved he was better armed this time. He and Kaitlyn remained cautious, looking around for trouble. They seemed about ready tae use the vessel.

Then two horses were right behind me.

The soldiers had their swords drawn and were bearin' down on me — fast. I pulled my gun and fired, hittin' one of the soldiers in the middle of his chest. He slumped over the neck of his horse and it careened away through the woods. I fired at the second soldier, but missed, only grazin' his arm and then he was on me, his blade swingin' in fury.

I bent low and ran for cover and twas when I saw a third soldier, his horse thunderin' down the slope toward Kaitlyn. And then behind me a fourth soldier and then a fifth.

I shot the soldier as he was swingin' at me and tried tae get a clear line tae shoot the soldier who was gainin' on Kaitlyn, but soldiers were convergin' fast behind me — the other Magnus fought a sixth man — Kaitlyn screamed a bloodcurdling scream.

I yelled, "Nae!" I shot the rider bearing down on me. I shot the next, injuring his shoulder so he fell tae his feet on the ground. He charged me with his blade carvin'. I dropped my gun tae draw my sword. One swing and I sliced through his arm. Blood gushed from his wound. He dropped tae his knees and I finished him with a blow tae the side. He slumped forward tae the ground.

The other Magnus yelled, "Kaitlyn!" I spun around tae take in what was happening in the clearing.

She dinna answer.

The last man charged the other Magnus, swinging his sword.

I grabbed for my gun, set my aim on Magnus's adversary, and fired — the other Magnus turned tae look. Twas a fatal mistake — the last soldier swung his blade up, and pierced the other Magnus through the neck. He crumbled tae his knees in the dirt.

Then slumped forward, dead.

Then the soldier charged me. I shot him again and again until he too was dead on the ground.

I raced tae Kaitlyn on the dock. Kaitlyn dead, run through with a sword, "Nae Kaitlyn, nae." Lifeless on the wood planks, her blood spilling. "Tis nae fair, ye canna—"

I picked her up and rocked her. "Daena go, please. I am tryin' tae save ye, mo reul-iuil. I daena ken how tae. I need ye tae help me. Tell me what tae do."

I cried there on the docks for a verra long time. Then I wiped my eyes and came tae a decision; I had tae try again.

PROLOGUE - MAGNUS

SUNDAY, NOVEMBER 25, 11:15 AM.

Near Gainesville, Florida
Third Try

The storm this time was wide and larger than before. I walked intae the wind and fury searchin' for the center of it, looking for the horses, any sign of the soldiers. I was hopin' tae cut them off afore they reached the spring. As I gained on an encampment, more storms formed beyond me. Then gale winds were buffetin' me from every direction and I could find nae sign of the soldiers.

Then I heard the Mustang drivin' down the dirt road in the direction of the spring. Twas earlier than last time. I raced through the woods as the car entered the clearing. My plan had been tae address the other Magnus. I would warn him tae be cautious. Then I would help him keep Kaitlyn safe, but as I raced from the woods tae intervene, the storm was ragin' above them. Horses were already bearin' down from the opposite direction. Afore I could get close, six men surrounded them.

I drew my gun and aimed. Kaitlyn was behind, protected by

the other Magnus, but they were backed up against the car. They each had guns and were aimin' at the soldiers, but there were men on every side. Kaitlyn fired, shooting one of the soldiers. Magnus shot another.

I barreled out of the tree line and shot a third soldier when another horse barreled from the trees behind me. A soldier, his sword held high, aimed for me, arcing down — I stumbled back two steps, shot that soldier as Kaitlyn, behind me, screamed.

When I turned a soldier was pullin' his sword from Kaitlyn's body, and Magnus was on the ground beside her. I watched as another soldier pierced him through too.

I shot every soldier left alive. Firing over and over until they were all dead upon the ground.

Then I raced tae Kaitlyn's side and pulled her into my arms. "Nae, nae nae, mo reul-iuil, nae. Daena — please." I kissed her hand and begged her tae move. I smoothed her hair and kissed her cheek and begged her tae come back tae me. Please — I held her close tae me and I pleaded with her tae come back.

There was so much blood. Twas everywhere.

My hand was covered in it, layers of it, all three deaths were splashed on my clothes. I wiped my hand on her skirts and felt her phone there in her pocket. I used it tae call Chef Zach.

He answered, "Kaitlyn?"

"Tis me, Magnus."

"Is everything okay?"

"Nae. Tis nae — Kaitlyn is..." My voice broke tae pieces.

"What happened to Katie?"

"Twas a fight, I... she is nae — can ye come? I need ye tae come and..."

"Fuck Magnus, okay, definitely. You're at my Uncle's property? I'm on my way, she's really?"

"Aye." Twas verra hard tae keep my voice steady. "I tried tae save her."

Emma's voice came from the phone. "Magnus, what happened?"

"She has died Emma, twas soldiers that came and they..."

"Oh no, oh, we're in the car, we're on our way, are you — stay there, hold on, we're on our way. I'm going to stay on the phone, okay? Just talk if you need to, we're right here."

I nodded and dropped my phone to the side and sat holding my Kaitlyn, nae longer livin', in my arms.

PROLOGUE - MAGNUS

It takes two hours tae get between the two places. I held her for most of the time. I rocked her and comforted her and for a verra long time I prayed. I asked God tae forgive me for it. For nae protectin' her and keepin' her safe, and then for strugglin' against it, for tryin' tae change what he had willed.

She died once at the hands of those men, but then by my hands, by my interference, she died again and again. Twas nae changin' the course of it and what had I done tae her soul that I pulled her back tae living only tae have her depart again?

There was nae peace in it. I had been playin' as God and each time had made it worse. The death had become more brutal. Her final breath more sure.

There was nae devotion in it tae do that tae someone I loved so much.

"I love ye, mo reul-iuil, without ye there will be nae peace, nae guidance, I daena..."

There were pains in my chest, and all I could do was try tae breathe.

~

Emma's hands were on my shoulder. "Magnus? Oh no, oh, Magnus, this is— " She clapped a hand over her mouth and stared around in horror. "Katie, oh no, not Katie." She started tae drop tae the ground beside me.

I shook out of my daze. "Och nae, Emma, daena touch me. I daena want ye tae have the blood on ye. Please."

She began tae cry, standin' near me, wringing her hands.

Zach had his hands on his head lookin' over the carnage. "Fuck, there are like — so many — Magnus, what the hell?" Emma reached up for him and he pulled her intae his arms while she cried. "You're here and also over there, Magnus, what happened?"

"There were three men. I wasna armed. I left her unprotected and they killed her on the dock. I dinna ken what tae do... I traveled back a day and tried tae save her but it happened again."

Zach groaned. "Twice?"

"Three times. Each time the storm grew in size, and twas hard tae find the center of it. There were more men and her death was more brutal and I am dead now... I canna—" I broke down again rockin' Kaitlyn in my arms.

Zach asked, "Do you think if you just changed it, tried again?"

"Nae." I gently shifted her from my lap tae the grass. I took a deep breath and stood. "Nae. I canna change it and forcing my will on it has made it worse. Ye were right on it when we discussed it the other day."

"But I didn't really know. I was just quoting Doctor Who. Maybe I was wrong. I can be wrong a lot, tell him, Emma. I fucking don't know what I'm talking about most of the time..."

Emma's face was covered in tears. "What is your heart telling you, Magnus?"

"That I canna change it. I prayed tae God and I ken it, she is lost tae me."

"Oh Magnus." She reached out for me, but I shook my head.

"I daena want ye tae have it on ye. Twill bring trouble on ye tae have it. Tis the blood of my own tae bear."

She burst into tears again, hiding her face against Zach's chest.

He ran his fingers through his hair. "What are you going to do now?"

I surveyed the carnage. There were bodies everywhere. Horses cantering around. "I will take it all with me. Tis too much trouble for ye tae deal with..."

"You have to get out of here fast. Emma and I will call the police. We can tell them we found your car and report you missing."

"Aye, Kaitlyn and I have provided for ye in our wills."

He groaned. "That's not — fuck, that's not what we — where will you go?"

"I will go get Quentin and send him home tae ye. Then I will decide — Kaitlyn wanted me tae fight for my throne. Tis what I must do."

"We won't see you again?"

"Aye, I think tis the end for us." I shook my head. "I am sorry, Emma, tae have ye see this."

She sobbed and said, "We'll really miss you. So much."

I nodded. "Take care of your family, Chef Zach."

He grimaced tae hold back tears. "I will, thank you for everything."

"Twas my honor tae do it." I began tae walk away tae gather the men, but felt the need tae say, "I spoke tae her as she left. My words followed her through."

Emma sniffled. "I'm so sorry."

"I am too."

Zach pulled his phone from his pocket. "I'll call the police as soon as you've left."

"Thank ye."

I dragged the bodies one at a time down the grassy slope and tossed them intae a pile beside the supplies Kaitlyn and I had planned tae carry tae the past. I dragged my own body through the mud, careful nae tae look. Twas awful tae see myself, as if my soul was divided. But lookin' on Kaitlyn was worse — I couldna do it without feeling' a pain so sharp I wanted fall tae my knees and beg God tae let me try again. I laid her body down on the blankets beside the pile.

Last I gathered the reins of the horses, wrapping them around my arm. I closed the case with the second vessel inside and stood with it between my feet. The supplies and bodies lay piled all around me.

I twisted the ends of the vessel, bringin it tae life, then I lifted Kaitlyn and held her in my arms as I recited the numbers, and left Florida and all that it meant behind.

This is the end of this small part of their story.
I know it doesn't make sense, not yet, but it will, I promise.
Now it's time to read the book.

ENTANGLED WITH YOU

PART I

1 - KAITLYN

"Mumblephnow?"

He took his toothbrush from his mouth. "What did ye say?"

I was sitting on the counter facing him. I giggled, dripping some toothpaste down my chin, my mouth full to spilling over, and giggling more. "Mumphleynoo. Lumneychon. Sphewskinnly."

His brow went up. "I haena any idea what ye are sayin'." He continued scrubbing the brush back and forth on his teeth and watching me.

"Sluuberlimnery."

He shook his head slowly and squinted his eyes. "Ye are nae usually so..."

I spit. Wiped my chin. And pretended to be exasperated. "I said, Lumneychon." And then laughed so hard I snorted.

Magnus laughed along with me. He spit and we passed a cup of water back and forth and both spit in the sink again.

He put his hands on my thighs and stood between them. "Twas fun watchin' ye race today."

"I came in sixth place in my wave." I stretched. "And every muscle is so sore I may not be able to walk for three days."

He shook his head slowly, sadly. "Twas nae the way ye raced. Ye splashed through that muddy pit with the skill of a warrior and took the prize as far as I could see."

"You're the best. I'm really glad to have you home. I mean, I know it's been a week but...still, we were moving our house through most of it."

He pulled my hips closer. "Tis good tae be home. Though it's a new home, you are in it."

I wrapped my ankles around his ass and pulled him closer. Leaned back on my hands, a smile and a raised brow. "Are we going to play here on the bathroom counter?"

Magnus smiled and looked around at the space, bright lights, giant mirror, cold surfaces. He said, "I daena ken if I could enjoy ye while starin' at myself."

"And we do have that big amazing bed to play on, you can enjoy me properly." I giggled again and slid off the counter, took him by the hand and pulled him down the hallway to the waiting bed. I climbed on and shoved all the decorative, damask, piped, brocaded pillows off to the carpet and sprawled caddy-corner and grinning. I was wearing a tiny midriff baring T-shirt with a pair of butt-cheek baring panties and quite proud of how cute I looked.

I could see it in his eyes — he was growing used to me in that loving husband kind of way, comfortable, but all I had to do was bare some skin and he was really really into me. Or wanted to be into me. I giggled again, so happy, and sprawled back as he dropped his uncomplicated modern kilt to the ground and climbed naked onto the bed beside me.

"So what next, Master Magnus?"

"I was thinkin' ye could introduce me tae your toys." He kissed me behind my ear on my neck.

My eyes grew wide. "I showed you last year."

His brow went up and his smile widened. "Ye showed me one toy, twas quite modest in size and function. I was surprised by it, I thought on it a great deal, but now I ken ye have a much larger collection."

"Magnus, you were gone for a whole year, so yes, I bought more, and have you been looking in my underwear drawer?"

"Aye, Madame Campbell, I missed the sight of your wee undergarments in all their splendid colors, laying clean and fresh in rows tae be worn. I find them tae be marvelous and there are so many now." His hand rubbed down my side and up under my shirt. He fondled my breast.

"I kind of got into a thing where I kept buying underwear while you were gone...." I arched toward his fingers.

"So I was lookin' at your undergarments and there beside them were more toys I haena met yet."

"You're serious?"

"Aye. " He grinned.

I said, "Are you sure? They don't freak you out? They are for when you aren't here, occasionally to play with when you are here — you are so much better — more fun. I don't want you to be worried about your manliness or anything."

"Have ye seen my manliness? I am nae worried."

I laughed, "Good point. Okay." I crawled across the bed to the dresser. I stood in front of my drawer and wiggled my butt for his viewing pleasure.

Magnus moaned happily.

I grabbed my three favorite toys and returned to the bed and dropped them beside him. "These are the only ones that matter." I sat cross-legged on the bed. "This is Pokey. Pokey meet Magnus, Magnus meet Pokey."

"What dost ye do with Master Pokey?"

"Oh really, you can't tell?"

"Nae, I can tell. Twas wantin' tae hear ye say it."

"You were gone a very long time. This is Nyum-Nyum." I held one that was small and curved in the palm of my hand.

"What does Master Nyum-Nyum do?"

I grinned. "Oh Master Nyum-Nyum does anything you want him to do."

"Aye." Magnus said simply.

I picked up the last, it fit on my palm too. "This is Eva. I met her on Facebook."

"What is Facebook?"

"That is unimportant, Magnus. The important thing is — Eva." I pulled my T-shirt off over my head and tossed it to the side. "I haven't been able to use her the way she is meant to be used." I stood up on the bed above Magnus and stripped my panties down my legs and kicked them to the side.

"She is a Mistress for ye? What does she do?"

"Guess." I dropped down to the bed, flat on my back, arms above my head, sprawled.

He held it in his hand above me. "She is the color green and would fit upon your ear, though I daena think tis the purpose."

He pressed it to my ear and I laughed.

He dragged it down my face to my nose. "Twould fit here, but for what fun?"

"I'll give you a hint. You have to turn her on."

He rolled onto his back and fiddled around with it for a moment, pressing and twisting, until it hummed to life.

"Am I goin' tae jump through time?"

"No, but we might have a little out-of-body experience."

"We? Verra interestin'."

His face was growing more serious. His breaths growing quicker. I could tell he wasn't as jovial anymore — more focused, more determined. He pressed the humming toy to my lips and slowly dragged it down my neck to my collarbone. I watched his face as he concentrated. His eyes taking me in. His lashes lowered on his cheek as he pulled the vibrating toy along my breast to the peak of my nipple and paused it there, watching. I arched toward it without even wanting to, wriggling and squirming to meet it. If he drew it away I pulled toward it. If he pressed it down I wriggled with it. Slowly it traveled down my stomach and across the curves of my pelvis and down, touching between my legs.

"There," I said with a breath.

His eyes closed. "I ken, but I daena..." I lowered a hand to fit it against me, nestled in my labia. His fingers followed it, and dipped inside me checking the placement. "Och, aye," he said and pushed my arms over my head and climbed onto me.

He winced a little, movements like this were still sore on his ribs. He kissed me and he flattened on me, a lovely pressure, holding me down, collected and settled, up on his elbows beside my shoulders. His hands resting on my arms, keeping them up above my head. He pushed his hips and himself, up and into me.

He exhaled in my ear. His voice low and rumbling against my skin, "I feel it."

I let out my air like a sigh as he filled me and the humming vibration played against me, almost more than I wanted, but oh, I wasn't going to — he held himself there, still and heavy and insistently inside me, filling me. I turned my head and with licks and nibbles pulled his thumb into my mouth and sucked it deeper against my tongue.

Magnus moaned and pressed his temple to my jaw, and we waited, pressed to each other, the intensity growing and spreading from between my legs and warming up my body. I adjusted my hips to press against him, pulling him in deeper.

He groaned low and deep almost a growl. Intense and tense.

My lips around his thumb, my mouth full, his other hand moved to my breast and squeezed.

The only thing on our bodies moving was my tongue flitting around his thumb, the vibration between my legs, his breath warm on the pulse point of my throat, the pressure of his fingerprints on my skin.

"God," he whispered and that syllable drove me to the edge.

My breath caught — ogodogodogodogodogod — I plunged over the falls and submerged under, as waves rolled up from between my legs through my stomach, I felt myself tightening and pulling and demanding and with a roar in my ear he rose up, held my hips and slammed against me over and over and over until he finished and collapsed down on my body.

The only sound was our panting breaths.

"Oh my god, that was awesome."

He rolled off me with a wince to his back beside me.

I pulled the toy from between my legs and turned it off.

"Och, aye. Every inch of ye was movin'."

"Really?" I laughed. "I thought I was completely still."

"You canna be when you are naked. Ye are writhin', corrachag-cagail, mo reul-iuil."

I curled up beside him, my head on his chest, his arm around. "Remind me what that means?"

"A flickering ember flame." He yawned.

"Oh." I kissed his chest. "I like that."

He pressed his lips to my forehead and said, "Aye. I need tae get up and check in with the guard." He sat up with a groan and then gave me a satisfied pat on my hip. "Stay here in bed I might..."

Exactly like Donnan patting me on the hip when he was finished with me before rising to dress. A memory flashed in my head — his shoulder butting against my mouth, his back bucking against me as he died.

I shoved his hand away — *whose hand?* "No no no no."

"Kaitlyn?"

I scrambled up, shaking my head, *no no no no —*

Kaitlyn?

I pushed my body toward the headboard and clung to it — *nononononono* — my bare legs a moment from being dragged down the bed. I pulled them under — nononononono

"Kaitlyn? Are ye okay?"

My hands clamped over my face. I curled in a —

"Kaitlyn? Look at me."

"I can't. I can't it's too..." I shook my head. "He did that. He patted me like that. He — oh god." I sank onto our pillows and tried to hide from him. If I hid he wouldn't be able to find me... I pulled a pillow around my face.

Magnus's voice, "Kaitlyn," sounded from very far away. "Tis me, Magnus."

He said it again and it took a moment more before I managed to say, "Magnus?"

"I am right here, mo reul-iuil, ye daena need tae be afeared." He lowered down beside me on his stomach, facing me. "Daena be afeared, mo ghradh, is ann leatsa abhios mo chridhe gubrath." Fingertips softly brushed my hair from my cheek and tucked it behind my ear. "You daena have tae be scared."

I grasped his hand.

"You are safe, mo ghradh."

I pulled my head up to see his eyes. Magnus. His eyes full of worry. I tucked his hand to my lips. "I'm sorry."

His brows drew down. His eyes squinted in concentration. His I'm-trying-to-understand look. "You daena need tae be sorry."

He sat there for a long moment quietly watching me.

He sighed long and rolled with a wince to his back and lay there naked, sprawled. Staring up at the ceiling he asked, "I ken it, Kaitlyn, but ye need tae say it tae me — he forced himself on ye? He was able tae before ye killed him?"

I clutched his hand to my face and didn't answer.

"I needs ken the whole truth of it. It needs be out in the open."

I concentrated on his fingernail. "He did. The first time was when I was coming out of the pain of time-jumping and I don't know how long I was there — or what happened before. I don't remember when he cut my face. So I don't know... The last time was when I killed him."

I watched the side of Magnus's face as he stared at the ceiling. His eyes darted back and forth, working out something, thinking it through.

"I told you that you didn't want to know."

"Tis a lot tae hear."

We lay there quietly for a few moments.

"Were ye — did ye... I am askin' if ye were takin' your pills... If ye still are."

"I was. I am. I don't think there's any reason why I should be—"

"When would we ken?"

"I could probably know in a few days? Maybe a week?"

"Good. If ye are... I daena..."

"I can't be, Magnus. It would be so..."

"Aye." The corner of his eye glistened. He spoke to the ceiling. "I daena ken what I have done tae ye, mo reul-iuil. I have brought so much despair tae ye."

"You warned me."

"Aye, but I also promised ye I would protect ye. And I haena lived up tae—"

I kissed his fingers and crawled from my position on the pillows, to his side, collapsing under his arm, over his chest, snuggled, afraid of his words, the words of defeat, terrible words, scared words, final kinds of words.

I clung to him. "I don't think that's what you promised me."

He lifted his head and looked down at my face. "I did. I promised ye protection."

"That's not what I heard. What I heard was that you would live your whole life always trying to protect me. That my life, my safety, would always be your first thought. And you haven't let me down Magnus, you have kept your promise to me. I know it. I'm scared when I think about what happened to me. I'm terrified when I think about what might be coming, and my brain is just like hiccuping right now, showing me things at really dumbass times. But when I think about you, here, I know you will always do your best to try to protect me. Because that's what you promised."

"But I am the son of Donnan. The son of Mairead. I have killed men for entertainment. What if I am nae the man who deserves ye?"

I circled my finger around on his chest. "You aren't his son. Or hers. You are my husband. Before god." I slid my thigh across his waist and his hand held it there. "We can't talk about deserving." I pulled his opposite shoulder up to turn him toward me and wrapped around him, legs entwined, arms wrapped, hands caressing. "Deserving is a deciding word. It's insecure, unstable... those kinds of words don't describe us anymore. You and I are decided. We are one, my love, stronger together."

His voice came from near my shoulder. "I am worried that I may have it inside me — an evil that I canna rid myself of."

"Oh." It was my turn to stare into space searching for the right words, finding them in a meme I saw months before. "Did you know that all the cells in your body have a lifespan and they die and are replaced by new cells?"

"The cells?"

"Yes, your entire body is made up of tiny cells and those each die and new ones take their place. Our whole body is completely new every seven years."

He pulled his head away to look at my face. "Tis true?"

"Science, maybe a little bit of myth, but that's unimportant. What's important is that you are what, twenty-three years old now?"

"I think I am twenty-two..."

"Oh no you don't. You were away for a year. You do not get to stay younger while I get older. You are aging at the same rate as me. This is not some Twilight bullshit."

His mouth turned up in the corner. "I haena any idea what ye are talkin' about, but I will say I am twenty-three years auld."

"My point is your body may have been originally built by Donnan and Mairead, but since then you have rebuilt yourself at least twice again."

His eyes squinted. "Really?"

"Really. Plus, if you think about it, you pray all the time asking for help and guidance. I think God has helped to build you into this big strapping man beside me. He doesn't want you to be evil. And Zach gets some credit, he feeds you every day. How can you be evil when you've got Zach serving you bowls of ice cream? Your physical trainer helped your muscles get all awesomely big. Me, I got you that oxygen tank. I made you take those vitamins. I tell you cool science-y things turning you into an awesome eighteenth century geek. We should get a lot more credit than those other two evil people."

"I haena thought of it that way." He tucked his head into my shoulder again and kissed me on my collarbone.

"It's a nice way to think about it right? We get to renew ourselves. Constantly shifting and changing. So don't worry about what you might become, just become the man you are. And you're a good man. And I love you so much."

"And I have kept my promise tae ye?"

"With every breath."

"Thank ye, mo reul-iuil."

"You're welcome."

"I do need tae check in with the security guard."

"Can I come with you? My heart is still racing. I don't really want to be alone."

2 - MAGNUS

The next morning Kaitlyn was still asleep when I jumped beside her on the bed and jiggled her awake.

"Kaitlyn, wake up."

She startled, "What — everything okay?"

"Aye, daena worry, tis just the day tae get Sunny. I am up already."

She groaned and patted the bed beside her. "You are not up already. It's too early for you to be up already. And definitely not because you're going to get your horse."

"I am standin' afore ye, dressed. Zach will have breakfast in a moment. Ye needs be up, ye have tae drive me."

She smiled. "Are you excited to get Sunny?"

"I am. I haena ridden for a verra long time."

She said, I think she was teasin', "You've been riding me, I'm not good enough?"

I had a memory slam intae me, Bella, sayin' — *My Magnus, are you comparing your wife to a horse?*

"You arna..." Bella, in my mind, leering up at me, tryin' tae entice me. I shook my head trying tae push the memory away. I took a deep breath. "You are more than good enough, but ye arna a horse. I need my horse. Can ye be ready soon?"

She threw the covers off sensing my urgency and went tae our bathroom to dress for our day.

3 - KAITLYN

We parked at the end of the stables and Debbie met us to show Magnus to Sunny. It was a blustery cold day. I was bundled in a sweatshirt and a knit cap, mostly because of the wind. Magnus was wearing his kilt and a white thermal henley-style shirt. I gave him a wool scarf that was green tartan plaid.

He said, "I daena think tis cold enough for this."

"Lean forward." I wrapped it around his neck. "You can take it off when I'm out of sight. I need to fuss over you a bit."

The plan was for Magnus to ride along the beach all the way to the north end.

We paid a builder to add a stable for Sunny at our house, so he could live there part time. We didn't have the permits, but the house was situated in a way that the stable was hidden from view, plus our neighbors were short-term rentals, mostly. I was sure no one would complain, at least for a while, and we would work it out if they did.

And when I saw Magnus nuzzling his face to Sunny's muzzle, speaking to him softly in Gaelic, I knew this had all been the right decision. Magnus was home. Our house was ready. Our lives were hidden. He needed his horse.

Soon enough his ribs would be healed and we would have to implement the next phase — rescue Quentin.

I hung out and helped Magnus a bit while he curried Sunny and saddled him up. Then I walked with him as he led Sunny down the path to the beach. "Twill nae take me long, mo reul-iuil."

"I'm nervous." We faced each other. "I want to come but I need to help Emma with her wedding plans and..."

"Aye," he smoothed the hair back from my face. "We have tae learn tae breathe again, both of us. We are holdin' our breath for what comes next." He tilted my chin up and kissed me. "I winna be gone long."

"Okay, definitely." He climbed up on Sunny and looked majestic and so freaking happy that I did breathe a little better. "Have a really good ride, okay love?"

"Och aye, tis a beautiful day. I will see ye at home, mo reul-iuil." My husband rode his favorite horse across the sand dunes to the beach and turned north.

I walked back to my waiting car and spoke to it. "Mustang, we will try our best not to let his love of Sunny make us jealous. You will always be my favorite horse." I slid into the driver's seat to ride home.

4 - KAITLYN

Zach and Emma were waiting for me in the kitchen to discuss the wedding plans, though talking with them about anything these days was difficult, because every waking hour with Ben was spent corralling, redirecting, watching, scooping up, and speaking to him in caveman-style sentences. "Ben doesn't want to put the key in the light socket, Ben wants to play blocks." Everything in the house that was breakable had been moved to waist level. Most of the floor was strewn with toys and cardboard books.

The night before we had given Ben pots and pans to bang and then he screamed when Zach decided the pots were too loud. Magnus joked, "Tis good to be at peace in our home." We all laughed. It was funny, but for Magnus it was also true. Even with the clamorous bang-banging of the pans this was the most peace in a long time. And for Magnus, Ben could do no wrong.

Ben was up in Emma's sling, riding on her hip for our discussion. Zach and I sat at the kitchen counter while Emma stood beside us, rocking, dancing, swaying, passing things to Ben hoping to keep him preoccupied.

"First, where do you want to get married?" I had a notepad in front of me. They were already planning, but my own list was necessary.

Emma said, "I heard the Ocean Club does it. A beach wedding with a place for dinner if we can book it on short notice."

"That would be perfect, we can call them next. How many guests?"

Zach said, "Us five."

Emma huffed.

I cut my eyes at him. "Now let's think about this, is that really the end goal here?"

"No, but that's all that I want."

Emma said, "By my count the number will be sixty-five guests: Immediate family, friends, some extras."

I stuck my tongue out at Zach. "I like Emma's number much better. So who will cater this extravaganza?"

"Me," said Zach.

"That's not really how it works."

"You tell him," Emma said, "I can't get him to listen to me."

I put down my pen. "It goes without saying that you could if you wanted to, but part of being Magnus's private chef is that you get to afford to have a wedding catered by someone else. He has a never-before-seen Picasso hanging on his wall and all he wants to do with his money is make sure his family is comfortable. You're a part of his family."

"There aren't any other chefs that I want, except — okay, I'll call someone, but I'm not happy about it."

I grinned. "Here's the thing, Zach, you love Emma right? You want to marry her. 100% of it is showing off to the world how much you love her and what you can provide for her. That's the whole purpose. You aren't supposed to have fun or even like the day much. It's not even for you. It's for everyone else."

"You got married in a small wedding."

"I didn't have to prove anything to anybody. As a matter of fact I didn't want anyone to know about it because the whole thing was crazy-town. You need everyone to witness your amazing wedding, because though you guys aren't crazy-town somehow you have to prove it."

"You're right, I'm just being..." He reached for Emma's hand.

I said, "So that brings me to this: Magnus and I discussed it and we have two gifts for you. You only get to take one. I'm going to tell you what they both are and you and Emma get to discuss them and tell us which one you want."

I drew the number one on a new fresh piece of paper. "Magnus and I pay for the whole wedding, everything. At the wedding we tell everyone that Magnus paid for it all because you are his star chef and he admires you so much that he wanted to. This makes Magnus seem very wealthy and powerful and your career seem important." I wrote 'We Pay' beside the number.

I wrote a two. "The second gift is Magnus and I don't pay for the wedding, you do. And Magnus tells everyone at the party that he wanted to pay for the wedding, but you insisted because you are that kind of guy and you make plenty of money. In this one Magnus makes a speech at the reception about how much he admires you and it brings everyone to tears." I wrote 'Big Speech.'

I added, "I don't know who I'm kidding though, Magnus is going to make a giant speech no matter what. He may cry too, so be ready. He's such a romantic." My eyes moved across the room to the tv. The weather channel flickered large on the main wall, the satellite imagery was clear.

Emma and Zach met eyes. Emma said, "We already discussed this. We didn't really come to an agreement, but I'm playing the Bride Card so I win. I think, if it's really okay, that Magnus should pay for the wedding. Nobody believes anything we say in regard to Zach's worth, hopefully they'll listen to Magnus on it."

I glanced at Zach. He looked surly.

I patted the back of his hand. "This is a gift. Magnus and I want to do this. This is not you asking, or needing, or because you can't do it. This is us giving you something and you can't turn us down."

"Fine."

"So we should call about the rental, go ahead and set the date."

Emma said, "What about Quentin, should we wait for him to come home?"

"I really don't think you should wait. You know what Quentin would say? He would say, 'It's about time.'" We'll go get him soon and we can celebrate it together, but he won't mind that you got married when you had the chance. Let's book it the earliest we can. Preferably before Magnus's ribs heal all the way, because once they do we'll need to begin planning our return to the past in earnest."

Emma said, "Okay, perfect. I'll call to book the space." While we had been talking, she raised her shirt to nurse Ben and was gently rocking him back and forth in the sling. I smiled at him as his eyes rolled back in his head and he fell asleep suckling right in the middle of our conversation.

"It's pretty amazing how that kid can go from a hundred to zero in three seconds."

"Don't I know it."

5 - KAITLYN

Magnus came home. I knew he would. Mostly. But I was also really nervous that he wouldn't. I was watching through the French doors in our bedroom and as soon as I saw him I raced down the boardwalk to the beach and arrived at the dunes breathless and over-excited. "You made it. And please don't think I was being overly needy by watching for you."

"Twas necessary, for many miles I was considerin' ye might be lost tae me again."

"So we are a fine mess, huh? Freaking out when we're apart, freaking out when we're together?"

"Aye. Better tae do it together." He dropped from Sunny's back.

"How was your ride?"

"Twas beautiful. Walk with me to the stable?"

"You haven't asked me that since 1703." I grinned.

~

That night's dinner was pasta Puttanesca, a meal Zach hadn't made in forever. Magnus talked about his day, the wind on the ocean, the houses he had seen. He asked us about Main Beach and the round house he passed. Zach and I did our best to explain how solar panels worked. He had seen them on a roof as he passed, but all the concepts were so foreign that our explanation got pretty silly, until we finally came up with "it's magic."

He shrugged. "It makes more sense that the sun's heat would warm us, than the wee holes in the wall." He pointed to the electrical socket. We agreed without mentioning that solar power also powered those "wee holes." He also asked about the palm trees and we had to google whether they were indigenous. We had such a nice dinner, talking and laughing and teaching Magnus about his small piece of the modern world.

It reminded me of those first days with Magnus, getting to know him, showing him the Island, falling in love. The scent of the sauce and the memories of that time, all conspired, causing me to feel like I was falling in love all over again.

6 - KAITLYN

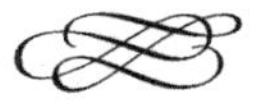

Thanksgiving was upon us and our chosen family was pulled in different directions. Zach and Emma and Ben planned to eat with Zach's family, joining Hayley and Michael. My mom and dad were the only parents who had other plans: a cruise they booked, which was absolutely fine by me. Someone needed to eat with my grandmother, also fine by me.

Magnus and I were invited to come after to the Greenes to eat with Zach's parents, but ultimately Zach was bummed he didn't get to cook. We made a deal, we would all eat early at other places, apart, and Zach would cook us our own Thanksgiving dinner together at about seven.

When we woke up that morning and I was putting on mascara, one eye closed, winking at the mirror, I asked, "Magnus, are you ready?"

"For the feast?"

"Not a feast, the biggest feast of the year, American-style. Wait until you try Green Bean Casserole — Zach is going to make it full of organic beans and portobello mushrooms and other things I couldn't talk him out of, but at Grandma's home they're sure to have the one from cans. We'll eat both and convene back here tonight to decide which one we liked better."

"I canna believe we are goin' tae have two feasts."

"Two turkeys, two big piles of potatoes, so much gravy, stuffing, cranberry sauce, any of this sound familiar?"

He grinned, "Tatties."

"Oh man, we are going to have so much fun."

The first part wasn't very fun. Grandma was loopy and confused the whole time. At one point in the lunch she startled at the sight of Magnus who had been there the whole time. "Who are you? Why are you here? You're so big you're terrifying me."

"Barb, I am married tae your granddaughter Katie. I am Magnus, you and I are auld friends."

She eyed us suspiciously and ate quietly.

It broke my heart a little and my heart wasn't wanting to be broken anymore. I tried to be cheery. I laughed it off and we talked about the food. I chit-chatted about the waiters we liked and the chef, and I asked her questions about her yoga class.

Magnus ate, but our eyes met over our plates. A wordless conversation — *This is hard. Aye. She doesn't know me. Tis verra difficult* — I told her all about the wedding plans but in many ways she wasn't really listening. And the food was delicious but really just another lunch because the conversation weighed it down.

On the way home, driving Magnus in the Mustang he held my hand and we talked about the Green Bean Casserole and the potatoes and then he asked, "Dost ye want tae talk of your grandmother?"

"No, not really. Not today. Today is for feasts and thankfulness. I'm filled with gratitude for all the years I have had with her, all the conversations, all the wise words. That's what I want to focus on. I'm thankful for you, too."

"I haena any idea why. I ate my tatties and tried nae tae scare her with my presence."

"Your fortune makes it so she is taken care of, close by, and I can share meals with her. So thank you."

"You're welcome, mo reul-iuil. I am glad tae bring her comfort."

I whacked my hand down on his bare knee, sprawled in the passenger seat, looking sexy under his kilt. "So, love of my life, now you and I are going to go for a long walk on the beach, maybe a nap, and we'll be ready for feast number two, Chef Zach's extravaganza!"

Zach's feast was amazing. The turkey was moist and seasoned with rosemary. The potatoes were fluffed with so much dairy that they were all I wanted to eat. The stuffing was crusty on the edges, but moist in the middle and the gravy drizzled over it was amazing and not gravy from cans either. This was gravy from the drippings as Zach pointed out incredulously when I asked. Also, Magnus thought Zach's Green Bean Casserole was much better. I wasn't sure, but I let Magnus win this one to make both of these important men in my life happy.

At my request there was even a can of cranberry sauce, plopped onto a plate, still in the form of the can. Because, as Zach grumbled, I was hopeless.

It was only the five of us, Ben banging on the table sitting on Emma's lap.

Finally Zach said, "Let me clean this up, Emma needs to nurse Ben to sleep. I'll bring drinks and pumpkin pie to the living room."

I said, "Can we help? If we all pitch in there will be barely anything—"

"Absolutely not. I just spent the day watching crazy stuff happen in my mom's kitchen. I'm grateful that I can run my kitchen the way I want. Alone. With no one putting pans away unpolished. Or the fucking knives in the same drawer with the spatulas."

I laughed. "Okay, Mister Control-freak, suit yourself." Magnus and I carried our wine glasses to the couch. He sat at one end, one arm waiting along the back cushions.

I checked the tv, set as always on the weather channel, and turned down the brightness so it wasn't as insistent. I turned on Spotify, the Ariana Grande station. I sat down and leaned against Magnus's chest. "How's this, painful?"

He winced, shifted, and adjusted my shoulder. "Tis better."

Zach walked into the room with a tray of brandy snifters and plates of pumpkin pie heaped with whipped cream. "This is Emma's favorite music."

"Cool, me too. And what's this?" I held up a chocolate rectangle that was leaned on my triangle of pie.

"Chocolate-covered bacon."

"Jesus Christ, are you trying to kill us?" I took a big bite. "Yum. Are there more, is this it, will we have to have a Hunger Games right here in the living room for the last one on Magnus's plate?"

"There are more. Eat that and you can have seconds."

Magnus said, "Hunger games, are they played with a ball?"

"The Hunger Games, let me see, it was a book series where young people were made to fight to the death to..." I checked his face, then squinted as I reconsidered. "Yeah, never mind. Let's call it a book series and I won't joke about it anymore."

Emma entered and plopped down in a chair. "He is fast

asleep. I want pie." She picked up a book from her pile on the end table. "I'm dying to get back to this, so don't mind me."

Zach passed her a bowl and we all ate happily with plates resting on our bellies.

I finished eating, passed my bowl back to the tray, took a deep breath, and jumped into a big important thing. "So, Magnus, I have something to discuss with you and... I — one day Zach and I were Googling the history of you, and we learned something about Lizbeth that I want to talk to you about."

"Lizbeth, what is...? You have a sad look tae ye, Kaitlyn."

"We learned that she doesn't make it through the birth, this December, I mean, in December of 1703, she dies."

"Och."

"I know."

"Can we go back and do somethin' tae save her?"

"I don't know, but I want to try."

Zach said, "Okay, wait, I don't want to sound callous, but we're talking about someone, your sister Magnus, I get that she's important to you—"

"She has raised me from a verra young age."

"I understand that, but she's been passed away now for three hundred years. She will die. Don't you have to get used to the fact?"

I said, "But when I go back there, to Scotland, she is alive. And she is amazing. I can't imagine Scotland without her."

Zach said, "I get that, but what about changing time? If you change the course of history, what will you change in the course of our present?"

Magnus asked, "What do you mean by this, Chef Zach?"

He leaned forward in his chair. "Like if you go back in time and killed someone, like a King, you would change written history. Maybe his death starts a war. Maybe something important that we need wouldn't be invented. Maybe the children of the king are important. Maybe you come back here and this present-day world has been altered because the son of the king wasn't born. As a time traveler everything you do might have consequences..."

Magnus said, "Kaitlyn has killed a king."

"That was in the future, we don't need to worry on that one much. Though what's happening there now should concern you."

"It does, verra much. So ye are sayin' we only need tae worry on our effect on the past? We left machines from the future in the past. We left a black man in a Scottish castle. I have already changed the story in 1703, and this world hasna changed." He looked around at us. "Has it?"

I shrugged. "I don't know. I don't think so."

Zach sank back in his chair. "But I guess if you think about it we wouldn't know. If the present was different from three days ago, we would be living in a different present with a different history. We would have no idea." He groaned. "I just totally freaked myself out. Hold that thought, I'm going to go check on Ben."

He jogged up the stairs and was gone for a moment and then jogged down to the kitchen. He called, "Sorry about that, got a little nervous."

Emma said, "I have the baby monitor right here."

Zach shook his head. "Sometimes you have to put your hand on his sleeping back to accept he's okay."

He opened the cabinet over the refrigerator. "I have a bit of a pot brownie. Anyone else wants a bite?"

"No thanks," I said. To Magnus I explained, "That's one of those cookies, like we ate that night, remember?"

"The one that made ye giggle like the ocean fish? Aye, I canna eat it. I need tae be ready in case there is a storm." Our eyes all shifted to the television screen. It didn't help, it was a commercial for Xanax.

I resumed our conversation. "And Zach, we have these paintings — they've been here for well over a year, but having them didn't change Picasso's worth or value or anything, right? I mean, if we killed a king that might have a ripple effect, but small things, in the scheme of it, might not be that big a deal."

"Yeah, you're probably right. Don't mess with big established important events and don't interfere in your own personal history. Like the time rules on Doctor Who—"

Magnus asked, "He is a physician?"

I said, "Doctor Who is a television show about a time traveler."

"Och, twas based on truth?"

"No it's completely fictional because time travel is fictional." I shrugged. "I mean, now that I've traveled through time I don't know what to believe anymore. Maybe one of the writers on Doctor Who actually had a vessel?"

Zach said, "Let's say the rules make sense — at least you'd have guidelines to behave by. The number one would be: you can't interfere in your own past or future."

Magnus said, "I came close tae that when I traveled tae see Kaitlyn at the bar."

I nodded. "Yes, you did."

Zach said, "While arguably a very fucking romantic gesture, it could have gone so wrong. What if you had gotten into a fight with her boyfriend? You might have ruined all of this."

Magnus said, "So we shouldna go back and fix what has happened to us." His brow was drawn down. "Or what will happen to us?"

"Oh, I think you can change course, but don't loop back on yourself and change what's already done. Like don't return to a year and a half ago, kill Lady Mairead, and call it good. I don't think that will work and it might set the world all spinning wrong. According to the Doctor at least."

Magnus said, "But that rule does nae mean Kaitlyn canna try tae save Lizbeth's life."

I pointed at Magnus in agreement. "True. I wouldn't be altering my past, just her future."

Zach said, "I still wonder though, that date has been set in the historical records, what happens if the records change — what else changes?"

Magnus stared down at his drink. "You think, Chef Zach, that if there is a written record of the birth and death there is nae changing it?"

"I just think you have to be careful changing it. Consider it carefully, make sure it's worth the possibility your actions may have a ripple effect."

Magnus leaned forward. "Chef Zach, Kaitlyn, what did ye discover of my own history?"

I gave him a wistful smile. "That's actually good news. The records we looked at didn't include your date of death. So nothing we do changes your history. We can do whatever we want." I took a sip of brandy and grimaced. "Ugh. Now I just want a soda or something."

Zach jumped to get me a fresh drink. I said to Magnus, "See, in the beginning you were telling me you were a dead man — you're not. You might be the closest to immortal of anyone. You've been alive for centuries."

Zach passed me a glass with coke and ice cubes.

Magnus asked Emma, "You have been quiet on the matter, Madame Emma, ye have thoughts on it?"

She put her finger in the page to hold it. "I agree with Zach, you have to be careful changing anything, but he's forgetting the biggest rule in Doctor Who — to act morally."

"I have killed men for entertainment."

She frowned in commiseration. "I know it weighs on you, Magnus, but soldiers have to kill under orders, that's what war is. You pray for guidance about it and you ask for forgiveness."

Magnus nodded quietly.

Zach said, "The other possibility is that no matter what you do, you might not be able to change what has already been recorded."

Magnus asked, "So if it has already happened we may nae be able tae stop it?"

Emma smiled sweetly at her husband and said to Magnus, "What my dear future-husband's drug-addled mind is not thinking about is you can't decide what to do simply because you haven't seen the record of it. You could just not look anything up and declare it okay. If you haven't seen it does that mean it doesn't exist?"

"Nae, ye are right, Madame Emma."

I asked, "Did you see my future, Magnus? Wait, don't tell me — no, tell me. Did you? Wait, don't tell me. Do — at least tell me if you saw a blank."

Magnus ran his hand over his head. "I dinna ask about it."

"Oh."

I gulped at the thought. "How weird would that have been if you had?"

"Aye. Tis why I dinna."

"Okay. That's good." I stared off into space. "I wouldn't want to know. I think..."

Magnus said, "So we daena ken whether we can change the outcome of a story..."

Zach said, "Nope, but that's cool right? It makes you exactly like every other mortal on the planet — just doing the best they can do." He gestured toward Emma. "Acting with morals as my sweet church-going wife would say and hoping it turns out fucking okay in the long run."

I said, "I think the one thing we are all saying is yes, we can go back in time and try to save Lizbeth's life. If I can, I have to, right? Don't even answer that. I know it. I have to do everything I can." I turned to Emma. "That being said, what can I do?"

"I can talk to my midwife about it in the morning."

Zach's phone vibrated. He picked it up. "Hayley is here."

He went to the front door and opened it as Hayley had her hand about to knock. She bustled in with a full bloom on her cheeks. She took off her jacket and tossed it toward the hooks on the wall, came to the living room, dropped on the couch beside my feet, and tossed a stack of mail on the coffee table. "Here's your mail. Don't worry about it. It's junk." She sighed loudly.

Zach followed her into the living room. "You look like you need a stiff drink?"

"I do. I need one. And you're partly responsible. But I'm not going to because that's not me anymore, in case anyone bothered to notice. I'd like a soda please." She jerked her shirt back, frustrated. "And why is Quentin still gallivanting around in the 18th century? He should be here to take me to a meeting."

I asked, "You could go by yourself?"

"Don't be ridiculous. I don't actually need to go, I just thought if Quentin was here I could be supportive of him going and that would be... Is anyone going to ask me what I'm doing here or do I have to talk about this bullshit the whole time?"

I said, "You are in a pissy mood, what's up?"

Zach handed her a drink.

"If you must know, Michael and I have just broken up."

"Oh no!" I left Magnus's side to throw an arm around her. "Oh no. Oh no, this sucks. What happened?"

Hayley waved her hand at Zach and Emma. "They happened, with all their love and marriage and having a baby and, ugh." She dropped her head to the back of the couch. "Right after the turkey, Michael gave me an ultimatum, marry him and start a family, or not."

I pouted in sympathy. "You chose not?"

"I did. Of course I did. Because I'm a dumbass. Probably."

I pulled her head to my shoulder. "You aren't a dumbass, you didn't want to marry him. That isn't dumb. That's what your heart is telling you and you have to listen to it."

She started crying. "I look at you with your awesome hunky husband and I want that, I mean, not him, he's prettier than me and I wouldn't be able to take the pressure, but someone who really likes me. And that I really like. I thought Michael was the one because I've been with him since I was seventeen, but maybe he's not the right one. He doesn't even really like me that much. Like not really. I want what you have."

"I have been crying for a year. You really want that? You really want to never know if you'll survive being apart? What I have might be a little too death-defying."

She looked at me with a red puffy face and tear-sopped eyes. "You missed him! You know what I think when Michael goes away for two whole days?"

I shook my head.

"'Eh. Whatever.' That's not who I should spend the rest of my life with!" She looked across at Zach. "Sorry, I know he's your little brother, and I don't mean to blame you guys, not really. I'm happy for you. Really. Your timing just blew my whole life apart."

"No worries, Hayley, I'm sorry about that. You've been my future little sister for years. I don't know what I'll do without that. Are you sure? You guys aren't going to get back together?"

"Nah." She waved her hand. "Kleenex please."

Emma brought her a box of Kleenex and Hayley blew her nose loudly. "When we were discussing it tonight it wasn't even sad, not really. It was like I knew it for a long time, but I didn't really know it." She sighed. "I guess now I can stop doing the races, though they were actually kind of fun."

"They were fun. Magnus and I will do them with you. Quentin will come and you can take him to meetings. And we'll all go out and do fun things together."

Zach began texting. "I'm checking in with Mikey now."

Hayley dropped her head back on the couch. "He's going to move his stuff out tomorrow. What am I going to do, sit there and watch him pack his stuff up? Plus I'll have to go get my stuff from his place." She was ugly crying now, full sobs.

Zach excused himself to go talk to Michael out on the deck.

The baby monitor beside Emma emitted a loud wail from upstairs. Emma said, "I might as well get in bed for the night. What is it eleven?"

I said, "Yeah, it's late."

Magnus whispered, "I have tae go speak with security." He kissed me on the cheek, squeezed Hayley's shoulder, and went through the French doors to the deck.

Hayley stopped sobbing enough to ask, "So what's happening with you guys, did I interrupt something?"

I held her hand. "You interrupted a philosophical conversation about the moral and ethical issues inherent in jumping through time. We weren't really getting anywhere on it. Except to justify what we want to do."

She sniffled. "You don't want to do that time-turning stuff like Hermione did, which Harry Potter book was that? Like the third — where she almost saw herself? I don't know what would happen but that part would probably be dangerous."

I took a deep breath. "I wouldn't want any of it to be dangerous. That would suck." We both chuckled. "Look on the bright side, Hayley. First, you get to be sad and I get to help you through it for once. Want to spend the night in our guest room?"

"Absolutely. Can we watch tv, like you on one end and me on

the other end of the couch with bowls of ice cream on our chest and talk about how screwed up our lives are like the good old days? I can tell you that Michael broke my heart and you can tell me that he's an ass and that I deserve better."

"That sounds good, we can focus on you for once. And I already ate some pie. But I'll get you a slice in a second. And yes, we can watch a movie." I picked up the remote control. "Are you sore? It's been a day and a half and I'm so sore I can barely move."

"Totally. Wait, look there, it's the newest Avengers movie."

The French doors opened and Magnus stepped in.

Hayley said, "Mags, you can come sit on the couch with us if you bring a blanket." Magnus disappeared down the hallway and returned with the scratchiest blanket in the linen closet, but I decided not to micromanage him. I sat in the middle of the couch. Hayley put her feet in my lap. Magnus sat at the other end. I leaned against him with his arm around me.

Zach entered from the deck. "Little bro is doing okay I guess."

Hayley said, "That sucks, he could at least be broken up about it."

Zach shrugged. "He is, but I'm not going to tell the ex about it. Want some pumpkin pie?"

"Yes, extra whipped cream because, you know..."

He left for the kitchen.

She said, "Did you hear that? Michael's upset about our break up."

"Of course he is."

~

The movie opened in the full Avenger style: battle, mayhem, chaos, jokes.

Magnus said, "Tis verra loud."

I said, "I know, movies can be so loud sometimes they even hurt my eyes. Want to go to the bedroom to sleep?"

"Nae, I want tae stay with ye." He turned sideways in the couch, his head back with his eyes closed. I snuggled against his chest.

Hayley turned the volume down a bit and activated the closed-captions.

Magnus quickly grew heavy and sleepy.

Zach brought Hayley a plate with pumpkin pie drowned in whipped cream. "I'm headed to bed, the kitchen is closed."

I whispered, "Good night, Zach, thank you for Thanksgiving."

"I'm glad you liked it, Katie, and it's good to have him, you, everyone home."

"Even me?" asked Hayley.

Zach chuckled and left the room.

She laughed, "He's glad to have me here, I'm so much more fun than Michael. He just doesn't want to pick sides."

7 - KAITLYN

"This is a marvel."

"What, this?" I sprayed a small mountain of shaving foam in the palm of my hand. I was sitting on the counter with my feet in the sink, slathering my leg with shaving lotion.

Magnus stood beside me with shaving lotion on his jaw. "Aye, and the... what did ye call it?"

"The razor?" I rinsed it under the stream of water from the sink and inspected it. "It is kind of amazing, see the tiny blades imbedded in there?"

He ran his own razor down his cheek, rinsed it, and clinked it against the side of the sink. "Tis sharp yet daena cut the skin."

I pulled my razor smoothly up the inside of my calf to my knee and gave it some extra twists there. "True, I never thought much about it. I pay less than $10 a month for new ones to be delivered."

He squinted at me, like he was considering, his hand paused halfway down the next section of his cheek. "Somewhere in the world there are men building these blades?"

"There's a factory, yes."

"Then they arrive here — how dost they send them?"

I rinsed my blade and ran it up the outside of my leg. "Through the mail, or wait, you probably want all the nitty-gritty. A man, or woman, picks up a box of blades from the factory, puts it in a truck, and drives it to the airport. The box is loaded on an airplane and flown to our airport, where it's loaded onto another truck, taken to the post office, sorted with all our other mail, and put in a smaller truck. Have you seen our mailman's truck?"

"I daena ken I have noticed it."

"Well our mailman drives it up our street and puts it in our mailbox."

"The box outside?" He lifted his chin and shaved around under his jaw.

I said, "Then Emma goes out and gets the box from the mailbox and voila — we have razors. You missed a spot right there." I pointed to a place close to his ear.

He grinned. "Ye missed a spot right there." He plunged his hand between my legs and tickled me right on the edge of my panties. They were cherry red. Because he liked them.

"Very funny." I swirled another mound of lotion in my palm and slathered up the next leg.

He was finishing up his jawline. "And the white cream comes from an airplane too?"

I thought for a moment. "Probably. But it was delivered to a store and we bought it there because I forgot to order it through the mail."

He picked up the can, investigated it and pushed the button to release some into his palm. "What is the magic tae this then?"

"That is air, a little air capsule, and it mixes with the liquid to come out as foam, you know, I don't know one hundred percent so it is a little magic, I guess."

He rubbed the foam on the inside of my thigh, groaned happily, then washed his hands in the sink. He leaned against the counter. "Zach is takin' me tae get some supplies for when we go back in time."

"And I'll be with Emma for our all day spa treatments. Phew, we're busy aren't we?"

"Aye, but the good kind. We will do everythin' tae get tae this, Kaitlyn, from now on."

8 - KAITLYN

I sat on our bed watching Magnus get dressed. "So you guys are really going to take Zach to a strip club?"

"Aye, his brother has planned it."

"I want to kill him."

Magnus raised a brow.

"Not really, but he should know better. Zach has a baby. Emma is worried."

"Emma has nae need tae be worried. Zach is goin' because his brother wants him tae act like a single man for a few hours. Zach will laugh and have fun, and I will be there and we will pretend tae look—"

"No looking."

"I will keep m'eyes closed the whole time."

He looked so freaking handsome. He was wearing a dark linen shirt, buttoned up the front, and a dark wool kilt. He had a new sporran and belt. His hair was a little longer than usual and a bit wet so it was back from his face, no curls coming forward.

He said, "I wish Quentin was here. I would have him drive ye for protection."

"I don't need a driver, I have a limo. You too. And ours is a bachelorette party. No protection, no boys allowed. It's going to be a rocking good time. Emma is a mom. I'm a married lady. Hayley isn't drinking. We're going to go crazy."

Magnus chuckled.

I added, "Quentin'll be here soon though. The Mustang is packed with what we need. We just have to get this wedding done first."

I lay back sprawled on the bed. "I'm still stuffed from the pretentious bridal breakfast this morning. All day spa. I'm exhausted." I opened my eyes to look up at him, stock still, appraising me.

"You likey? I got my nails done, a facial, the full massage." I held up a hand to show off my nails and put a leg up in the air. "Feel it, soft and silky." He ran a hand down my leg and sighed.

"I like ye verra much. This dress is verra..." He shook his head.

My dress was a soft shimmery filmy little party dress. Seemed a shame to waste it on strangers in a nightclub in Jax, but also, it would be fun to dance in a night club. I hadn't gone dancing since I lived in Los Angeles.

He pulled me to standing. "But I am runnin' late for our limo."

I took a deep breath. "Okay. I'm running late for our limo, too."

He put a hand on each side of my face. "You arna frightened?"

"I'm not. Not really, just nervous. A little, yeah. I'm scared."

He smoothed my hair back. "We will be separated for a few hours, mo reul-iuil, tae have some fun with our friends. I will see ye tonight." He kissed me on the lips.

"Tonight."

9 - KAITLYN

We were at the Myth nightclub in Jacksonville. There were ten women. Some of Emma's friends from high school were there and some of us were drinking a way lot. Hayley had a couple of drinks because she justified it as people were "counting on her." I had too many drinks, but in the fun way.

It was good to relax.

The music was so loud, the beat pounding into my bloodstream, the lights strobing. Hayley ditched us to dance with some guy. Another man tried to dance in the middle of our circle and kept rubbing up against us, all handsy and stupid.

Emma was having a blast. One of her drunk friends kept drunkenly declaring how much they loved each other. There was a very handsome hipster sitting near the bar checking me out—

My eyes swept across the floor.

Magnus.

Zach was pushing through the crowds, scanning the room. Magnus followed him.

I jumped and waved. "Zach!" I danced up to Emma and yelled in her ear. "Zach is here!"

"Zach?" She stood on tiptoes. "Aw, Zach came to see me." She smiled. "He's the best."

I hugged her and announced, "I'm so glad you're in my life," crossing over into drunken love declarations.

A second later Zach snuck up behind her and swooped her in his arms and nuzzled into her neck. "Hey girl."

I turned to my guy. Magnus — hot, magnificent, but also, you could tell, kind of freaking out a little. Glancing at me in pieces, wincing at the lights and sounds. Trying to smile, but a little like a grimace. I put him out of his misery by throwing my arms around his neck, pressing up on him and saying, "I missed you."

"I missed ye too."

Zach leaned in. "We're going to dance to two songs, then head home, cool?"

Magnus said, "Aye, tis okay with me, Chef Zach."

Hayley danced over. "Are you ditching me?"

"I'm totally ditching you. See this hot guy in the skirt? He wants me. He wants to take me home. In a limo. So yeah, consider yourself ditched." I grinned. "Besides, there's another limo outside that will take you and the girls home."

"If I go home!" She waved over her shoulder as she danced back to the floor.

I turned to Magnus. "Will you dance with me? We can do that swaying thing we did at our wedding reception before we were so rudely interrupted?"

"Nae, the music is much louder and faster, we should partake of some real dancin', my lovely wife."

"Oh we should, should we?" We wound our way to the crowded dance floor and faced each other.

"You put your arm up like this." He ran a big hand up my

side so that it was over my head. It was a sultry move, looking into my eyes, stroking up my skin — a 'wanting me' kind of move.

All around us jostling, gyrating people bumped and tousled. The music was hard and loud, the strobe lights flashing. I could only see him in tiny half-second beats.

He said, "Now put your leg out like this and a hand on your hip. Then we..." He began hopping with his leg kicking out, so awkward and silly. I started giggling.

I kicked my leg in and out and did a couple of spinning pirouettes, not beautiful like my former dancing days, but passable and dorky. His hand on my hip, we jumped and jostled and occasionally clung to each other when people in the crowd bumped too close. It was aerobic and sweaty and hilarious. When the song wound down I threw my arms around his neck. "I love you so much."

"Aye, ye must, or my dancin' would have scared ye away. Tis nae as wiggly as the others."

Another song started. I yelled, "One more!" and we did it again, more, faster, until finally near the end of the song, he shook his head.

"The ribs are achin' a bit, Kaitlyn, I need tae rest."

I pulled him through the pressing crowd to the back of the room. A second later Zach and Emma appeared and a moment later we were all outside climbing into the limo.

Magnus helpfully pointed out, "We have beer."

"That's so upscale, we had champagne."

He drunkenly opened two bottles.

Emma and Zach passed because as Emma put it, "I planned to stay out later than this but now that we're headed home I really want to see Ben."

Zach said, "Me too."

"Want us to pick him up in the limo on the way home?"

Emma laughed, "Yes, but not actually, I'm not crazy. I want

to go home for a little while without Ben, then call grandma and make her get up in the middle of the night to bring him to me. She promised she would. That way I get the best of all worlds." She snuggled under Zach's arm.

"Wait! What's this?" I spied a can of spray cheese in the fridge. "Spray cheese!" I asked Magnus, "Did you have some?"

Zach answered, "Michael brought it, I wouldn't let him serve it. It's gross."

"Is it?" I ripped the plastic cap off the top. "Or are you jelly because you can't recreate the awesomeness that is the taste?" I raised my brow at Magnus. "Tilt your head back, Highlander, let me turn ye on to spray cheese."

"Tis in a spray can? Tis food?"

"Och Aye," I joked.

He tilted his head back. I sat up on my knees over him and sprayed cheese all over his tongue.

He closed his mouth, smiled and swallowed. "Tis good!"

I opened my mouth and sprayed it on my tongue and fake-groaned with pleasure. "Yum. I mean, that taste? Rubbery aged-cheddar cheese-food? Delicious."

Zach moaned and joked, "I can't even watch this, but I have to because I'm facing you in the car. This is a nightmare."

Emma tried to hide his eyes.

"Emma, you want some?"

"No, never, unless it's organic?" She giggled which was fun, I rarely heard Emma giggle.

I stared the back of the can, a little bleary at this point. "I can't tell."

"Oh what the hell. Close your eyes, Zachary."

Magnus and I both laughed. Magnus said, "Chef Zachary, I dinna ken this was your full name!"

Zach moaned, closed his eyes, and pulled his gangly body into a fetal position while I piled spray cheese on Emma's tongue.

I squirted some on Magnus's tongue again, then my own. Emma grimaced. "Ew. I forgot. That's not good."

Magnus laughed, "Tis delicious, but I prefer Chef Zach's cheese bread food, what was it called?"

"My grilled cheese sandwiches?"

"Aye! Verra delicious."

Magnus and I leaned together drinking from our beers. He said, "I rather like travelin' this way, I canna see the road."

I giggled. "This is the longest you've had your eyes open in a car."

"Aye, I can relax back here. I canna see the trees hurtlin' by, and nae one thinks me weak because of it."

"Men in the back of limos are generally seen as pretty intriguing. What did the boys say when you and Zach left the strip club?"

"They questioned my manhood. Twas an incredible amount of insults hurled at Zach and I, caused me rather tae miss my clan back home."

Zach said, "They're going to really be pissed when they remember we left with the limo."

"Och, aye. And when they are verra drunk and stumblin' home, they can consider the wisdom of callin' me Kaitlyn's whippin' boy." He chuckled. Zach laughed.

10 - KAITLYN

In our bedroom Magnus scooped me into his arms. "I dinna ken I could wait for ye this long." His hand rubbed up under the back of my dress, dove into my panties, and clutched my ass brusquely. "Och, aye." He pulled me closer and kissed my neck. He picked me up. I wrapped my legs around his waist and he carried me to the bed. He dropped me down.

I bounced and squealed. "Whoa, you want me."

I swear I saw him flinch. He shook his head and took a deep breath. His easy smile was gone. "Aye, I want ye."

"What just happened there?"

"Nae matter in it. I thought of somethin' I dinna want tae..."

I looked at him trying to tell what it was.

I sighed and lay back on the bed. "Was it something or someone that doesn't matter to us? Like a stupid brain hassle from the past like I get sometimes? Or is it bigger and we need to talk it through?"

"Twas much less than that, Kaitlyn. Twas nothin' tae talk through."

"Good, because that was the best date of my life. And it was with my husband. And it wasn't even a date, he came and picked me up in a limo. I want this night to keep going like that because we deserve some happiness: a night without the past, or drama, or tearful discussions. But if it is important, if it's something that you need to talk about, I will try to listen. Or Zach. Maybe Zach would be better if it involves..."

"I daena need tae talk of it. I will if I need tae, but I daena, I promise, mo reul-iuil. And it has been one of the great nights for me too."

"Okay, good. Then let's get back to it." I climbed to my knees and started pulling his shirt off over his head. I kissed his chest and felt him relax, his arms went around me.

His fingers fumbled with my zipper. "I daena — can ye turn around?"

I turned and swept my hair over my shoulder.

He pushed and pulled on the top of the zipper and mumbled, "Tis a marvel."

"What is, the zipper?"

"Och aye," he pulled at the top. "But..."

"Having trouble back there? You have to pull the lever up. That unlocks it and you glide the whole thing down."

He jiggled for a moment, then I felt the zipper pull down. He chuckled. The zipper went up and back down as he investigated it. Then with a quick scoop my dress was off and tossed across the floor. A hand on my breast the other arm around, lips on my neck.

I turned and started working on his belt but had trouble concentrating because he was super handsy — touching me everywhere, I couldn't get his kilt freaking off. "I can't—" I pulled away to focus on the belt.

He chuckled and helped me fumble with it. "I daena ken the sense of it."

"We're drunk."

"Aye, but tis necessary tae—" His belt pulled away and his kilt dropped to the ground.

"Jesus Christ, Magnus."

He looked down. "I have a terrific need for ye, mo reul-iuil."

"I can see. I thought you weren't wearing your sword to the strip club tonight?"

He scooped me down to my back on the bed. There was no pressing against him, he only fit between my legs, which was hilarious. I stifled my giggles. "Have you had this boner the whole night, is this what seeing strippers does to you?"

His mouth against my neck he chuckled. "I dinna open my eyes in the club."

I swatted his back playfully.

He said, "I want tae spend some time on ye, I also daena have the time—"

I squirmed up a bit pulling away from his insistent prick. Putting him at chest-level. "I don't know, you've been in a club all night—"

"Twas nae all night." His voice came from his chest, like from within a struggle, holding himself back, fighting to stay on top of it. His breath through his nose, came bullish and desperate. He kissed my breast, closed his eyes. "I left early tae come for ye, I dinna—"

"But still, you might have to beg nicely, Master Magnus. I might not be in the mood."

He groaned and placed his lips around my nipple, his fingers flitted and played between my legs. I watched his face, the struggle on it, and ran my hands down his shoulders. He closed his eyes and moaned.

"You want me?"

"Och, aye."

I sighed over-dramatically. "Convince me..."

His fingers dipped and played between my legs, I lost myself in it, my breaths coming faster, my—

"Ye are ready for me..."

"I am, god I do, but not yet..."

I arched my other breast toward his mouth. He sucked and nibbled then shook his head and dropped his forehead to my breast. "Please, Kaitlyn..."

I arched toward his mouth more. "You know it takes me twice as long..."

His mouth closed over my nipple, his eyes closed, his breath panting. He pulled away from my breast. "I ken tis true, but I canna — I need..." His dismay was evident.

I wrapped my legs around his back, tantalizingly close. I shifted down a bit, closer closer — he moaned and it was almost a growl — until I was a second away from him. My arms wrapped around his head, fingers wound through his hair, I whispered, "Say something in Gaelic."

His voice was wet, hot, breath and vibration, "Chan eil an t-sìde cho..." He paused and adjusted his hips edging closer.

I tightened my legs, holding him still, separate, apart. "More."

With a breath of air he said, "...math an-diugh 's a bha e an-dé."

"Oh god, Magnus," I whispered in his ear. "More."

He nuzzled his forehead to my shoulder. "Tha droch shìde ann — dreich."

I gasped, *okay*, and he slid into me with another groan. He rose up above me and drove into me over and over, delicious and desperate and intense and very very very fast. A few moments later and he was done. Collapsed on me. I felt his gratitude in every inch of his body, especially between my legs where he was finally calmed.

We kissed long and slow. "God, you were frantic for me. That was very hot."

"Aye." He kissed me. "I like ye verra much, mo reul-iuil, even when ye are tryin' tae kill me." He rolled off me onto his back and pulled the covers over us.

I laughed. "I hardly think you'll die just because I make you give me a little foreplay first. What were you saying in Gaelic?"

He chuckled. "I was speakin' of the weather."

"Oh my god, Magnus, I thought I recognized one of the words, the weather!"

"Twas all I could think on in my desperation for ye. I was talkin' about the weather in my head."

I laughed. "That is the freaking funniest thing I've ever heard."

He curled his face into my shoulder laughing. Then abruptly stopped, leaned on an elbow and watched the door.

I stopped to listen.

Zach's voice.

"Zach's mother is dropping off Ben, probably."

"Aye, I will rise tae check with the security." He went to his drawer and pulled on a pair of pajama pants and pulled a T-shirt over his head.

"That didn't look painful at all."

"I feel much better."

I sighed. It was good news, but also meant we had a lot to do.

I heard the indistinct mumbling of Zach and Magnus in the living room. A few chirps from Ben. Emma's whispers and the soft footsteps of Emma carrying Ben upstairs. But then Zach and Magnus continued murmuring.

And a moment later, they continued.

They were in the living room, near the tv. I pulled on a pair of sweatpants and a T-shirt to go join them.

I wish I hadn't.

They were both facing the weather channel and a dramatically red-colored blotch of radar-imagery over the center of Florida.

"What is it, a storm?"

Magnus put out an arm for me.

Zach said, "Yes, I noticed it as I was answering the door. This was a few hours ago, a big storm they didn't see coming. It lasted for a half hour and then dissipated quickly."

"That's right above Gainesville."

Zach said, "Yep."

I asked, "Do we go get the vessels?"

Magnus scrubbed his hand up and down on his face. "Twas just the first look for it. How many days did the vessel in Scotland take?"

I said, "There was a storm every day for almost two weeks before we got to it."

"Aye, we have some time. We have a wedding tomorrow, and I am too drunk tonight tae time journey."

"I agree. On Sunday we'll deal with it." We stood nodding at the screen as it changed to a car commercial. "That being said, Zach, I'm sorry, we probably shouldn't watch Ben tomorrow night after the wedding. Just in case."

"Definitely. No worries, we get it. I actually don't think Emma could leave him anymore anyway. That was a long time tonight. We've got the hotel tomorrow night. We'll take Ben with us."

"Thank you for understanding. Now get some sleep you're getting married tomorrow."

"See you in the morning."

Magnus kissed me on the forehead. "I need tae speak tae security on the back deck. Will ye return tae bed?"

"Actually, I'm kind of awake now. I'm going to sit on the couch and watch tv."

11 - KAITLYN

A wind pushed Magnus in through the door. "Tis cold outside tonight."

I was snuggled under a blanket, one of the soft fluffy ones, at one end of the couch. The tv softly flickered with an infomercial. I had been searching for something cool to watch, something entertaining. Instead I found mindless: an ad for a super strong tape. Magnus joined me on the couch, leaned on me between my legs. I placed a pillow under his head on my stomach and we pulled the covers up over both of us. He asked, "What is this then?"

"Shhhhh. It's an advertisement for a super strong rubber sealer." I twisted one of his curls around my fingers. "The guy on the tv cut a boat in half and now he's going to use the tape to seal it up."

Magnus watched the ad, his brow lowered, eyes squinted. "How much does this cost?"

"It's not that expensive, actually." The man tossed the boat in the water, got in it, and floated around. The boat was cut in half a second before, but now it was seaworthy. "If it works that good, it's cheap."

"We should order some, have it come by airplane."

I gave him a sad smile. "Yeah... But we don't really have a need for it. That's the thing about infomercials you have to use your willpower and not order stuff while you're drunk." I sighed. "I'm nervous."

He shifted to look up at me. "I ken ye are, mo reul-iuil."

I stretched his lock out long and twirled it back into place. "Grandma says when my stomach feels this way not to think of it as fear but excitement. She tells me I have nothing to fear, only things to do. I reminded myself of that when I walked down the aisle to you on our wedding day. But now — now it really is fear. I can't convince myself that it's not. I don't know how to talk to myself about it."

Magnus solemnly nodded. "Perchance ye need tae stop talkin' tae yourself on it, mo ghradh. When I am preparing for battle, I have tae ready myself with tasks. I sharpen my sword. I dress carefully so I daena forget anythin'. I ready my horse with attention and care. I focus on those tasks so I daena have time for the fear. Though tis there just behind my stomach."

"You get scared?"

"Aye. Sometimes. Mostly for ye. I am scared I winna be able tae keep ye safe."

We looked long into each other's eyes. I fiddled with his hair and took a deep breath. "So yeah, on second thought, we need to order some Flex Seal. Can you get me my purse from the counter?"

Magnus retrieved my bag from its spot beside the stack of books on childbirth. "I'm going to teach you how to drunk-order products we don't need."

I called the number on the screen and ordered two rolls of Flex Seal tape.

"Who are ye callin' for it?"

I pressed my hand to the bottom of my phone. "It's a lady somewhere in the Midwest, she's taking my order, then asking for my credit card number. Someone in a warehouse will put it in a box and mail it to me."

Magnus shrugged, "Och, so much."

While I was ordering it, I changed the channel. There was a commercial for an upside-down tomato plant grower-thingy. "Want one of those, Highlander?"

He watched for a moment. "Tis a plant that grows upside down? Aye, tis magical."

I dialed that number too. While I had that service rep on the line I changed the channel again. A man was selling chamois rags. I gestured toward the screen and Magnus smiled. "Och aye, ye see what it can do?"

"I do and it's only two payments of $19.95."

"I have nae idea if tis good."

"Trust me, it can clean that mess? It's good." I changed the channel while I gave that service rep my credit card number and found an elderly woman selling copper-bottom square pans.

"Order that one for Chef Zach," Magnus said.

I giggled. "Oh yeah, he'll love it." He would hate it. His pans were special, awesome, chef pans, definitely not infomercial pans.

Finally we came to a channel where a man was selling knives by cutting through tomatoes.

I said, "I don't know if it's because I'm drunk, but he looks drunk." He spun his knives and tossed something in the air and sliced through it but looked a little slurry while doing it.

"Aye, he's had a nip of the whisky before he came intae the tv."

I giggled. "Do you think he's inside the tv?"

Magnus laughed. "Tis the only explanation."

"Yeah, I guess so. Should I order the knives?"

"Aye, the man has almost chopped off a finger, perhaps if we order the knives he will climb out of the tv and go home tae bed."

I called the number, ordered the knives, gave her my credit card number, and Hayley's address and hung up the phone.

"I love you Magnus."

"I love you too, mo reul-iuil."

"That helped a lot. I'm almost tired enough for sleep. But there's one more thing to watch." I switched from the television channels to YouTube and searched: funny cat videos. I found a twenty minute compilation. "Settle in, Scottish Highlander, I'm going to introduce you to the best my culture has to offer."

A minute later we were both laughing. A few minutes past that sleep was on me, pulling me down, knocking me out.

I do remember this: the strong arms of Magnus lifting me from the couch, carrying me to our bed.

12 - KAITLYN

I entered the kitchen and announced, "Zach cover your ears. Maybe go la la la."

He dutifully covered his ears. Emma and Magnus turned to me. "There's good news and bad news today. Both are that I just started my period." I pulled down the Midol bottle from the cabinet and dropped three into my palm.

Magnus said, "Aye."

Emma said, "I was wondering, but didn't want to ask." I shot all three into my mouth and swallowed them down with water.

"Yes. The whole sordid thing is completely behind me, so we don't have to wonder or anything." I hugged Magnus and kissed him and said directly to him, "And I literally don't have to talk about it anymore, okay?"

"Och, aye."

"Good, I need coffee pronto." I smiled at Zach. "You can stop now." He dropped his hands.

"I just announced that I'm PMSing on your wedding day, and that I need coffee to try to get on top of it." I turned to Emma who was rocking Ben on her hip.

"Emma, I promise you, I'm on top of it. Not trying, I am. It's just you, only you, today." I pulled out my notebook. "Your appointment for your hair is in one hour. Then we come back here to get into your dress. Then the limo will take us to the – what's the weather?"

Zach said, "A fucking nightmare."

"See, that's why we got the booking on such late notice, because everyone knew the weather would suck. We won't go out to the beach. We'll do it in the reception room beside the dinner tables. It will be fine, right, Emma?"

She grinned as Zach brought her a big plate of waffles covered in strawberries and whipped cream. "It's already bigger, more magnificent than any wedding I ever thought I'd have."

"See, Zach? That's why you're marrying her, she's perfect. She sees gloomy, windy, stormy weather on her wedding day and she calls it magnificent."

A stack of waffles appeared in front of me. "...and you and Magnus will take Ben to an indoor gym to wriggle around on mats and beat pans against a wall, then you meet us here, give us Ben, and you go and we'll meet you there." I placed a line of checks down the list.

These weren't my 'finished' checks, these were the 'nervously checking' checks. But the good news was I had nervously checked them all. One task, done.

13 - KAITLYN

"You look really beautiful." I fluffed the simple veil down her back.

"It's not too much?"

"It's the perfect amount of much. Perfect."

Ben said, "Ma-ma!" And patted her on the breast.

"I've got to get married fast, this dress does not accommodate a breastfed baby." I put my arms out, "Ben want to go dancing?"

He climbed into my arms and I started dipping and swaying with him like a maniac before he figured out I wasn't as cool or as milky as Emma. "The music starts in three minutes. I'll leave you with your mom." I swooped Ben out the door. He was giggling. I was barely cramping. This wedding had been pulled off. In two weeks we had done it, beginning to end. Well not end, yet, almost end. Okay it hadn't started yet.

I met Magnus in the front row of the hastily arranged chairs set up in a square in the middle of the room. The tables were pulled away to the side and the guests would have to help us rearrange the room after the ceremony. No one could complain because there was a torrential downpour outside — sheets of rain, sideways, and everyone was on their best behavior about it so Emma wouldn't freak out. Of course Emma never freaked out. It was one of the great things about her.

Most of our friends stood along the edges of the room, around the tables, cramped in corners. The chairs in the middle were for family and that's where Magnus and I sat because we were family too.

Ben spied Zach standing at the front of chairs with the minister, and called, "Da! Da!" And everyone collectively oohed and ah-ed because that was really freaking cute. Zach chuckled. I jiggled Ben a bit to keep him happy and gave him his favorite chewy-teething toy.

The music started and Emma walked in. I clutched Magnus's arm. "Isn't she beautiful?"

"Aye, he is a lucky man."

"He is, he's so lucky. And we are too."

Magnus kissed me on my forehead and pressed his cheek there, making me feel just so loved.

The ceremony was simple and special. I could tell that Zach's family didn't think it was lavish enough. Emma's family didn't think it was religious enough. So I concentrated on Zach and Emma's faces: nervous, excited, in love. That was all I needed to see. They said they would love each other forever and ever until "death do us part." Tears welled up in my eyes.

Zach's lower lip trembled, Emma's eyes sparkled, and they nervous-laughed when Ben called, "Mama!" while they held hands. And that was it, they were declared married, officially a family though for years they had been one anyway.

Ben had enough of me. His arms outstretched I excused myself through the audience and handed him off to Emma after they 'kissed the bride' which was apparently a thing in their ceremony. I came back to Magnus with a smile.

~

With everyone pitching in it only took a moment for the tables and chairs to be set up again for the dinner. Magnus and I milled around talking to everyone. The only sucky part was Hayley and Michael were determined to stay on opposite sides of the room, so I had to choose my conversations. I said, "You're going to have to be a grown up here and at least let me talk to James."

"Fine, as long as you tell him to tell Michael that I'm fine, that I'm moving on, that I danced with a guy at the club last night. I almost stayed the night. I even thought about bringing him to this wedding but that would have been awkward, 'Hey, one-night-stand, want to go to a wedding with me tomorrow for my ex-fiancé's brother?'"

"There is no way to make that un-awkward."

"True that."

14 - KAITLYN

Magnus stood to make his speech.

He looked nervous and commanding at the same time. He wore a dark tuxedo coat with a white shirt and a kilt in deep colors of green and blue, his family tartan. He had a basket-handled sword strapped by a leather belt to his hip and his sporran was silver and fur. I was super proud of him and so glad he was home. This wedding was for Zach and Emma but there had been whispers for so long about me and my mysterious Scotsman that I was so glad to put them to rest, here, now.

"When I arrived on these lovely windswept shores..." He gestured toward the French doors. Outside the beach was being pummeled by sideways rain, whipping wind, and the sea grass was horizontal. A few people laughed. It was a truly crappy day to have a wedding.

"I had the good fortune tae meet my wife, Kaitlyn, on that first day and my life was changed forever. She introduced me tae an American grocery store, the controls for the winds in my house, and she brought Chef Zach intae my life. And Emma."

He spoke directly to Zach. "Ye have been a friend, a confidante, and a brother. And through the years ye have become like family tae Kaitlyn and me, with Emma and your son Ben who has made our lives so much noisier and more joyous than before. I find it hard tae imagine my life without ye."

He looked around the room with a warm smile. "I am only regrettin' that I have nae control on the weather, I would have wanted clear skies for him on this happy day."

He raised his glass toward Mr and Mrs Greene, "It has been a pleasure meetin' ye, ye've raised a fine son." He raised his glass toward Emma's parents, "A congratulations tae ye for gainin' such a caring son for your daughter." He raised his glass to Emma. "I dinna mean tae leave ye from it, Emma, goes tae ye as well."

Tears were streaming down her cheek, I could barely see them through my own. "That's okay, Magnus, that was enough, it was awesome."

He raised his glass higher and said, "This next part is a toast my Uncle Baldie has said at every wedding since I was a wee lad." His voice became so Scottish it was almost unrecognizable. "May the best ye've ever seen, be the warst ye'll ever see. May the moose, nor Magnus, ne'er lea' yer pantry wi' a teardrap in his eye." Zach laughed. "May ye all keep hail an' hearty til ye're auld enauch tae die. May ye be jist as happy as we wish ye now tae be. Slainte!"

We all raised our glasses, "Slainte!" We drank as Magnus sat down.

I called across the table, "Zach, do you have something you'd like to say?"

He half-stood and grumbled, in the tux we made him buy, and waved his hand. "No. She knows how I feel, I don't need to waste your time watching me fucking cry like a ba—" He started to sit back down but looked at Ben in Emma's lap and shook his head. He stood with fits and jerks. "Okay, yeah, I will." He looked down on Emma. "You know I love you?"

She nodded her head looking up at him, crying. Ben looked from her face to his.

"I love you because you're the best person I ever met. Ever. Without question. And thank you for Ben. He's awesome. I'm grateful every fucking day for both of you. You know it?"

She nodded.

"Good, because I'll say it in front of everyone but I want you to know it already. This is just a party. I love you every other day too."

"I know it every day."

"Good. Let's get on to the drinking and dancing, people. Thank you for coming." We all raised our glasses and again chorused, "Slainte!"

I rolled into Magnus's arm and kissed his neck. "That was awesome, Magnus. And you didn't even have to mention that whole part about paying for the wedding. I liked it better. And Zach was practically sobbing."

"Och, aye, today is a day tae honor Zach and Emma, not the great and mighty Magnus, there is time enough for that." He grinned.

"True that." He jiggled my face with his shoulder so that I met his lips with a long sweet kiss. I sighed as warmth flowed from my heart. "I love you."

"I love ye too, Madame Campbell. You are a bonny lass and a fine wife."

"Why thank you, Master Magnus, you are a pretty great, dreams-come-true Highlander, and I'm kind of a little hot for you right now, too bad I'm on my period and sort of in a cramping, grumpy, funk."

"There's always tomorrow."

"Yes, I like we can think that way." We kissed again.

15 - KAITLYN

A DJ played music. Zach and Emma danced to Oasis's Wonderwall and it was a little awkward, but there was no way Zach would dance to anything more pop than that. They invited more people to the dance floor as the song was very long. Magnus slow danced with me, my hand clutched his, his hand on my back. I whispered, "Just sway like this."

He listened to me perfectly and I melted in his arms. Slow dancing with my husband was a lot like being in love with him, like he filled my lungs with air but also took my breath away.

Then he stood to the side and looked handsome while I danced with Hayley and looked, I hoped, adorable. My dress was a deep gray tulle with simple rhinestone straps over my shoulders. My hair was swept into an updo. I wore simple diamond earrings and strappy rhinestone heels.

After three more songs. Hayley and I collapsed in chairs at one of the tables. She said, "I am exhausted, dancing last night, now tonight..."

"Are you going to see him again?"

"Well, I don't know if you noticed, but he was shorter than me. Not a big fan of that. But we'll see."

Tyler dropped into the seat beside me. "Katie can I talk to you?"

My eyes went big because he startled me. I hadn't crossed paths or even needed to say a word to him for weeks. I glanced over at Magnus's back, not sure why, but he was in a loud jovial conversation with James and Michael.

Hayley said, "Fine, I guess I'm unwanted. You look great, by the way, Tyler, the tux suits you. I'll go talk to the other unwanted ladies." She gestured with her head to the tables that seated Emma's aunt and Michael's cousin and grabbed the half empty bottle of wine off our table. "If I take wine maybe I can get them discussing dirty scenes in that raunchy show I watched last week, they totally look the type." She literally cackled as she walked to their table.

"What's up?" I asked Tyler.

"Have you been watching the news?"

"No, I've been in wedding mode — what do you mean, the storms?"

His eyes squinted. "What storms?"

"Nothing, no storms, I mean — the hurricanes, just with the weather outside and the flooding and — what did you mean?"

"I heard your name on the news last night—"

"What the...?"

He glanced around the room. "I was feeling everyone else out about it, no one else heard the story, so I don't know, maybe you can hire a lawyer..."

"What are you talking about?"

He pulled out his phone and scrolled down a page. "There's a big YouTube feud going on, that guy you used to be engaged to—"

"Braden?"

"He and his girlfriend broke up."

"How do you know all this?"

"When I met you I thought I recognized you, I follow lots of YouTubers, mostly the gamers, but this feud involves some gamers so..."

"Okay, they broke up, good."

"Well, they're being real assholes to each other. Now they've got other YouTubers joining in, and they're really playing dirty against each other. She's pulled you into it."

My eyes went wide. "YummyBabe? Why?"

"Because she's not nice, but she says he beat her. He says she cheated. They're both saying terrible things and she's released some of his private videos and photos. You're in them."

My stomach sank to the ground. "Oh god, what kind of videos?"

But I knew.

Tyler took a deep breath. "With a quick search of your maiden name, you can find them, but I don't recommend it. Braden didn't call you about it? He's lawyered up."

"Crap, crap, crap."

"The case is going to be a big one because it's about privacy, videos, the #MeToo movement, what's publishable, and a big issue right now, revenge porn—"

"Holy shit, Tyler, did you just say revenge porn, porn?"

"I didn't watch it but it looks like it's kind of porny. I don't think you filmed it to be shown to the public."

I didn't. Years ago, so sure Braden and I were going to be together forever, I let him film me while we had sex. I said dumb things. I did stuff pretending to be sexier and more raunchy than I actually was. Embarrassing, pornstar kind of bullshit. Because he loved me and we were going to get married and he was never going to betray me with...

And now it was public.

Now it was not only public but part of a ratings war between children pretending to be influential and important influencers. With brains the size of walnuts.

I glanced over at Magnus. He was still in conversation but his eyes flitted to me in discussion with Tyler. I decided, a split second decision, to go for the coverup.

So I smiled.

Tyler followed my eyes to Magnus and back.

I said, while smiling, "So what are the odds that I can ignore this and it will go away?"

"If no one watches Fox and Friends then you're cool."

I groaned, still trying to smile. "Mom and Dad will know by the end of the day."

"You need a lawyer. I researched it, you can file Take Down Notices with the websites carrying the videos."

"I'll probably need a public relations person to get on top of the story."

"Maybe... How will your husband take it, he seems pretty traditional?"

I stared at Magnus for a moment.

"I have no idea..."

Magnus was watching me, his eyes squinted.

"I'll figure something out."

"Sure, I wanted you to know in case someone blindsided you with the information. The press is involved, which means they might want to talk to you—"

It hit me that someone might be looking for me, lawyers, or a reporter, or Braden might want to try to explain.

"Crap, this is coming at a terrible time."

"Anything I can help you with?"

I shook my head. "No, not, no, not at all. I'll figure it out, thanks." I excused myself to go to the restroom to try to get on top of my heartbeat.

~

"What was Tyler sayin' tae ye?"

"Tyler? Oh, nothing, not really. Just something he saw on the news, I'll—"

Emma's mom came up just then. "Should we do the cake now?"

"Of course! Yes, let's do the cake!" I rushed to get Emma and Zach for the cake cutting and to tell the DJ to fade the music. The whole time I was smiling like crazy, trying to mask my internal freak-out. What had I done the night I was filmed? What had I shown? I didn't remember watching it after, but I do remember really getting into it and god — I was so embarrassed. All these people, this whole wedding full of people could all watch it by tonight.

Emma's old uncle Jim, he could have already watched it. I could never show my face in public again. Why did I do shit like that? I was young, but still, here I was a married woman, to a 'traditional' man, and I was a freaking porn star.

"Emma, want me to hold Ben while you and Zach cut the cake?"

"Sure!"

She passed me Ben and I could barely focus on him, my mind was whirring so much. Was my name on the video? Was my face visible? The camera hadn't been on a tripod, Braden had been focusing and pointing it all over me and — I was beginning to wonder if I might pass out. My head was tingling and my mouth was dry and my hands were shaking.

I found Magnus and wordlessly handed him Ben.

He watched my face. I ran a trembling hand down my neck.

What if someone was snooping and found out my address? What if my sex tape exposed my private details and the guys from the future found us? What if Magnus was captured because I was on YouTube writhing and moaning in bed with another man. Shit. Blackness swooped around the edges of my sight, like a tunnel, I was going to—

16 - KAITLYN

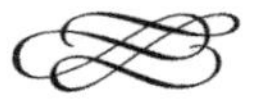

"Katie?"

Emma was hovering over me.

Magnus's worried face was over her shoulder.

"Why am I on the ground?"

"You fainted right as we were about to cut the cake."

"Jesus Christ, why am I such a freaking drama queen?" I sat up. "It's all the Midol I took. Probably." I dusted off the front of my dress.

Magnus said, "Go slow gettin' up."

I gave him my hand. "I'm cool, just having a moment." I looked around at all the faces. "No worries, just Katie trying to be the center of attention as usual." With Magnus's help I hefted myself to my feet. "You try to dance in shoes this high, it's a wonder we can stay upright at all."

Emma said, "You're sure you're okay?"

"One hundred percent. Sorry about that. Go back to the cake-cutting. It's probably low blood sugar, I need cake."

Once all the focus turned away from me, towards the cake, which was a beautiful round three-tiered number, and I could allow myself to look weak again, I rolled up in Magnus's arm and clutched his strong shoulders. He kissed my hairline. He kissed my ear. He kissed my temple.

What if this was too much for him to understand? He thought tiny men might live inside our television — how would he grasp the nuances of 'Hey, your wife once fancied herself quite, um, acrobatic in the bedroom and allowed a man to film her performance. Now that man has released that video into the public. Men can watch your wife for pleasure.' How would he feel about me then?

I held on to him blinking back my tears.

"Kaitlyn, are ye okay?"

I nodded my head, pressed to his shirt, and took a deep breath. Then another. I said, "You smell good. Like soap and incense and the love of my life."

"Aye, Kaitlyn, and in a moment I will smell of vanilla cake too."

I smiled. Behind me the guests were laughing. I turned to see Emma and Zach with cake smeared on their faces from the traditional 'first bite gone wrong.' I joined the applause, the laughing, and did everything in my power to put my worry aside.

I would Google the video later. And I would talk to Magnus, tonight. At the latest I would talk to him about it when we jumped to 1703. That way he wouldn't be able to see the video even if he was curious.

No sense dwelling on it before then.

The cake was delicious and helped a lot. I ate my slice, standing face to face with Magnus, looking up at him, my mouth overly full of cake and frosting and he sweetly kissed the edge of my lips for a bit of the crumbs there.

I felt a lot better actually.

Fuck Braden. Fuck his girlfriend and their whole sordid

mess. I was a rich, mature, married woman. I was beyond sex tape drama. Whatever.

Music started and Hayley rushed me. "Dance with me?"

"Yes! I thought you'd never ask. But how did Ed Sheeran end up on Zach's playlist?"

"I think Emma decided there was too much Blink-182 for this crowd."

I kissed Magnus on the cheek and turned to the dance floor as the doors at the far end of the room opened, our security guard stuck his head in, and gestured for Magnus. Magnus crossed to the door.

I watched him while the world slowed down around me.

Hayley had a full-blown dance floor wiggle happening. The aunts, an uncle, a few cousins, and Emma were dancing while I stood stock still watching Magnus approach the security guard and, oh crap, their faces intent, their discussion fast and serious. Magnus looked over his shoulder at me as he stalked out the door.

I followed.

17 - KAITLYN

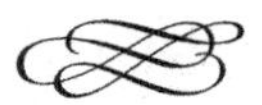

When I made it to the front hallway of the Ocean Club, the door at the far end was closing. "Where's Magnus?"

Jimmy, the security guard, said, "Lady Mairead is here, he went into that room to speak to her."

"Oh no, oh no, oh, crap."

I timidly knocked. "Magnus, it's me."

Magnus opened the door.

"She's here?" I could see her over his shoulder. The room was a sitting room that Emma had used for dressing. Her dress-bag, makeup kit, and Ben's diaper bag were on the coffee table.

Lady Mairead said, "Good evenin', Kaitlyn, I see ye are barging in where ye are nae wanted." She dropped a raincoat to the ground and leaned a dripping umbrella against the wall. "I was hoping tae speak tae Magnus alone."

I shook my head. "No, that's... no. I want to hear what's happening, it involves me."

She raised her brow and smiled, her greasy, malevolent, twisted smile. I used to think it was a condescending smile, a little overly pretentious because of her placement in life, but now I knew it was a true 'bitch smile'. And I wanted to knock it off her face.

Magnus had a sword. I could yank it from its scabbard and swing it at her.

She said, "Not really, but suit yourself."

Magnus wasn't speaking. He looked like he was trying to get on top of his fury.

"How did you find us?" I asked.

Her outfit came from the future: filmy material, slacks, a jacket with fur at the collar and wrists. It was punctuated with diamonds at her ears, twice as big as mine. She looked regal and wealthy, pilfering from history was paying off very well for her.

Another knock on the door, I opened it. Zach was standing there. His eyes flitted around the room and fell on Lady Mairead and stayed there though he spoke to Magnus. "How's everything, you cool?"

Magnus didn't take his eyes off her. "Aye. I am sorry for the trouble, we will keep it confined tae this room."

Lady Mairead rose. "Chef Zach, I was verra pleased tae hear of your wedding today. I have brought ye and Emma a gift." She leaned over a burlap sack, ran her fingers over five different frames, eyeing them, then pulled out a rolled-up piece of paper. She held it out for Zach.

He said, "I don't think..."

"Daena argue, Chef Zach. Whatever your feelings for me, tis a once in a lifetime drawing and ye should accept it in the manner tis given, with your best future in mind." She untied the piece of twine and unfurled the paper. It was blank. "Tis one of Leo's invisible maps. You will see if ye shine it under a light."

Zach held it up to the lamp in the room and tried to look through the paper.

I said, "By Leo, you mean...?"

"Of course," she smoothed the front of her jacket. "Now, Chef Zach, can ye leave us tae our discussion?"

"Sure, um," he was still investigating the paper. "Thank you, Lady Mairead. Um, Magnus, need me to stay?"

"Nae need for it, ye can return tae your wedding."

"Okay, sure." He rolled the gift and departed while retying the twine around its middle.

Lady Mairead said, "Remind me, I have some art for you as well, Magnus. You should call the head of collections at the National Gallery to have them appraised."

I asked, "Do you have the provenance for the paintings? I was told I need the history to get them appraised and confirmed, I—"

Lady Mairead curtly said, "I've got letters from the artists, giving the works to me. Will that help?"

"Yes, maybe, yeah."

Lady Mairead crossed her arms and tapped her chin, appraising me.

I looked away, but decided that made me seem weak, so I looked back.

I asked again, "How did you find us?"

She looked at me pointedly. "It was easy enough tae, as you know, Kaitlyn, ye art oft in the news stories this week."

I huffed.

She watched my face and Magnus's in turns.

I was feeling squirmy under her gaze. Now I wished I had pulled Magnus aside and told him as soon as I heard.

Her smile widened. "You haena told him the truth of it I see. I imagine ye daena want him tae ken it. Tis sordid the way ye have carried on with other men—"

Magnus's jaw set. "She has told me of it." His eyes cut to me quickly. "We daena have secrets, she tells me everythin'."

She made a humphing noise. "Well, I believe your trust is misplaced, but how you run your household and keep your wives is your own business I suppose, Magnus, though divorce is an option. It wasn't in 1703, but you could now."

"What is your business here then, if ye arna involved in mine?" His chest was rising and falling fast with his breaths. He stood at one side of the room, I stood two feet away.

Lady Mairead stood across the space.

She said, "We should sit, I have come tae see ye from a great distance and I am feelin' the pain of it. I daena mean tae disquiet ye, but tis time tae speak on the matter. We have much tae discuss." She dropped to the couch and gestured toward the chairs across from her.

I glanced at Magnus. He shook his head. I stepped closer to his side.

"There has been much disorder in your kingdom, Magnus. Twas quite a predicament ye left. I have been feeling the misfortune a great deal. Your ribs have healed?"

"Aye."

"Losing Donnan was a true blow." Her eyes fell on me. "Kaitlyn has told you the full story of it? How she ended up and where?"

Magnus sat down in the chair opposite her and leaned his elbows on his knees. "I said we have nae secrets."

I didn't want to sit in the other chair, it felt too gosh darn far away. I perched on the arm of Magnus's chair.

She nodded. "I see. I will get on with it. Your Uncle Samuel has decided tae take your throne. He is lobbyin' the governors tae allow him tae ascend and without ye tae argue against him, they may well allow him tae take power. He is formidable. He has killed or dismissed most everyone that was favorable tae ye. When ye return twill be quite—"

"I daena intend tae return."

She leveled her gaze on him, "He wants tae kill ye. What would ye do, hide? I found ye as soon as I decided tae. The only reason he hasna found ye here is because he hasna the brains tae think on it well. But he will find ye. He will kill ye and Kaitlyn will be taken tae the future and punished as the murderer of Donnan. You would never be safe from it."

A growl came from Magnus's throat.

She continued, "Since ye have abandoned me tae deal with the troubles ye left, I have kept him from findin' ye. When I realized he sent men tae attack my brother's castle Balloch, I proved tae him that ye were nae there and encouraged them tae withdraw. I have kept your home here in the New World a secret from him. It has been a dreadful amount of work tae accomplish this."

She paused and watched him for a moment.

I could hear the faint beat of a Katy Perry song through the door. It was incongruous to have a party in the other room, and a meeting like this about futures and battles and death and 'no where to hide,' happening here.

"I daena have control of the situation as I did with Donnan. With Donnan in power I simply had tae deliver ye and the throne was yours. Now I must accomplish a great deal more."

"Twas nae so simple. I had tae fight. I almost lost my life."

She shrugged, "In comparison our current troubles make those battles seem easy.

"You are speakin' using 'we' and 'our'. I am nae a part of it."

"You have a death wish. It pains me tae hear ye say it." She stared into space for a moment. It didn't seem like she was listening to the songs, but she asked, "Magnus, have you become accustomed tae the music?"

"Tis still verra loud, but I have grown used tae it."

"I have as well, twas Chef Zach that started us on it, you remember. I haena gotten used tae the images though. The lights bother me greatly. I greatly prefer the turn of the twentieth century, twas verra civilized and nae quite so loud."

They both sat quietly for a moment.

Why the hell didn't I wear a dirk under my dress? I could spring on her, stab her through the heart, become a double murderer. I might of course not survive the trauma.

She said, "Since ye seem intent tae break your vow tae me, Magnus, I have been considering my paths forward. As I see it, I have two. Samuel is married, but she is a ridiculous woman. I should bed him I think, become his mistress, then his wife. He is verra stupid and I could easily convince him of my worth."

"You wouldna do it."

"Oh I would. He has a son. I could throw my wisdom and protection behind his bloodline and ascend tae power in this way. Twould be comforting, I suppose, tae use my skills in service of someone who would be grateful for them. I wouldna have tae listen tae them say they daena want the throne."

She shifted in her seat, irritated at the thought. "The problem with this scenario is my own son would be an enemy of the throne. Samuel wouldna trust ye tae remain uninterested. He would want tae kill ye and if I protected ye twould be my death warrant. This path for me, taking Samuel's side, guarding his bloodline, would mean I canna protect ye as I have been accustomed tae do and ye would have tae remain hidden for all your days without my help."

Magnus scowled.

"The second path before me is one where ye accompany me tae the future. You secure your throne. And ye protect your own bloodline and mine."

Magnus said, "But—"

"Before you speak on it, Magnus, I want ye tae understand, you arna only speakin' for yourself. Tis easy for ye tae hide. You could even hide Kaitlyn if ye could keep her under control. But there is the matter of your child."

Magnus stared down at his hands. "I will protect my family."

"Will ye? Because if you and I choose tae allow Samuel's bloodline tae take the throne, your son will be a direct threat to Samuel's son. I daena ken how Samuel would allow your son tae live. Bella is in hiding, but—"

My heart dropped to my feet.

Oh god.

Magnus's head shot up, his eyes focused. "What are ye...?"

She smiled, nodding her head as if pleased. "Ah yes. And have ye told your wife about your mistress?"

I drew in air and my back went completely straight. I stiffened. I stiffened so much I might never relax again.

"She was nae my mistress."

"Oh really? She lived with you. Donnan said he was oft in your apartments and would see her unclothed in your bed. You haena shared this with your wife? You daena keep secrets from her?"

Magnus said to me, "Daena listen tae her, Kaitlyn, she is tryin' tae start trouble between us." He reached back for my hand.

I brushed it away and did the only thing I could do, fold my hands in my lap and stare at the wall across from me. A watercolor painting, a common one here on the Island, a local artist who painted beach scenes, a wash of tan, a blur of blue for the ocean, a flick of a tiny black brush for a flying seagull — what the fuck was I thinking about while my husband discussed his son by another woman?

I emerged from my mind-freak to see my husband run his hands through his hair with a groan. "How do we — tis mine? It could be Donnan's..."

Lady Mairead said, "Tests have been run. The baby is yours nae Donnan's. Ye can see for yourself."

She held out a bundle of white paper, folded in thirds. Magnus unfolded them and smoothed them out to read. I looked over his shoulder. There were three columns of numbers and letters and at the top Magnus's name, another name, Bella, and a third column, Unborn Child. I was looking at my husband's paternity test, but I couldn't see it because my vision was swimming in and out of focus with the tears that were filling my eyes. Furious tears.

Plus Magnus's hand was shaking.

He said, "I canna tell what it..." He looked confused and dismayed by all the numbers that meant something important but wouldn't outright say it.

Lady Mairead said, "It says that you are the father. The DNA markers connect ye directly."

Magnus scowled down at the page. He flipped to the following page. Donnan's name topped a column of numbers, a few with minus signs. He flipped back to the top page, none of the number and letter combinations in Magnus's column had minus signs. He tossed the papers to the coffee table.

I tried to swallow my rage.

Lady Mairead said, "Bella has gone intae hiding because Samuel meant tae kill her." She pulled a square pale pink envelope from her pocket and held it out. "She sent this for ye, Magnus, so you would ken where she is with your unborn son."

Magnus refused to take it. "I daena—"

I leaned over the coffee table, and snatched it from Lady Mairead's hand.

She looked incredulous. "You want tae read what the mistress says tae your husband?"

"No. I don't." I folded my arms with the note under them pressed to my chest. Petulant. "But Magnus will, and it's for him to read, not you."

Lady Mairead scoffed. "I have always said I rather like you Kaitlyn. You haena been the best wife for Magnus, I do regret the alliance, but I see a great many familiar qualities tae myself."

"I'm nothing like you." I continued staring at the painting, my trembling hands stuffed under my arms, the note sealed by another woman gripped in my fingers. I didn't want to touch it, but what if Magnus reached for it, wanted it?

I would probably totally freak out. And by freak out I meant, I had no idea, but it would probably be freaky.

I could feel him glance at my face, but I kept my eyes averted. Fury was riding my breaths. But I didn't know who I was most furious at — Lady Mairead and her evil, malicious ways? Magnus for breaking his vows? Myself for being here in the middle of this nightmare without a good escape route? Nothing to do but sit here and take this?

"So I have two choices, Magnus. The one, I back Samuel. You and Kaitlyn hide together, live your happy life here in Florida, or anywhere really. Bella would be left tae protect your son alone. Samuel winna want him tae live, but twould be none of your business tae worry on it. Or two, you come take your throne and protect your son as your heir. I ken which choice I prefer, but I need ye tae decide which one ye will be able tae live with."

Magnus's hands were clasped. His mouth was pressed to them. He looked about to explode, holding himself back. His face held a storm. A lightning storm, wind and rain, torrents of it. The kind of storm that bent a human to its will.

He couldn't think with that kind of storm inside.

I couldn't think watching the torment buffet him.

Magnus.

He just heard he has a son.

I wanted to kill him.

My heart also broke for him.

"No." It was from inside of me, so abrupt and sudden I didn't really understand why I said it. No, to what? To whom? Just, no?

Lady Mairead leveled her eyes waiting for an explanation.

Why was I speaking out of turns? Again. And I wasn't even part of the conversation, not really. I was just one of the choices.

"You can't make this choice, Magnus. Don't."

"I have—"

I turned to Lady Mairead. "He can't make this choice."

"He has tae."

I turned on the arm of his chair and spoke directly to him. "You can't make it. How can you? You can't. And I can't watch you make it. No matter what you choose I can't let you make that choice — whatever you choose it won't be the right one. It will kill me to see you choose it. You can't. But I can, okay?" His brow drew down even more.

"Magnus, you have to let me make this choice for you. It has to be mine." I clutched his hand. "I know the man you are, you can't make it."

"But I—"

"I'm serious, if you choose me, what becomes of us? It's us, alone, hiding forever? Could we even have children? What if I can't? How long before you hate me for having chosen me?" I pulled his hand closer to my heart and held it against my chest.

"And if you choose her, if you choose your son... I can't ever forgive you for that. There isn't a choice here for you to make, but there is a choice for me to make. Let me."

"Kaitlyn, ye canna leave me."

I stroked down his jawline. "I can't leave you. I won't. But let me decide for you. Trust me in this. I'm the only one who can do it without tearing us apart — if you'll let me."

He searched my face for a long moment then nodded. "Okay, mo reul-iuil, okay you decide."

Lady Mairead asked, "You would live by Kaitlyn's wishes?"

"Aye, I live by my wife's wishes, I serve as she decides."

I took a deep fortifying breath. "Magnus will fight for his throne. He will come to the future and he will be the king. He will protect his—" The word caught in my throat. "Son. And... Yeah. He will."

"You heard your wife, Magnus, do ye agree?"

His pause was long and worrisome. He stared down at the carpet before him, then said, "Aye."

"Good. I do need tae rest before we go tae your kingdom—"

Magnus said, "I have made a promise tae Quentin that I will bring him home. I must do that afore anythin' else."

Lady Mairead sighed. "Fine, I suppose it can't be helped, you can handle that first, though I will need a gesture from ye tae prove ye will comply with your wife's decision. A promise that you will come tae the future ready tae fight."

"You have my word."

"Your word isna good enough."

I stood. "What do you want then?"

Magnus said, "Daena, Kaitlyn."

"It's fine, Magnus, really. I'll agree to just about anything to Get. This. Bitch. Out of our lives."

Lady Mairead pulled a small leather-covered book from her pocket. She placed it on the side table, opened to a blank page, and placed a ball-point pen across the pages. The pen was printed with, "Loving Amelia Island!" down the side.

"I would like ye tae write here, Kaitlyn, where ye were on — let's see, the mornin' of the third day of November, the year 2019?"

I said, "That was a couple of weeks ago. I woke up at home—"

"Please write there the time you woke up and the address of your bedroom."

"Oh." My heart sank. I scrawled the address of our home.

"Then where did ye go?"

"I was in a race, in Jacksonville."

She gestured for me to write it down. "The time and the address."

I wrote that down too.

"And then?"

"I ate dinner at home with Magnus and then—" I glanced over my shoulder at him. "We went to bed early because I was tired."

"Write the time ye were home for dinner and the time ye went tae bed." She watched me write. "Put the date at the top. Include the year. Now sign the bottom of the page."

I signed it. A possible death warrant for myself. I had to comply or I would be dead two weeks ago. There was no way I could go back and warn myself without throwing everything that had happened, all the happy moments between then and now, out of whack.

Lady Mairead picked up the book, closed it, and pushed it into her coat pocket. "If ye daena come tae the future, ye canna hide from me. I will go tae this date and Kaitlyn and I will discuss the issue. Dost ye understand me, Magnus?"

Magnus said, "Och, aye."

I raised my chin. "Yes, we understand."

Lady Mairead returned to her seat.

I drew a deep breath and another standing between Magnus and Mairead. "And about you needing a place to rest tonight." My words started faint, but I made them louder and more firm to make up for a weak beginning. "There is no way in the world that I am allowing you to come to my home. It's my home, not yours. You aren't welcome. I will call and get you a hotel room. The security guard will take you."

Lady Mairead said, "Aye Kaitlyn, keep your home tae yourself. You should enjoy the peace of it. Twill be a matter of days before your past catches up tae ye and the press is on your doorstep. Then all of Samuel's army will arrive soon after tae bring ye tae justice."

Magnus said, "Call about the room, Kaitlyn. Security and I

will take Lady Mairead there. She will leave first thing in the mornin'."

"Yes, she will." I smoothed down my dress. "Yes. She will. Magnus, can I speak to you in the hall?"

In the hall Magnus pulled me into his arms. I cowered there against his chest and let him surround me. We didn't say a thing.

There were too many emotions and things to say, but it all had to wait.

Finally I pulled off and stepped back.

He held my face and wiped my tears away with his thumbs.

"I'm probably a mess and there's a whole wedding reception to deal with."

"You look beautiful and..."

I showed him a sad smile. "What should we do with this?" I held up the envelope.

"I daena want it."

"I get that. Me too. But you might need to know." I tucked it into his chest pocket. "You're going with her to the hotel?"

"I should. I will guard outside her room. You and I have a lot tae talk of, I daena want tae go without speaking tae ye on it, but I daena trust her tae..."

"Yeah, me neither."

I watched his face. "Magnus, come home in the morning. After you see her off, come right home. Even if you—"

"Even if I — what?"

"If you travel with Lady Mairead, if you need to go see the woman who..."

"I daena. I winna go."

I straightened his tuxedo jacket and his tie. "But if you do have to, come back in the morning, November 25, so I don't worry."

"Aye. I will be home in the morning."

"I'm going to organize the hotel room for her. Then there's the rest of this party..."

"Aye, ye should do that. We daena want tae ruin the night for Chef Zach and Emma."

"Okay."

He kissed me once on the lips and left to speak to the guard.

18 - KAITLYN

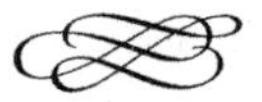

Hayley rushed me as soon as I returned to the reception. "What did she do? What did she say?"

I adjusted a gift that was shifting from underneath the pile of wedding presents. "I had to make another bargain with my creep-tastic mother-in-law and yeah, it's life and death and this is how she rolls."

"I'm sorry honey, but at least you have Magnus now, where is he by the way?"

"He's leaving with her, but not in a bad way, he's taking her to her hotel. Because she is not staying in my guest room."

"That is the truth. I don't even think she should get to stay on the island. So we get to dance now?"

"Yes. Let me hug the bride first."

I found Emma at a table laughing with Zach. I leaned down to speak to them. "First, I'm sorry I was gone for so long. Magnus has taken her to a hotel."

"Jim drove them?"

"Yep, so for now, we're unprotected, like the old days before life got all drastic and insane. But hey, enough about me, how's the wedding so far?" I looked at my phone. "It's almost over actually, we only have the place booked for another thirty minutes. I'm going for a drink and I'll be dancing with Hayley, but I'm totally at your service — anything you need?"

"No I'm perfect Katie, thank you so much, the night was really great."

"Good." I hugged her because I felt kind of overcome. I went to dance it out to pop wedding music on a dance floor crowded with Emma and Zach's relatives.

Two songs later we watched Emma, Ben on her hip, and Zach rush out the door with umbrellas over them to their waiting car. We maybe should have thrown something at them for good luck but they were pelted with rain and none of us wanted to go out in order to manage it.

Hayley hung around for a bit and helped me load the presents into garbage bags to protect them from the rain and Emma's dad and uncle raced them out to their car. They were planning to give me a ride home because Magnus and the security guard, Jim, left in mine. Hayley asked if I needed her to come home with me and I told her no Magnus would come home. I just didn't tell her when he was coming home.

I hugged her goodbye and we all rushed to our waiting cars.

Emma's dad helped me cart all the presents to the house and then left me for the night in my big new home, all alone.

I changed into pajamas and grabbed a beer from the fridge.

I opened the rain-dripping garbage bags, pulled out the presents, and stacked them on the dining room table. I made it pretty. I toweled off the ones that were wet. I played my Spotify, 'I'm doing great!' Playlist with lots of Ariana Grande and Katy

Perry. About thirty minutes later there was a soft knock on the front door. Jim's knock.

"Katie I wanted you to know I'm back. I'm checking outside. I'll be on the back deck."

"Thanks Jim."

"Magnus was set up outside of her hotel room. He said he'd be back first thing in the morning."

"Sure, of course, thank you Jim. Need any food or anything?"

"Nah, I ate, see ya in the morning."

He left to walk the perimeter of the house, keep me safe, surround me with protection. All I could do was sigh. I turned on the television and watched The Office, season 3, an episode I had watched too many times before. I still laughed and that felt good.

Magnus and I had been looking forward to a new kind of night, taking care of Ben, just the three of us. It would have been a chance to be 'parents' even if it was just pretend. And that was... I really really wanted to take care of a baby, like I would have been if I hadn't lost ours.

Plus we were going to be mostly alone in our house, something we rarely got. I thought back on that first night, when I spent the night in Magnus's room, while he slept in the chair.

That had been a lovely night full of fresh hope and getting to know each other. We needed more of that. Our time together was always brief and too far apart.

But he would be home tomorrow morning.

I went to the laptop on the kitchen counter, a stack of midwifery and birthing books beside it because I had been researching, and googled my name, Kaitlyn Sheffield.

I was in the news.

There was a screenshot: me, a little out of focus, in the midst of writhing, my lips parted sexily, a blur applied to my naked parts, because this was the 'news' after all. The caption said,

"The private videos of former YouTuber, Kaitlyn Sheffield, are released as part of a YouTube ratings battle."

"Fuck you, I'm not a ratings battle."

I checked YouTube and the live links all said, "We are unable to show this content." Someone had taken the videos down already.

Unless of course I kept looking.

I didn't want to, but I did, scrolling deeper into the Google search results until I found a link on page two. And there I was having sex with Braden. He was talking to me, saying sweet, stupid, and sometimes sexy things, and I was nodding and acting like I was turned on. I closed my laptop lid. I opened it again and cleared my search history.

I started a list, number one, hire a lawyer.

I didn't think I would be able to sleep.

Magnus had a son.

He might right now be in the future seeing her. The mother of his son. Probably not. But he could. I didn't really understand what he thought about her, felt about her. He hadn't given me a clear explanation. And now there was a child.

I kind of wondered if I was in shock because I was taking it really well considering.

But maybe it was a little like being up on a shelf, there would be a time coming to deal with the emotions of all of this.

Was I abandoned again?

I didn't feel like it, maybe because I had made the choice.

Ultimately from now on, this was what I decided to do.

That was a relief having decided.

I finally curled up on my bed and fell asleep.

19 - KAITLYN

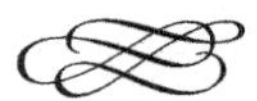

I woke up very early. I opened the curtains and looked out on a brisk, windy, but clear day. The day after a storm was usually a pretty good day. There would be a lot of rubbish to deal with, but yeah, the air was fresh. The sky blue. Wisps of clouds racing from horizon to horizon above.

I padded into the kitchen and put on a pot of coffee and in the fridge found the breakfast Zach had left me — plain yogurt. A note in his scrawl said: the granola is in the pantry. I had never once liked granola. Unless it was on ice cream and that was only because the ice cream masked the taste.

Irritated, I checked the pantry. The granola box was on top of a box of brand new mixed-fancy donuts. With a note: a heart, signed 'Emma and Zach.' Under it, in parentheses it said, 'You should really eat better,' in Zach's scrawl.

I said to the empty room, "Well, you're my chef, if I eat badly who's to blame, really? See how I got you there?" I opened the lid. The assortment was magical: frosted, sprinkled, glazed, baked. I decided which ones Magnus would like and I picked the ones I would eat and while the coffee brewed, I took a bite of each of them. Because it was an empty house and I could.

I pulled a sweatshirt on over my head, a pair of flannel pajama pants on and a pair of wool socks on my feet, and carried a stack of cloth napkins under my arm, the box of donuts, and two mugs with a carafe of coffee out to the deck. I returned for the jug of milk. There were two wooden rocking chairs out there, close to the house, right beside each other, protected from the wind. It was eye-level to the beach. My views stretched to the windswept sea grass and the frothy foaming deep green sea beyond. Actually the color was more like that Gingham filter on Instagram, like a deep green but with most of the green taken away. It was beautiful. The direction of the wind was perfect for keeping my hair out of my eyes. Three birds were flying and swooping and cawing out over the beach.

I took a long edifying drink of coffee, warm, half of it whole milk like a hug on my insides, and ate a bit of the chocolate-frosted chocolate cake with chocolate sprinkles donut and tucked my feet up into the seat and enjoyed the view.

I marveled at the scenery outside and the peace and quiet in my insides.

How was I so calm? I thought through the last few weeks. Magnus, doing everything in his power to help me heal. Magnus, constant and kind. Magnus, dealing with his own shit too, and overwhelmed by it all, but still — trying.

Maybe it was, like I came to last night, that I had decided for Magnus and me. I chose. And his words, "I live by my wife's decisions, I serve as she decides," he hadn't meant that as some kind of flowery 'win me back' kind of bullshit. He meant it. I watched his face as he said it, the words came from deep down near his bones and marrow.

He loved me so much.

He kept proving it to me.

From his romantic speeches to his every day laughs.

That was what was keeping my emotions at bay. After a long year without Magnus I had him back. He had a ton of baggage but he was back. I had baggage too, but mine was inside. Mine would get better if I could stop everything from happening to me and be the one who makes things happen.

Step one, decide for once, check.

And I would help Magnus carry his baggage.

Step two, do that, check.

And helping the love of my life deal with this heavy burdensome pile of awful? I could do that.

He was worth it. And it was within my skill set.

I watched one of the birds swoop down into the shallow parts of a wave as the door opened from the living room and Magnus's footsteps came across the boards of the deck.

He wordlessly sank down in the other chair and his hand wrapped around mine on the side-by-side armrests. He sighed and looked down at our hands, clasped tightly. He looked over at me. "Good morning, mo reul-iuil."

"Good morning, Magnus." I rubbed my thumb along the back of his hand, watching his familiar strength as his muscles simultaneously relaxed, but also held comfortingly close.

My voice was quiet when I asked, "Did you go?"

"Nae, I dinna go, Kaitlyn." He brought my hand to his lips and brushed the back of my fingers. "I dinna. I will tell ye if I do."

He took another deep breath. "I want ye tae ken I would have chosen—"

I shook my head. "I meant it when I said I don't want you to tell me. Because I know what you would have chosen, Magnus, because I know you. I know the kind of man you are. But I also know you couldn't live with it after. You would have regretted what you didn't choose. That's why I intervened."

He watched my face as I spoke.

"This is something we need to leave unsaid, okay?"

"Aye, mo reul-iuil. I will listen tae ye on it."

I pulled the box of donuts from under my chair and held it open for him. He picked a long maple donut with a piece of bacon across it. He ate half of it in one bite. I handed him a mug with black coffee. He finished the donut with the third bite and we both leaned in our chairs and our hands found each other again.

We watched the seagulls dip and dive in the wind on the beach.

Magnus said, "We have much tae speak on, mo reul-iuil." He focused on our hands again. "I said twas the truth that we tell each other everythin', yet we have heard much that we dinna ken. We may want tae begin again."

I clasped his hand and pulled it to my chest, a tear slid down my cheek. "Can you tell me about her?"

"Aye. I will if it will help ye on it."

"It will. I really don't want to be surprised with anything anymore. She lived with you, like really lived with you?" My voice broke. "She slept in your bed?"

His thumb rubbed along my knuckles. "Did I tell ye, Kaitlyn, that I never got tae go outside?"

I shook my head.

"In the arena, when I was fightin' was the only time I had the sky above me, the sun on my face, the air. Twas hard tae have the one, the battle, the near death, tae get tae the other, the open sky.

He brought his other hand to clasp it around mine. "Her presence was the same, I had tae put up with it tae get tae the freedom she promised me. She arrived one night as a gift from Donnan and we were locked in together. There was only one bed, mo reul-iuil, but in the beginnin' she kept tae herself. So I let down my guard. I kent she was a prisoner too and I kent that made her dangerous, but I was desperate about havin' tae give ye up and I dinna guard against her well enough. I slept beside her, yes."

"What was, I mean, is her name? You aren't saying it..."

"Her name is Bella."

"Is she beautiful?"

He took a deep breath. "Yes. But she wasna... I daena ken how tae describe it — I dinna like her, she wasna the same as—"

"I really don't want you to compare us, Magnus. I understand. But I need more. Donnan saw you together?"

"Bella had a way of sayin' and doin' things that made it seem as if I belonged tae her."

"Like what?"

"She called me, 'My Magnus,' and would touch me in a way tae show tae Donnan that we were together. Though we werena."

"Did she know about me, that you were married?"

"She asked about ye and I told her the truth of it, that I was married and I wouldna be hers." He ran a hand through his hair and seemed upset. He let go of my hand and reached in the donut box for another donut. He ate half of it in a bite and put the other half back, wiped his hands on a napkin and took a drink of coffee.

"What did she say?"

"She told me ye were dead. She said it again and again."

I took a deep breath and nodded.

"So tell me about when it happened."

"Twas the night before Donnan's Gala, she told me she wanted tae be with me and when I reminded her I couldna she refused tae listen tae me on it. She threatened tae tell Donnan about our plan tae overthrow him. Donnan kent where you lived, I told her that Donnan would kill ye tae get back at me and it—" He shook his head, staring out over the sand dunes to the ocean. "Do ye want me tae keep tellin' it?"

"Yeah."

"She was pushin' me tae bed her. Twas all verra confusin', she said ye were dead, but I also kent that Donnan would kill ye — twas hard tae worry about those two things at one time. Tae mourn ye and feel desperate tae protect ye, and both of them filled my head so that I couldna think straight, and she was taking off my clothes and — that's when I took her tae my bed. Twas only once. I ken it daena excuse it but I want ye tae ken, twas only once. When Lady Mairead called her my mistress twas nae the truth of it."

I clasped my hand tighter around his. "I knew that wasn't the truth of it. Thank you for telling me all about what was true."

He nodded.

I pulled his hand into my lap wrapped in both of mine. "So you have a son." My next breath caught in my chest three full times while I gasped in enough air to swallow down the tears that wanted to come. "I wanted to be the one who did that for you."

His face broke, tears pooled in his lower lid. "I ken ye did, Kaitlyn. I ken it." His head bowed and I pulled his arm and his shoulder and his head to my chest and held onto it. I pressed my cheek into his hair and held him while his shoulders shook from the grief of it. It took a long time of holding him. A breeze ruffled my hair. The wind was calming as the morning sun brightened and warmed on our deck.

Slowly he raised his head and I pressed my tear-covered cheeks to his and we kissed long and sweet and sad. His breath on my skin, my fingers on the pulse of his neck. And slowly he pulled away, we passed a cloth napkin back and forth between us for our tears, and returned to clasping each other's hands, watching the dunes and the ocean beyond.

"So I will be a king then, or die trying?"

"Please don't die."

He took a deep breath. "It canna have been easy for ye tae

hear all that Lady Mairead said and make the decision ye made..."

"It was easier for me than it would have been for you. It's the kind of man you are. You are bound with honor. And Lady Mairead and — others, they are trying to destroy that part of you, to what — make you decide between me and someone else that deserves your protection? Your child? I won't ever make you choose like that. I won't." My lower lip trembled. "Because I'm safe for you."

"You mean tae be my protection, Kaitlyn?"

"Always, as you are mine. I'll always be your safe place."

He covered my hand with his. "I like tae think of ye as my home, Kaitlyn."

"It is always true."

A wispy cloud raced across the sky and we watched it for a moment.

Magnus said, "Have ye forgiven me on it?"

"I do. My forgiveness happened slowly, moment by moment, but it's fully here. I might be angry sometimes as we live the rest of our lives dealing with your son. The world seems pretty unfair to me right now — that might make me really really act out... I would like to punch someone and my list of someones is getting much longer. But, you, my love, I just want to wrap around you and keep you safe."

He wrapped his hands around mine, drew my fingers to his lips and kissed my knuckle.

"I will teach ye tae punch."

I chuckled. "It's a deal."

"Tis your turn tae tell me of what happened tae ye, that Lady Mairead was speakin' of."

I said, "This needs another donut." I pulled out the box and we each took one. I poured a little more coffee in our mugs. We chewed with moans of pleasure and we took long drafts of the warm liquid. I wiped my fingers and mouth and began. "Years ago, when I was with Braden, I made a mistake and let him film me, with a camera, while we were having sex."

Magnus's brow drew down. "Why would ye?"

"Why did I do anything between the ages of sixteen and twenty-two? Because I was a dumbass. A not thinking dumbass. I don't know. It was the stupidest thing in the world. But at the time—"

"Twas Braden's idea?"

"Yeah, it's like a power thing, now that I think about it. It's like 'look what I can make my girlfriend do.'"

"So twas tae show other people?"

"I didn't think so at the time, though in retrospect I should have made him destroy it, but I didn't and I never thought about it again. It definitely wasn't for him to watch, it's just weird."

I checked his face, concern and concentration, trying to understand what I was telling him.

I continued, "Recently he was breaking up with his girlfriend and she was spiteful so she went into his videos and photos and released a bunch of them."

"Explain what ye mean by this?"

"Remember those cat videos we watched? Like that. People watching tv can watch this video of me." I decided to spill the rest of it. "And the worst part, it was on the news. That means my name is connected to the video and from the sound of it, from Lady Mairead appearing on our doorstep, my personal details will be released because of it. My past has caught up to me and now it's put us both in danger."

"Twas this what ye learned of last night at the reception?"

"Yes. Tyler told me, he saw it on the news."

He stared out at the horizon as he asked, "Did he watch the video of ye, Kaitlyn?"

"No, I don't — he said he didn't, but the truth is, everyone can watch it and I just, I'm so freaking ashamed. Telling you, I don't know how you can even look at me right now, I'm such an embarrassing wife."

He winced. "By my accounts ye misplaced your trust, but ye canna hold yourself tae blame for the actions of a scoundrel."

"Really? You're not furious? Ashamed of me? Embarrassed?"

"Nae, for what purpose, tae hold ye tae account for his wrongs?"

"Wow, I thought you would be totally upset by this information."

He shrugged. "Tae me, tis all just shiftin' light and colors, ye tell me ye are in there, but ye also told me just two nights ago, that there arna real people inside the tv. Isna that what ye said?"

"True, real people aren't inside the television, but—"

"And ye are here in front of me, flesh and blood, nae there in a bed with another man. I daena ken what those lights mean but they arna real, we shouldna worry on them much."

"And you aren't mad that it's exposed us to being found by Lady Mairead?"

"We are found, mo reul-iuil, because the future has been lookin' for us. Twould have happened soon enough. My ribs are healed. Lady Mairead has been bargained with, Samuel is comin' next. We have tae rescue Quentin and then we will do what comes after."

"None of this is what I thought you'd say."

"I am tryin' nae tae be a barbarian. I want tae kill him, but ye winna let me. Will ye?"

I shook my head. "You'd go to prison. Or me."

"Aye. I daena like the sound of that, so instead I am bein' reasonable on it."

I dropped my head back on the chair and let out a long breath in relief. "I feel so much better now that you know. But I'm still embarrassed. I'm naked for the whole world to see."

"I think when Braden loved ye he wanted the video tae keep ye close. You are verra beautiful, Kaitlyn. When I am away from ye, I am verra glad tae have a photo. I canna forget ye, but a photo helps tae keep ye clear in my eyes, as it is in my heart."

I smiled. "Thank you, I don't think it's quite the same, but thank you for telling me I'm beautiful. That goes a long way this morning when I'm all overwhelmed."

"You are also a terrible arse."

I went incredulous. "A what? What the hell does that...?"

His face screwed up. "I daena ken if I said it right, it means ye are good, by speakin' the opposite. Ye ken it, you and Hayley say it often tae each other?"

"A terrible arse — you mean a bad ass?" I giggled.

"Tis nae the same?"

"Nope, but that's cool. You meant bad ass and I'll take it. I'm a beautiful terrible arse. I've been called far worse."

Magnus kissed the back of my hand as he yawned. "I need tae sleep."

"Me too, can we cuddle through it?"

"Aye."

20 - KAITLYN

We woke up groggy past lunch time, discussed the matter, decided that we would leave tomorrow, but today we would go downtown to a restaurant to eat. I couldn't remember the last time we ate out together, so I was pretty psyched. It was a blustery fall day, so I pulled out the fall day clothes: a pair of jeans that were curvy on me, a long sleeve shirt with a scoop neck for cleavage. A jacket and a scarf in a tartan plaid. It was Magnus's and fun when I wrapped it around my neck to see how his eyes lit up. "I like ye in the tartan, Kaitlyn, it reminds me of my past home."

"It reminds me of your past home too. And we'll be back there tomorrow."

Jim met us in the garage. "Hold up Magnus, there's a car outside. It's parked. A rental."

Magnus said, "Stay here, Kaitlyn."

Jim drew his weapon and they both left me standing quietly, heart-racing, in the garage. A minute later I heard my maiden name, "I'm here to see Katie Sheffield, she..."

I peeked out of the door.

Braden was standing in my front yard.

"Braden, what the fuck are you doing here?" I crossed the driveway.

"Katie?"

The most common question I had been asking, "How did you find me?"

Jim stepped in between us, Magnus stepped to my side.

"I called your parents and told them I needed to speak to you." He stepped toward me and Jim stepped between us. "Who the hell are these guys?"

Magnus said, "I am her husband, and you are?"

"I'm Braden, I was her fiancé—"

I said, "Key word: was, and not that it's any business of yours, but this is my husband Magnus Campbell. This is our security guard."

"Oh. A security guard? For what?"

"To keep assholes like you off my property." I looked at Magnus. "My parents told him. Great. This means our address is out."

Magnus said, "Aye."

I asked Braden, "What do you want?"

"To talk to you."

"You flew to Florida and drove to Amelia Island to talk to me? You must be fucking desperate. You could have begged my phone number out of my parents and let me hang up on you and it would have saved you a lot of effort. I remember how much you hated effort. I've got nothing to say to you. And frankly I don't have time, Magnus and I have to deal with something right now, that's urgent — or wait. Are you here to apologize? Because I'll listen to an apology but absolutely nothing else. My guess is an apology will take five seconds. Go."

"I am sorry, but—"

"Great, thanks. See ya." I grabbed Magnus by the elbow and

pulled him toward the garage asking, "From this moment they could come right?"

Braden followed us still talking. "I just need five minutes, I — you heard about the videos?" His eyes cut to Magnus. "Maybe we can talk somewhere alone?"

Magnus said, "She daena want tae talk tae ye alone."

I nodded. "Magnus can hear anything you want to say. And yes, we know about the videos. I said it before and it's totally true, you're an asshole. I can't believe you let her have them."

"I didn't know she had them. I didn't even know I had them still. Look hear me out, okay? She found them and I guess was holding onto them for this — I just wanted you to know, remember Ulysses Lovell? We met him at VidCon?"

"Yeah, I guess?"

"He's doing a story about me — he's working with Yummy-Babe. He's asking a lot of questions and really being an ass—"

"Whoa, that's rich coming from you, the king of assholes."

Braden looked uncomfortable the way Magnus and Jim were glaring at him.

I said, "Just to get you out of my driveway, what is your point?"

"I was going to ask you not to file a lawsuit and to, you know, say nice things."

"Not? That's classic. I'm filing a lawsuit so big that it will threaten to bring down the entire porny-YouTube industry. Better hold on tight."

"But I didn't do anything, maybe just—"

"It was your camera. Your idea. Your video that has existed in the cloud for three years. And guess what? It was your terrible choice in a girlfriend. And now because you don't treat anyone around you with respect and dignity, your payback that the lawsuit is getting bigger the more you talk to me. How did she find the video?"

"She was looking for it..."

"So it was also your flapping jaw that told her it existed." I gestured at Magnus. "My husband has taken this news in stride, luckily for you he isn't that concerned about the implications, but you're seriously delusional if you think I won't use all the lawyers I can afford to come at you for suffering and damages."

He said to Magnus, "Sorry man, about the trouble."

Magnus grunted, a noise that came from his chest. His arms crossed, he glared at Braden.

Jim glanced in the front seat of the rental car. He leaned in through the open window and pulled up an iPhone.

"Katie, this is recording."

"What is, his phone? His fucking phone?" I turned to Braden. "Your phone is recording?"

He shook his head. "I was on Instagram Live while I was waiting to talk to you, I guess I forgot to turn it off.

Jim said, "Looks like a location marker too."

"Did you use my name, Braden, were you talking about me?"

"I was talking about coming to see you, yeah."

I looked at Magnus, wide-eyed.

He said, "We will need tae go today then."

"Great Braden, now I'm suing your children and your children's children. You suck." I yanked the phone from Jim's hand and threw it on the ground and stomped on it. It made a very satisfying cracking noise. I ground my heel into the top of it. "We're done here. Don't ever come to me with your petty YouTube troubles or your fake pleas for ratings help, as far as I'm concerned we don't know each other anymore. We never have. Get off my property."

"Fine, but if you wanted a court case, I'll give you one."

"For what? Name one thing you can sue me over?"

"You broke my phone. That's part of my livelihood."

I shoved him in the chest toward his car. "You shut up. You

stole my livelihood from me. And I freaking left and moved to Florida and now I have my happy ending and you get the hell away from it; you're ruining it!" I all but forced him into his car.

He climbed into the driver's seat, started the car, and rolled down the window, "You know what, you deserved it. You're a cold-hearted bitch—"

Magnus grabbed the door handle and yanked it open. His voice was deep and guttural. "Get out of the car."

"No."

Magnus's face was terrifying, dark and angry. "You heard me. Ye get out of the car and we will discuss—"

Braden looked terrified. "Hell no." He spun out of our driveway, slamming his car door as he drove, spinning up a spray of sand, and sliding a bit as he turned onto the main road headed south.

Magnus watched him leave, shaking his head. "Why canna nae kill him?"

I stood beside him. "Because it's illegal."

"Tis hard tae understand when he deserves it."

"Well, I doubt he'll bother us anymore, but man, it really bothers me that Braden is the one who leaked our exact location."

"We are fully found, Kaitlyn, tis time tae go."

21 - KAITLYN

Magnus tugged my bodice down my arms to my waist. We tucked in all the layers of my long underwear. I gathered my hair to the side while Magnus tightened the laces one after another and tied them. He rested his hands on my waist and pressed his lips to the back of my neck.

"How come as soon as I finish tyin' your lacings I want tae take them off again?"

I wrapped my arm around his head and held him embracing me from behind. His arms around. I loved this position. Wrapped, pressed. His strength was a shield around me, enveloping and protecting. His voice near my ear, his breaths, now sure and healthy, warm and deep, filling the air around me. The scent of him on me. I pressed back and nestled to his chest. He kissed my ear and ran his hands up and down my tight bodice. This position was protection and desire, both, wrapped.

"Can we stay here, like this?"

His arms wrapped tighter around. A hug that warmed me. We held it for a long time. It was very much like a parting embrace, though we weren't, but what we were doing was so full of uncertainty that we held each other like a goodbye anyway.

His voice rumbled up from his heart. "I want ye tae ken, mo reul-iuil, that I love ye beyond what I have the words tae say. I canna describe the depths of it, but I need ye tae ken that I will live my life tryin' tae speak tae ye on it."

I pressed against him. "Then I will spend my whole life listening."

"Aye, I thank ye for it."

Finally we pulled away.

Magnus strapped a knife to my leg.

And he finished dressing, quietly, methodically. It was how I knew he was scared.

We drove through McDonald's for three combo meals, one for me, two for Magnus, and we, with the ac blasting, were headed south to a few acres of unused land outside of Gainesville, where we had hidden the vessels.

I needed to call Zach and tell him we were gone.

"Hey, how's the honeymoon?"

"Good, except, um, Katie, hate to tell you this but I heard about a video—"

"Oh god, don't watch it!"

"I didn't. But what are we—"

"Magnus and I are leaving, we're headed to Gainesville right now to get the vessels. I don't think you can go back to the house. We have to move again."

"Tell Magnus I said hi."

"His eyes are closed I think he's sleeping."

Magnus said, "I am nae sleepin', but ye are hurtlin' the car down the highway and tis too fast."

"It's not too fast Magnus, I'm only going 65." To Zach I said, "I need you to hire me a lawyer, I mean besides the one I already have, he's a family lawyer, I need a not family-friendly lawyer, a mean ass lawyer, one that will sue the hell out of Braden and restore my good name."

"Good, Okay."

"Plus you have to move the whole house again."

"Fuck Katie, seriously?"

"Yeah, I'm really sorry about it."

"I mean we just got settled. It's our honeymoon. This danger bullshit is getting really old." I heard him huff through the phone and Emma asked in the background, "What's happening?"

I said, "I'm so so sorry."

"I know you are, it's just — I'd like some peace, you know? Sorry, I know you know, you want it too. This is just hard."

"I know. I agree. I'm dumping a lot in your lap and—"

"It's not that it's too much work. I don't mind the work, hell, I want to be useful. But can't we all have a home for once?"

I sounded like Magnus when I answered, "We're going to do everything in our power to get to that. I promise."

"Yeah, I know. I just needed to vent." He blew out some air. "Where should we go?"

I looked over at Magnus, "Where should they move to?"

"It needs be somewhere desolate and quiet, without so many storms."

Zach said, "Look, I'm sorry, don't worry about it. We'll figure something out. I'll call Hayley, we'll brainstorm again. I've got this."

"We'll try to get back in one week — with Quentin."

"In time for Christmas, sounds great."

Zach hung up.

I looked over at Magnus.

"Zach is upset about having to move."

"I daena blame him."

"Yeah, me neither."

None of this was optimal, but though we had been planning, ready to go, aware that it was coming, it was still shocking that here we were — found. Suddenly we had to go. Right now.

An hour into the ride, Magnus asleep, an Ed Sheeran song came on the radio. I cranked it up, because I was bored and sang, loudly. Magnus opened one eye. I turned and sang dramatically, directly to him, emoting, wailing. He smiled and watched me for a moment.

"What is this then?"

"This is one of the songs Emma snuck onto the playlist last night, I danced to it with Hayley, sing with me. Listen to the words. It's talking about weddings and love and how beautiful she is..." I tapped on the dashboard during the music, then pointed at him when the chorus started. I sang and Magnus sang some of the words, watching me for cues to them. The song wound down. I tapped Spotify and Bluetooth on my phone and pulled it up again. "Again!"

We both started singing, I was belting out, Magnus a beat behind for the words. "Okay, chorus again, do this with your hands." I reached out and pulled the air and clutched it to my chest while I got all emotional to the song and then looked over as Magnus grinned watching me.

I smiled, "You sing it to me." He sang the chorus, deep baritone and vibrating sexy yum.

"Whoa, that was... awesome. I really like your singing voice. You can do that anytime."

"Thank ye, I like singin' on how beautiful ye were on our wedding day."

I blushed. "That seems like a long time ago."

"Twas only yesterday when I watched ye walk down the aisle, tis still fresh in my eye and my heart." Then he joked, "The song was almost as good as the songs back home." He began to sing. "I heard the liltin', at the yowe-milking, the lassies a-lilting afore the dawn o' day; but now they are moaning on ilka green loanin', the Flowers of the Forest are a' wede away."

"What is that one about?"

"The battle of Flodden, a verra long time ago, and the men haena returned from the war."

"A tragedy, we have to be dramatic for it, sing more."

Magnus sang, "We'll hae nae mair liltin' at the ewe-milkin', the women and bairns are dowie and wae. Sighin' and moaning, on ilka green loanin', the Flowers of the forest are all wede away."

"That's beautiful."

"Aye. But do yours once again, m'fair lassie, I have a need for the loud music of the time tae keep my mind off the comin' storms."

I picked up my phone to push play again. "That's actually a great way to describe rock and roll." And we sang.

22 - KAITLYN

I pulled the Mustang down a dirt road that wasn't marked. It had a decrepit mailbox and a broken-down rusted gate. The gate didn't do anything but pretend to be a gate, sort of, just by looking like one. Magnus jumped out of the car, swung it open. I drove through, and he closed the gate across the road behind me.

The dirt road was super muddy because of the storms yesterday. I drove around the deeper puddles spraying mud behind the wheels, unsure if the Mustang would get stuck. Our car would need a really good washing when we got back. The tires slid a bit on a wet patch. "Come on come on come on." I did not want to deal with a car stuck in mud while wearing all of these layers of woolen clothes. Plus it was growing dark out here on this dirt road in the woods near sunset.

We finally made it to the small grassy slope near the small dock at the edge of the freshwater spring. We parked our car to the side of the clearing under some trees.

I popped the trunk. Magnus strapped his scabbard and sword across his back and then we made a trip carrying our supplies. I had a leather backpack that looked antique. We had a couple of wool blankets. I had some protein shake mix in a ceramic jar with a cork lid and some protein bars wrapped in waxed cloth. We had a water filter. I had a small leather kit for medical emergencies, and it included a midwifery kit along with pages of directions and a small book called Emergency Childbirth. I had a bag of antibiotics and other medicines all wrapped in parchment paper and sealed with tape, plus the herbs and homeopathic remedies that Emma sent. I of course had my period stuff too, a menstrual cup and period panties. This time I was on top of the situation though: the PMS symptoms were mostly gone anyway. We also had a small stocked tool box.

"Well this is a fine load of stuff." I stood appraising it in two small stacks. I joked, "If you can't bring the eighteenth century into the modern age bring the modern age to the eighteenth century. The only thing we are missing is the cart and the horse."

Magnus said, "I am missin' the horse. We could go back for Sunny?"

"You don't want to accidentally leave Sunny in the 1700s. Keep reminding yourself, 'Sunny will be waiting for us when we get home.'

The corner of his mouth turned up in a smile. "And when we get home, I will teach ye tae ride. We will get a partner for Sunny and name her Osna."

"Remind me, what does that mean?"

"Tis the sound ye make when ye are happy in my arms."

"I make a sound when I am happy?"

He grinned. "Aye, when I have bed ye well, ye sigh."

"I do, I really do, I really like it when you get me there. And you have a deal. I'll have a horse named Osna." I checked through the pile. "The guns are still in their box in the trunk. Can you get them?"

Magnus returned up the grassy slope to the car. I checked the front buckle on my backpacks for the fifth time when suddenly from the dirt road came the sound of a car engine. "Crap."

A silver Toyota pickup spun into the space and pulled onto the grass dividing me from the Mustang and Magnus. The truck's headlights were shining at me so I was momentarily blinded. A dark figure stepped from the car. "Katie?"

I shielded my eyes. "Tyler? What are you—"

He slammed his truck door shut. Then opened the door and turned off his headlights. "Michael asked me to come check on his Uncle's property, because of the bizarro storms — why are you here?"

"Um, because, um." I gestured at Magnus. Tyler turned to see him. Magnus had his hand on the door of our car: frozen, calculating, watching. I waved my hand like it helped me to think. "We came to see the land too. I used to come here all the —" I had no idea what I was talking about. I was dressed like I was headed to a Ren Faire. I had a small pile of blankets and first aid supplies like I was headed on a Doctors Without Borders trip or something. Plus I was trespassing.

Tyler said, "The storms are really big and they're happening at regular times." He checked his watch. "About an hour from now..." He looked me up and down. "You really shouldn't be fooling around out here. And have you guys seen or heard the horses?" He looked around the space. "I heard horses."

Magnus's hand moved to his sword hilt over his shoulder. "Horses?" He began walking our way.

And that's when I heard them thundering through the underbrush. Horses. Men making that, "Haw!" sound. Right then, horses, ridden by soldiers, barged through the underbrush, over the bushes, through the dark trees, and down the slope. They descended on Magnus, trampling all around.

"Get behind me, Katie." Tyler dragged me behind his truck.

He craned around the truck to see. "Who are they?"

"I don't know." They weren't from the future, but they also didn't look like they were from Magnus's time period either. The horses had an armor on them and the men were in unfamiliar costumes, they were yelling like crazy without any familiar words. "How many are there?" I could hear the clanging and crashing of sword blades and I didn't want to look.

"Three."

I had to look. Magnus was fighting blade to blade against three.

"Shit shit shit, oh my god, they've surrounded—"

Tyler said, "I see it." He opened his truck, dove across the seats, slammed open his glove compartment and pulled a gun.

I said, "Hurry, please hurry, they're going to kill Magnus. Please help."

He put his hand on my shoulder, keeping me down. "Hold on, I don't have a clear shot and I can't leave you—"

"Help him!"

I shoved his hand off and stood to look over the hood of the truck. Magnus's sword arced down but a soldier behind him was swinging toward him. "Shoot them. Go run over there and shoot them. My husband is fighting for his life—"

I scrambled back up to see what was happening. One of the men dismounted. He prowled around Magnus in a circle. The two other men circled him up on their horses, their blades held high looking for an opening. And then, another man on horseback galloped from the woods.

"Oh my god, Tyler, do you see it? There's more."

He said, "Look, stay here, don't move." He crouched and ran around the front of the truck leaving me to myself.

My view was the dock. If I could get there. I could pull up the vessels and get us away. Tyler fired. I raced to the dock hunched over. *Shitshitshitshitshit.*

I dropped down on the dock, grasped the long chain hanging

over the edge, and began tugging it up, hand over hand over hand from the water. It was heavy and long. The water was ice cold. Within a second my hands were ice-cold-freezing-rigid-painful. "Fuck." One hand and another up and up. The chain dragged splashing and splattering. I took glances over my shoulder at Magnus — fighting for his life.

My eye caught as Magnus swung, misstepped, and stumbled forward. "Please, please, God, please let him live.

One of the soldiers jumped off his horse and charged me on the dock. Swinging his blade. Coming fast.

Tyler was a few steps behind, yelling wildly.

There was nothing I could do but cower in a ball. He would be on me in a sec—

Tyler fired, the man jerked, stumbled forward and collapsed on top of me. I shrieked and shoved him off.

Tyler made it to me just as another man was running at us. Tyler said, "Get back man, Don't come another step. I'll kill you if you come closer."

The chain felt even heavier as the safe box rose to the surface. I tugged and tugged and finally got a hand on the case's handle and lugged it onto the dock.

Behind me Tyler fired. I turned to see the second soldier whip back, yell, clutch his stomach, and drop to the ground near our pile of gear.

Tyler stood over me, arms locked, pistol aimed. He fired toward the soldier Magnus was fighting and missed. "I can't get a clear shot."

Magnus's blade sliced deep through the soldier's arm. Blood gushed from the wound. The man dropped to his knees and then slumped to the ground. The last soldier charged Magnus, swinging. Magnus fought him in a circle, blow for blow, his sword swinging down and arcing up. He was growling and bellowing as they fought.

He had to be exhausted. I was exhausted watching it.

I dialed the number into the combination lock on the case. It took two tries before I got it open. Inside were the two vessels wrapped in waterproof bags. I opened one of the bags as Magnus took a blow that knocked him to the ground.

"He's tired, he's going to get killed."

"I know, I need to get closer, stay right here, don't move."

"What's going to happen to me? He's the only one left."

Tyler said, "We don't know that." He raced toward the truck to get a better shot as Magnus got back to his feet and swung his blade up knocking the man back.

Magnus swung at him again and again and again forcing him up the slope until finally Magnus arced his blade down bellowing and cut the soldier between the neck and the shoulder with a burst of blood. The man dropped lifeless to the side.

Magnus held his heavy sword tip to the ground, leaned forward, breathing heavy.

I watched from my place on the dock, on my knees, my skirts wet from the splashing. Tyler rushed back to stand guard over me. I was watching Magnus from around Tyler's legs. How were we going to get rid of Tyler before we jumped? How were we going to explain all of this insane crazy bullshit violence and swordplay?

Magnus swung his sword over his shoulder and into its scabbard. He grabbed the reins of the horse closest to him and a strap on a dead soldier's armor and pulled the horse and dragged the body down the slope toward us.

I jumped to my feet and rushed to the other horse and led it to our gear. Tyler followed me. I asked, "What are you doing?"

"Nothing, just—"

Magnus dumped a body on the pile. "Are ye okay, Kaitlyn?"

"I'm okay."

Tyler said, "Was that it, all of them? Are you sure?"

Magnus shook his head. "I daena ken—"

"There are probably more."

Magnus eyed him suspiciously. "Och, then we needs tae go fast." He went to drag the last body down to our gear.

Suddenly from the woods more men on horseback, charging from the trees, bearing down on Magnus.

"Magnus! Run!"

Tyler pulled me behind him.

I turned away so he couldn't see what I was doing and twisted the two halves of the vessel so it hummed to life.

Magnus was hurrying down the slope dragging a body behind.

"Hurry, Magnus, hurry!" My heart was racing.

Four horses were thundering behind him.

He yelled, "Say the numbers, Kaitlyn!"

He reached me, dropped the body onto our pile, and wrapped the reins of the horses around his arms. I said the numbers. He threw his arms around me as the soldiers roared down the slope.

I reached the end of the numbers as horse hooves were about to crash down on us and then I felt the ripping of my body as the vessel hurled me through time.

23 - KAITLYN

The pain was so intense my body was tight frigid stiff while my mind writhed in agony.

Magnus's voice close by, "Kaitlyn?" I peeled my eyes open. Frosty breath came from my mouth in puffs. Part of my rigidity and pain was shivering because of the ice forming on my skin. Magnus tucked a wool blanket around my face, tight. He pushed the ends of it under my hips and around my feet.

He pulled another blanket around his shoulders, sitting beside me, head bowed, icy air around his cheeks. I slid into unconsciousness again.

24 - KAITLYN

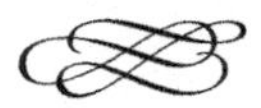

I didn't think the pain was gone, or if it was it had been replaced by a new pain. Freezing cold air pain. A chill that had entered my bones and was making it hard to think. Like frozen all through. Magnus's voice came to me from a distance. "...who are ye?!!! What are ye doin' here?" He sounded enraged.

I tried to peel open my eyes.

Tyler's voice. "...I was checking on the property, man, what the fuck?"

Magnus and Tyler were arguing. I groaned, opened my eyes and tried to focus. Magnus was standing over Tyler, a wad of Tyler's shirt in his hand. Red in the face, yelling. Scary yelling. "Tell me what ye are doin'! Are ye a brother? Dost ye plan tae kill me?"

"No — what? No."

Magnus shook Tyler. "What dost ye want with Kaitlyn? Why are ye surroundin' her?"

"I'm not, what?"

Magnus drew back his fist. "Tell me what ye want with her or

I will kill ye where ye lay. Tis nae difference tae me, ye are a dead man now any way ye think on it."

Tyler's hands were up trying to protect his face. I groaned again and struggled to my feet. It was so freaking cold out here. I shuffled over to where Magnus was standing over Tyler. "Magnus? S-s-s-stop—" My voice was weak and shivery.

His eyes were so full of fury they didn't see me.

"Stop." I grabbed his sleeve on his fighting arm.

He shook my hand off. "What dost ye want with her? Explain it, now, or ye will lose your life because of it."

Okay this was getting heated. Magnus was red-faced with the look he carried when he found the men who abducted me.

One word slammed into me — 'bloodlust.' I grabbed his arm and clung to it. "Stop!"

He swung my hands away.

Tyler said, "I saved your life, Katie — get this fucking barbarian off me."

Magnus turned on him again, past the point of stopping, "What did ye call—"

I threw myself back onto Tyler, my body between him and Magnus's fist and I begged, "Stop, please, Magnus. Stop."

He dropped Tyler's shirt with a shove to the ground, causing me to fall backward on top of him.

With his chest heaving and an expression of shock in his eyes, he shook his head and stepped backwards. He took another step backwards, watching me try to pick myself up off of Tyler.

I asked, "Tyler are you okay, also what are you doing here?"

He brushed himself off. "I don't know what I'm doing here. Where even is here? Why does my whole body hurt? Why the fuck is it so cold and you need to tell your husband..." He glared at Magnus. "To never lay a hand on me again."

"He won't. Right, Magnus? He won't."

Magnus was glowering, his chest rising and falling in heaves.

I pulled the blanket around my shoulders. "And to the other stuff, you've just time-traveled with us to the 18th century. Seriously. I don't know the mechanics of it, but Magnus is from 1703."

"Bullshit."

"No, it's not." I shook my head. "It's too cold out here to explain what I barely understand myself, but it's the truth and you'll know once you're here for longer than ten minutes. For now, let me get you a blanket and Magnus and I will discuss getting you back home." I limped, stiff from cold and fear, over to our pile.

There was a dead body on our blankets. I pushed its shoulder trying to move it but it was way heavier than it looked. Magnus came to my side and pushed the body off. I carried a blanket to Tyler. "Wrap in this, it will help."

"There's blood all over it. There are dead people. We might catch some—"

"You know, there's blood on all of them. We were lucky we weren't killed. Wrap up in the freaking blanket."

"Is it dark to you? Really dark?"

I nodded. "Yeah, it's very dark."

I returned to Magnus. He was standing staring at the ground, incapable of speaking, trying to pull himself back from the edge. I pulled a blanket around his shoulders. And looked up into his eyes. "Come back, Magnus."

"I canna trust him."

I pushed a lock of his hair back behind his ear. "But you can't kill him. He's here accidentally and we're responsible for it. We have to get him back."

"He called me a barbarian." He glanced at Tyler and shook his head.

I smoothed down his chest. "I've used that against you before. I know—" I took a deep breath. "You aren't. You can't let him get to you." Magnus was looking everywhere but at me — "Magnus."

He looked into my eyes.

"I need you to get on top of it and listen to me—"

"What if he is here tae kill me? He could be a brother, or — he could be here tae take my throne, and I daena have a way tae stop—"

"He had many opportunities before, right? He didn't. He's just a know-it-all and a control-freak who's bordering on a death wish. We have to get out of the cold, into the castle. We have to decide what to do about Tyler. Not killing him."

Magnus scowled. Then nodded. "Will ye be careful around him? I daena what he is up tae but I think he is of a danger tae—"

I shook my head. "He's not a danger to me, but I'll be careful."

"I was goin' tae say a danger tae me."

"Well that, my husband, is literally the same thing. If he's a danger to one of us, it's to both of us. I'll be careful. You be careful. But we need to get ourselves out of the cold. And him out of the cold. He has a mother and a father back in 2019, he can't disappear here, imagine what that would do to his family?"

He ran his hand through his hair. "So now I am responsible for Quentin and Tyler and—"

"We are responsible. Plus he might be helpful. He was military. He could drive one of the machines, help us get them out of here."

"Och, aye. I will accept your word on it. Do you think he can ride a horse?"

"I hope so because we aren't all fitting on one."

25 - KAITLYN

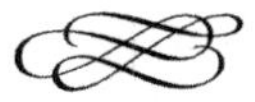

I returned to speak to Tyler.

I explained to him we would get him back to Florida very quickly, but, and he agreed, we couldn't do it yet because that shit hurt. And we needed to get out of the cold. I mentioned that we were here to pick up Quentin. I spoke fast and sure and managed to convince him that he didn't have any more questions.

Frankly it was like he was in shock.

Much like how I felt after every time jump.

Magnus assigned us jobs and Tyler went straight to being argumentative about the 'how' of packing up our gear but overall he was helpful. Magnus ignored him mostly and I had to be the go-between. We unpacked the saddlebags on the horses once they were subdued enough from the pain of time-jumping and kept everything that looked expensive or important. My guess is that the men had been from the past. Their clothes seemed like it, but then again they were well fed, good teeth, clean. I couldn't place them in any part of history.

We packed our stuff onto the horses. Tyler did luckily know how to ride.

Magnus made Tyler follow, but said, "I will have my back on ye, but also, Kaitlyn is on my horse. I am trustin' ye nae tae try anythin' dangerous while she is close."

Tyler scowled. "I won't try anything."

We, Magnus and me on one horse, a horse full of our supplies, and Tyler in the rear, headed in the direction of Balloch Castle.

It wasn't far.

But near the end of the trail, Magnus slowed our horse.

"What's happening?"

"Shhh. I am listenin'."

I listened too, but it was all very very quiet. Nothing to actually listen to. Magnus looked left and right and around and behind us. He said, quietly, "Move from the trail." He turned our horse toward the woods and Tyler expertly moved his horse from the trail as well.

We all went still in the midst of the trees. Listening. Waiting.

Finally Magnus gestured with his head away from the castle, and he silently moved our horses the opposite way we came. I held on with my arms around his back. Scared by his silence. Waiting for what would come next.

"What happened back there?"

Magnus said, "The castle has been captured."

My voice went quiet. "How did you know?"

"Twas verra quiet. Without the sounds of the usual day."

Tyler said, "That's the way it sounds right before an ambush."

Magnus said, "Och, aye." We rode quietly for a moment. "We

will go to the village, see if my family has gone there, find out what has happened. Twill be a cold ride. Can ye accomplish it, Tyler?"

"Yeah. I can do it."

Magnus urged the horses and their pace quickened.

26 - KAITLYN

I looked back at Tyler. "You warm enough?"

"Yeah, thanks for the wool socks that helped."

We could see our breaths. Frost covered the trees. We passed below a ridge of snow-covered mountains, our horses picking a path that had frost-covered mud banks to both sides.

Tyler asked Magnus a few questions about the mountain ridge and the trees we were passing under. Magnus answered his questions curtly, his body tense, his back stiffening. I tucked my face to his tartan and squeezed.

I didn't know 100% what he was so worried about with Tyler. He had never been jealous for one minute with James. He had restrained himself with Braden. He usually trusted me, completely. But his concern over Tyler interfering in our lives was new, unexpected, and it should have bothered me — jealous husband wasn't something I wanted, but the truth was, he wasn't wrong. Tyler had been overly familiar since I met him. And I didn't want to tell Magnus this, but I was worried about Tyler's motivations too.

Because in all this time since we arrived here, he hadn't really asked any big questions as if this was normal. Or expected. So I was in complete agreement with Magnus – Tyler wasn't to be trusted.

Our only disagreement was that I also thought we *needed* to trust him. We could use his help.

But Magnus had to be on guard and I needed to accept it.

Magnus had suspicions and I trusted him, that was the thing. His suspicions were mine, too.

I asked, "Where are we going, how far?"

"Not too far, there is a village, a tavern I am headed tae."

"I can't feel my toes. It's so cold."

Later we pulled our horses up in front of a two-story stone building in a village farther along the River Tay. Magnus dropped to the ground and held his arms up for me. I landed on the ground with a groan. My legs would not go straight. I was stiff and my hips ached. Plus my thighs. Magnus tied off the horses and led us inside. It was warm and dark, just a couple of small lanterns. A crackling fire at one end. Six tables and some chairs. So dark. I could barely see the shifting forms of people near what looked to be where the drinks were served. At one of the other tables a couple of men looked bleary-eyed and leering.

Magnus spoke with the man at the bar and came to me with a whisky. "I will be back in a moment, stay here, daena talk tae anyone. Tis ruffians about but I have tae get the horses tae the stable. The owner is watchin' over ye."

"Okay, sure." I was happy to have a whisky that would go a long way to warming me up.

Magnus grunted at Tyler, "Come with me, we have tae see tae the horses."

Tyler glanced at me, around at the room, then followed Magnus out the door.

I swigged from the whisky. It was smooth and warm and filled me with strength. We were good. Unfound. Now we were rescuing Quentin, it was all part of the plan.

Sitting and waiting in the 18th century was so bizarre. Like what I imagined a sensory deprivation tank to be like. My sight was barely working. Darkness closed in all around the edges, I had to squint and concentrate to make out the details. My hearing was muffled, except my internal body sounds: they were too loud. I put both hands on the whisky glass and concentrated on it. The table top. Waiting for when Magnus would return. Wondering briefly how I would manage without him.

Finally they did return and I was relieved again that I wouldn't have to deal with being alone here. Because I had already dealt with that once before. To punctuate the precarious position I had been in, one of the men leaned in, his head wobbling, spittal flying from his lips, "What a bonny lass issshee — want tae sssshhhh — ye doin' ashhsum—"

Magnus brought his whisky to the table. "Would ye speak tae your own wife with such a smooth tongue? Or are ye merely practicin' with my wife? I canna say tis improvin' ye, and I ken tis makin' my wife quite damp from the spittle and your want of mastery on it."

The man's head wobbled quite comically. He muttered something then passed out with his head on his arms.

Magnus sat down with a laugh. "Tis a quiet night at the tavern. I suppose the weather has kept the regulars away tonight."

Tyler blew on his fingers. "I can't get the heat in them. This is like New York City."

Suddenly the front door blew open and Uncle Baldie, Quentin, and Liam, Lizbeth's husband, blew through with big voices and boisterous slams and thuds.

Magnus jumped up so fast he tipped his chair, not a hard feat, the legs barely matched and my chair was rocking on three long legs and a short.

Magnus hugged his uncle Baldie and his brother-in-law Liam, and then he and Quentin were hugging and beating each other's backs. Magnus said, "You are half the man ye once were!"

Quentin laughed, "Peril and Starvation have knocked about thirty pounds off me." He turned left and right. "I'm on the Medieval Diet plan."

I rolled my eyes and laughed. "It's not medieval times, I keep telling you, plus..." I came around the table and threw my arms around him. "I don't think you look that bad, what are you, forty-three now?"

"Ugh. I'm twenty-four. Or am I? You guys were gone so long I might be seventy-four. Why the hell is Tyler here?"

We hid our voices from Baldie and Liam. "Sorry about that. We took a month. Magnus's ribs are much better, Zach and Emma got married—"

"He finally did it?"

"He did. We came back on this date to be here for Lizbeth's birth. Sorry we left you for so long. There's a lot more to tell you about — we were found and Tyler was there and we had to jump — he's here accidentally."

Quentin squinted his eyes in Tyler's direction. "I don't trust him."

"Join the club, but he's here and he's going to help and—"

"Well, we can use it. This here is a shitstorm of epic proportions."

We all pulled chairs up to the table and Magnus ordered a round of whisky. "Where's Sean?"

Liam gruffly said, "He has taken the Earl's side in it. There is a man there, Commander Davis, he says he is from Donnan's kingdom. He is here tae arrest ye for crimes ye committed there. He'll be wantin' your wife too."

Magnus leaned forward. "The Earl means tae turn me over?"

Baldie said, "The Earl wants the weapons, we could use them in the comin' wars. Davis has promised more weapons if they will turn ye over. We have had a rift in the family over it."

Magnus scowled. "And Sean is with the Earl on this?"

"Och aye, Sean is with the Earl. Lizbeth tried tae persuade him tae see the reason of it, but he sent us away, and is convinced the weapons will bring the Campbells to power. He winna listen tae reason."

I asked, "Where is Lizbeth now?"

"We had tae steal her away tae the home of McClelland. His wife, Madame Greer, is carin' for her as the bairn is near."

Magnus and I looked at each other. Magnus said, "Kaitlyn would like to see her, she has brought medicines and trained with a—"

Liam's brow drew down. "I canna let ye use your witchcraft, Magnus. There has been enough of the work of the devil here already."

Magnus said, "Tis nae the work of the devil. I promise ye, as a brother, my wife can help bring Lizbeth through tae safety. My Kaitlyn is a god-fearin' woman and..." He looked around searching for words. Then focused his speech directly to both Baldie and Liam, "I ken tis mighty devilish the weapons that have come, but they arna mine. They belonged tae Donnan and they have chased me here. I came askin' for refuge. I dinna mean tae bring such destruction. I will fight with everythin' I have tae bring our family back taegether."

Liam looked skeptical.

Magnus continued, "You remember they were nae with me, they were against me. They were nae with Kaitlyn, they were used against her. We escaped with no more than our lives. I had tae depart tae be healed, but I am home now tae fight or if tis the only way tae remove the weapons I will turn myself over tae the Commander, what was his name?"

Baldie said, "Davis."

"Aye. Are there more men?

"He makes the number six."

Tyler said, "That's not that many."

Baldie said, "They have the weapons of a larger army, they daena need tae waste the souls on us."

Magnus hung his head. "You have tae believe me, Liam, I am in earnest. I will lay down my life if I have tae, tae undo what has happened here. Please allow Kaitlyn tae see Lizbeth."

Liam sat quietly for a long dreadful moment, then said. "Aye, Young Magnus, I will."

Baldie said, "And though ye say ye are willin' tae lay down yer life, I ask ye tae remain alive long enough tae rid us of these weapons. If they arna yours, I surely hope ye can remove them and turn Sean's mind back to his former self."

Quentin said, "I thought he was on our side too. I was in charge of the weapons. He helped me keep them locked up. We had a deal, use them if the castle was attacked. Then this Commander Davis strutted in and gave the Earl this whole bull-shit story about you. Sean believed it. He all but forced Lizbeth from the castle."

Magnus asked, "Maybe he was getting ye all out tae safety."

Quentin shook his head. "He said some shit though, made it sound like he had gone to the dark side. He said you should have fought for your kingdom, and now he would ally with Samuel since you weren't capable of ruling."

Magnus scowled.

Liam said, "Lizbeth is devastated that Sean has left us, she dinna want tae leave his side. We had tae drag her away. I think ye may be the only member of the family he will listen tae about it."

"I will talk tae him." Magnus's face was pensive. He took a deep breath and then patted Quentin on the shoulder. "How did it go with ye then?"

Quentin shrugged. "Twas life and death for a bit there but I have managed it—"

Magnus laughed. "You sound Scottish in your tongue, ye are truly a part of the family?"

Quentin grinned. "They dropped the Magnus from my name and now I'm just Black Mac. Still not sure how I feel about that."

Baldie threw an arm around Quentin boisterously. "He is a Campbell now, he has shared the whisky, the brawls, and the foul winds of the—"

Quentin joked, "Campbell men."

Baldie laughed, "I was goin' tae say the Scottish winter, but that will do tae answer Young Magnus."

I said, "So all we have to do is secure the weapons, retake the castle, kill the commander, and change Sean's mind?"

The corner of Magnus's mouth turned up in a smile. "That's all we have tae do, mo reul-iuil."

I swigged from my whisky glass and grimaced from it. Feeling quite tipsy I said, "Easy," and snapped my fingers.

Through all of this Tyler drank. He slammed another long draught of whisky, banged the glass on the table and said, "I don't know what kind of crazy-ass Jumanji-bullshit role-playing D&D thing this is, but whatever you just decided to do, I'm game. But how about another round first, I'm finally feeling warm."

27 - KAITLYN

I bundled up and hugged in under Magnus's arm. We left Tyler and Quentin to sleep in the bunkhouse at the tavern and walked through the dark down a village path to the McClelland house where Lizbeth was bed-resting. We would stay there with her. Liam walked a bit ahead of us showing us the way. I was a bit tipsy. I had let down my guard because this had been an insane few days and it looked like insane days stretched into the future. And whisky had been put in front of me. Plus it was cold outside.

It was a frosty, cold night, our breaths puffed. I clung to Magnus for warmth but I was weaving a bit from the drink and when I bumped him I giggled. He said, "You arna walking well, Madame Campbell."

I said, "Me thinks, hiccup, Madame Campbell has had too much of the whisky." I stumbled against him again. "Ugh, why do I do this? What if Lizbeth goes into labor tonight?"

"Sleep on it. If somethin' happens ye will be fresh enough."

"God, you would say that. You can drink and it doesn't affect you. Except that one time..." I wrapped my arm around him, our feet crunching on the frosty ground. "You like me a lot, don't you, Master Campbell?"

"I adore ye, ye art the beat of my heart, mo ghradh."

Liam pushed a door open and slipped into the house.

"I have to pee." I wobbled to the edge of the path, hiked up all my skirts, pulled down my long warm pants exposing my bare bottom to the elements, and peed on the frosty ground. Magnus stood beside me and peed in a graceful arc into a ditch. "How come mine takes every thigh muscle I have and you can just do it like it's the easiest thing in the world?"

"My parts are made tae be simple because I have one purpose. Ye have been cursed with the weight of womanhood, mo reul-iuil. You have many purposes."

I sighed dramatically. "What are my purposes?"

He adjusted his kilt. "Bairns and..." He stopped. "Taking care of everyone." He straightened my tartan on my shoulders, kissed my nose, "We are here." He led me into the house. I only tripped on the stoop a little bit, but it wasn't really my fault, it was an uneven stoop.

Lizbeth was asleep and wasn't in labor. So with quiet whispers Liam led us into a very small room, with a wooden bed and a straw mattress. I said, "This is going to be uncomfortable. I call tops."

He said, "I canna sleep with ye tonight, I must join the guard at the door."

"Oh. It's like that?"

"Tis like that."

"Aw man, I shouldn't have drunk so much whisky." I hiccuped to punctuate my distress.

"You deserved it after the days ye have had..."

"You too though, and now you don't get to sleep?"

"You will sleep for both of us, I will take mine when I'm relieved." I dropped my backpack off my back to the ground and scrounged through it. Here's your walkie-talkie."

Magnus chuckled. "Tis a funny name."

"You remember how to use it?"

He nodded and clipped it to the belt across his chest.

"Okay," I pulled my tartan around my shoulders and climbed into the bed. It was more uncomfortable than it looked, being not much wider than an ironing board. Magnus tucked my blankets in around me. "G'night, mo reul-iuil."

I asked, "You aren't going anywhere? Just outside?"

"Aye, just outside. And we will speak on the walkytalk."

"Perfect."

He left the room and it was pitch black and so quiet I couldn't hear a thing at all. I clutched the walkie-talkie to my chest. And though I tried to be a big girl about it I turned it on and pressed the button. It made a loud squawking sound that threatened to wake up the whole house. I scrambled to turn down the volume and whispered. "Hi."

There was a second of waiting, longer than I thought I could bear, and from the static-y inside of the apparatus, Magnus's voice. "Sleep well, mo reul-iuil, I am just outside."

A tear rolled down my cheek, but I found myself able to sleep.

28 - KAITLYN

When my eyes opened in the morning it was ice cold in the room. Ice cold. Shivering. I tightened my blanket, my head was pounding. I needed aspirin and water, pronto. A deep breathing met my ear and I looked down, Magnus was on the ground beside the bed: flat on his back, his tartan wrapped around his shoulders, frosty breath coming from his mouth.

I decided not to wake him especially because I had no idea how long he had been there. I quietly stepped across his broad chest and pulled open the door with the loudest god-dammed creeeeeeak. I checked him.

He groggily said, "Where?"

"I'm going to see Lizbeth, keep sleeping, I'm sorry I woke you."

He mumbled, "Good," and threw his arm over his face and went back to sleep right there on the floor.

I tiptoed down the hall. There were three closed doors.

I crept down the stairs and found myself face to face with an older woman in the kitchen. She was plump and grey haired, dressed in a wool dress and wrapped in a shawl with an apron over the whole thing. She drew down her brow. "Ye must be the Young Magnus's wife then?"

I nodded.

She looked at me skeptically. "You are quite young tae be the cause of all this devilishness. I have heard ye called many a name, but here ye stand afore me, a young bride, not much older than m'self at the beginning."

I mumbled, "What kind of names are they..."

She threw down a dish towel. "Tis nae important the flappin' mouths of simple minds, daena ye worry on it. Lizbeth Campbell says, and says it quite loudly and firmly that ye are a godly woman, as pious and good as they come, and I have a mind tae help her in the cause of it. I am Madame Greer. You and I are friends from this day forward. You need a friend, I can see it."

I smiled widely. "Okay, definitely. Friends, yes."

"I have been told that I can think what I want and because I daena shut up about it I get my way in most things, so I want ye tae listen tae me on this: Tis your life we are speakin' on. You are a guest in my home, but I'll see ye pray here every mornin' beggin' God tae look after us all." She gestured to a small bit of wool fabric on the stone in a corner in front of a small cross.

"Oh, yes, of course." I went to the corner and knelt on the fabric.

"Now ye begin and I will direct ye on it if I feel ye needs be directed."

She began wiping out a large pot with a grimy towel. She waved her hand at me, "Go on then."

I started with "Dear God..."

She chimed in with "Good good, an excellent beginnin'."

I asked for forgiveness and she chirped about how my soul would surely receive it. She prompted, "Your Young Magnus will be wantin' guidance leadin' the men against this evil."

I prayed for guidance and for God to use Magnus as a tool for his good works and Madame Greer nodded sagely. She added, "Magnus will need wisdom to deal with this mess, tis family against itself, he will need God tae protect him." She wiped at the counter while I prayed for guidance and protection for Magnus and when I included Lizbeth's coming birth, I asked that she be delivered of the baby safely and Madame Greer said, "Amen, Madame Kaitlyn, include my sister, Morag, she has a tendency tae seein' the worst in people. She may need ye tae show her a bit of kindness. She does feel the winter weather in her bones."

I prayed for her sister's pains and included Madame Greer, without being asked, and her husband Ailbeart for good measure; for Lizbeth's husband, Liam, and Uncle Baldie, and I included the Earl and especially Sean, that he would be guided to come to peace with the rest of his family. And when I ended and looked up, Madame Greer beamed at me. "Now see, ye are just as Lizbeth has said. I will remind the others that Lizbeth does ken the measure of ye." She thrust a bowl toward me with some mealy substance at the bottom. "Eat your fill and up the steps tae Lizbeth's room, she has been waitin' on ye."

While I ate she carried on with her chatting. "You also haena complained once about the beddin' in your room, I will be addin' that tae my list of your fine qualities." She twittered like a bird, then said, "Aye, have ye seen Young Magnus this mornin? The men were up verra late, with the guard. We haena had this much activity in a long time." She huffed. "Trouble is the men are all in an uproar and haena had the good sense tae work the fields the way they ought. I think we will be havin' a few years of trouble for it. But I said tae my Ailbeart, twould happen when the trouble started on Lughnasadh. I said, 'Ye canna wage war during a harvest festival and expect the crops tae flourish.' Och, we will be feelin' it." She stopped hustling around the kitchen to turn to me with a sigh. "Have ye a bairn, Madame Kaitlyn?"

"I lost my first."

"Och." She shook her head sadly. "Well, ye are young yet." She cleared my empty bowl. "I am afeared for Lizbeth, tis a troublin' time tae be bringin' a bairn tae the world."

"I hope to help her. I have had some training with a midwife from back home."

"Good. Lizbeth trusts you, and the bairn will come on the morrow, ye mark m'words. I have been meanin' tae call the physician but I daena want him in m'house. I will continue tae mean tae call for him. Now get ye upstairs. The men will be wantin' tae eat next."

29 - KAITLYN

"Lizbeth?"

I crept into her room, but I didn't need to. Her smile was wide and she looked fresh and rested like she was about to bound from her bed. "Kaitlyn!" She gestured for me to come to her and hugged me happily.

I said, "I have been so worried about you, but you look great."

Her rounded stomach jutted under the sheets. Her bed was big and comfortable.

"Have ye met Madame Greer? She has sent me here tae rest though I daena need tae. But she is wise on everythin' and whatever she tells me tae do, I do."

"She made me pray this morning."

She leveled her gaze on me. "Good," she brushed her covers. "You listened tae her on it, she seemed pleased?"

I nodded.

"Good. She is on your side, Kaitlyn, she will protect ye as she can, but daena cross her. There are rumblings about ye. That Young Magnus is bein' controlled by ye and ye are the cause of the Campbell war. But I am doin' my best tae keep ye safe."

"Thank you." My mind was rolling with the trouble of it, what did they mean? Were people calling me a witch? I couldn't even imagine what that meant – like a *witch* witch? But I was grateful to Lizbeth and Greer for their protection.

Lizbeth said, "Tell me what ye know of the weapons?"

I moved off the edge of her bed and pulled up a chair. "They're from Donnan's kingdom. Magnus's father. I don't know anything about them. He doesn't know anything about them. I knew how to drive them only because my father taught me to ride a vehicle similar to that. It wasn't a weapon, it was something to ride. It's hard to explain. In the islands, where I'm from, they use something like that — teaching me to ride was like teaching your daughter to ride a horse. But the weapons, the men, I didn't know them, and I didn't know they would follow us with so much destruction. I am so sorry about it."

Her hand went up to my cheek. "I imagine ye are, sweet Kaitlyn. I imagine ye are. I have seen ye chased with horrors that I couldna imagine and now I have seen them with m'own eyes. Tis terrible what they can do. And this is the same history Black Mac has told us, he was greatly missin' ye both. How is Young Magnus?"

"His ribs are healed, but he is very worried about his family, especially Sean."

She sighed. "I am worried about him too. He sent me from the castle though I begged him tae leave with us. He would nae listen tae me, twas the first time he wouldna listen tae me."

"Magnus was wondering if he sent you away to protect you?"

She sighed again. "It has crossed my mind, but his place is with us, nae with the Earl and his aspirations, nae with this man, Commander Davis. His place is with us."

"Magnus will meet with him, he will try to straighten it out."

"Good."

"Where are your bairns?"

She laughed. "They are safe. They are with their nurse. I see them when I am up tae it. There are so many now, three, tis exhaustin' tae think on it."

"There will be a fourth soon."

She widened her eyes swallowed some air. "I keep remindin' m'self, every bairn is a blessin'."

"I have been wanting to talk to you about something... I asked a great many questions of a physician that I trust and I have brought medicines. I would like to be here for the birth. If you will have me. I think I can help."

"You hae been tae a birth before, sister?"

"No, but—"

"Tis the kind of carryin' on that might scare ye from the joy of motherhood for good. Magnus is okay with ye bein' here for it?"

"He is, he knows I have some knowledge on it now."

"Well, I would wish tae say I daena need ye, but Mildred Campbell dinna survive it nae three months ago. The physician attended her, he is more likely tae deliver one tae the grave."

"Oh god, don't say that."

"I have tae be ready, Kaitlyn. Tis possible that these days may be my last."

"Well, I don't think we should be so dark about it. This might not be your last days, this might very well be some of your best days if I can help it."

Lizbeth smiled. "Tis good tae have ye home, sister. Tis ice cold outside and rainin'. What will we do with ourselves?"

30 - KAITLYN

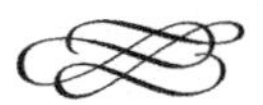

Magnus knocked on the door. He set down a few boxes of my equipment and medicines and kissed me on the cheek. I gave him my chair and he sat down by the bed. "Hello Lizbeth, are ye well?"

She sprawled back her arms and said dramatically, "I am barely able tae manage, I fear my end is near."

Magnus's eyes went big.

She grinned. "Tis nae true, Young Magnus. I am fine, I am only in bed because Madame Greer is makin' me intae an invalid because it will be better for my reputation tae barely survive the birth than tae be my mother's daughter and survive everythin' with the help of the devil."

Magnus shook his head. "Ye scared me."

She patted the back of his hand. "Twas nae fair of me, ye have had too much fear these days. I am sorry for it."

He said, "You canna talk of leavin' us, we need ye."

"Sean daena, he has turned his back on the family."

"I daena ken what is happenin' with Sean, but I will learn it. Are ye havin' a bairn this morn?"

"By the morrow, tis the new moon tonight."

I asked, "Why? What does that have to do with it?"

She laughed merrily. "The moon has always got some mischief tae it, and will likely call the bairn out in the middle of a darkened night. Also Madame Greer told me the bairn would be born on the New Moon and I daena hae the will tae argue with her."

We all chuckled about it.

Magnus said, "Lizbeth, I intend tae leave Kaitlyn with ye today but I need tae speak tae her on some things first."

"Of course."

I followed Magnus to the hall.

In the hall he ran his hands through his hair. "Have ye heard what they are saying about ye, Kaitlyn?"

"Yes, but don't worry about it, Magnus. Madame Greer and Lizbeth are protecting me. I spent the morning in prayer. Don't worry." I smoothed my fingertips on his temple.

"Tis hard tae trust anyone, they are all at odds with each other and—"

"We've caused it, we're going to fix it. Has there been any news about the castle?"

"Nae movement, but I have tae believe they ken we are here. The men want tae storm the castle tonight..."

"Oh. I thought—" I thought I would be with them, because of our whole 'Magnus won't leave Kaitlyn by herself' thing, but there wasn't anyway to reconcile the two missions. He had to storm a castle. I had to help deliver a baby. And how could I help with the storming? I didn't have the right skills.

He said, "I wanted tae wait, but the truth is, Kaitlyn, they could bring the fight here, to these village men. They shouldna have tae fight for their homes. These are peaceable people. Lizbeth is here, we daena want a battle in the streets while she is deliverin' a bairn."

"I don't think it will be helpful to deliver a bairn when she knows her husband is fighting at the castle either."

"What would ye have me do, Kaitlyn? Your word is my command."

"You don't have to say that. I actually don't want to be your commander. I just want to make sure we've thought this all through." There was a humming sound outside the house.

My eyes went wide. "What is that noise?"

"The drones. They send them regular tae look around the village. There have been many since we arrived last night. Daena go outside, Kaitlyn. Stay from the windows."

"Oh. Yeah, okay."

"I have the men, tonight will be dark. We can take the castle and time-jump the weapons tae Florida."

I stared over his right shoulder, nodding, thinking it through. "Who will time jump with the vessels?"

"Quentin and Tyler. I will give ye the other vessel."

"What if you're in danger? You'll jump with them?" We were back here, in that place where there were too many possibilities. We couldn't come to an agreement on where to meet because there wasn't anyway to meet. "Be back by tomorrow. No matter what. Tomorrow, so I don't worry."

He nodded. "And I'll have my walkytalk. You will ken what is happenin'."

"Of course. Okay. This is good."

He pulled me into his arms and we held each other for another long time.

He whispered, "I love ye," into my hair. "I have tae meet the men. We have tae discuss the plans. And we have tae get our weapons and men tae the castle, there is much to do."

I held tighter. "I can't let go. Can you hold me a little longer?"

"Aye."

He cradled my head to his chest and I didn't think I could ever let go. It was another one of those moments where I felt like this was it — the last time. I breathed in, the cloth spread across his chest full of the scent of him.

I didn't want to break the silence, but I had to say how I felt. "I love you my husband. You are my everything."

He squeezed me closer. His voice vibrated his chest against my ear. "As you are mine, mo reul-iuil. For a time we will have only the voices from these small boxes, but you will ken that my voice is from me, near enough, doin' everything I can tae come home."

I hugged him again and stepped back. I patted my waist belt with the two-way radio on it. He patted his two-way radio in his leather pouch, strapped to his sword strap, situated over his heart.

"I'm going to go back to Lizbeth."

"Your gear is in the room. Everythin' ye need."

"Did you have something for breakfast from the supplies?"

"I did. I will see ye soon."

And then we both turned and walked toward our different journeys.

31 - MAGNUS

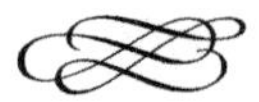

The afternoon had been long. We gathered supplies, weapons, and men and met in the woods to formulate a plan.

We knew Commander Davis's men would have seen the storm that announced our arrival. The drones were here, watching the village.

We were scourin' the woods searchin' for the men navigation' the drones. And we kent Commander Davis would send more men tae the village tonight. We had tae cut them off before they made it there.

The meetin' had been difficult — Quentin and Liam and many of the other men were convinced Sean had turned a traitor.

I thought he was pretendin' the part.

I wanted tae count on him. We were brothers and I had grown used tae thinking of his life as my own. We had fought together. We had celebrated and mourned and we had gotten intae a great many scrapes together. I couldna believe he would turn his back on me.

But I especially disbelieved he would turn on Lizbeth. She

had been like a mother tae him, a friend. He trusted her in everythin'. If she told him tae come away from the castle and he refused, he had a reason. I was sure of it.

Also I couldna believe he would ride against the village. Twas full of family. Friends. I couldna believe it.

So I thought he would remain at the castle.

It nagged at me though, some of his last words, he wouldna listen tae me about the throne. He had seemed irritated that I wasna wantin' tae take it.

I thought twas brotherly advice, but perhaps twas somethin' more ominous?

But I could nae reconcile it with the man I grew up with.

32 - MAGNUS

Quentin and Tyler and I rode tae the castle, crossing the River Tay at the old bridge and following along the river banks. We hoped tae have the element of surprise. Quentin was verra good at ridin' a horse. Tyler was good enough.

In the far distance we could see the smoke of the camp set tae draw Davis's men away from both the castle and the village. As we drew nearer tae the banks of the river, I tapped the button on my walkytalk. Kaitlyn's voice came through. "Hi."

"Good evenin', mo reul-iuil. I wanted ye tae ken I was arrived at the river. We will be goin' through the tunnels tae the castle now."

"The baby is coming tonight."

"Tell Lizbeth God speed."

"She says the same to you. I love you. Be careful."

"I love ye too. From now on I will send ye the signals tae ken I am a'right."

"Thank you. I'll see you soon."

And that was it. We dropped from our horses and left them tethered tae trees.

I had a miner's lamp on my forehead and though twas dark I found the tunnel entrance easily. I had spent much time here with Sean.

Which meant Sean kent about the tunnels, too.

~

Tyler asked, "So we're going to go into this dark as shit hole?"

Quentin was loading weapons. "Yep, and you're going first."

Tyler joked, "I'm the new guy, why do I have to do anything first?"

Quentin said, "Because you know how in all the movies the black guy dies? I am not dying. I've been stuck here eating crap food for four months. Trying to keep a bunch of medieval white guys from accidentally blowing themselves up with weapons way past their brainpower to comprehend. And I'm not dying now. Not this close. So you, my new friend, are going to do all the bull-shit tasks, not me—"

I said, "I will go first. Tis my hole. My death tae meet."

Quentin said, "Well that got dark fast, boss. I didn't mean it like that."

I strapped a gun tae my waist. "I dinna take it like that. I will go first so the black man and the new guy both winna die." I patted the walkytalk and joked, "Unless of course the death comes from behind."

Tyler and Quentin both groaned. I led the way intae the tunnel.

~

The tunnel was smaller than I remembered and I was bigger than I'd been when I was young. As a boy this had been fun but now bendin' under the low ceiling was exhaustin'.

I tried tae keep my light off, but beamed it every few feet tae check our progress. Then I banged my head, hard. I groaned.

Quentin's voice was a whisper. "You okay, boss?"

I held my hand tae my head and tried tae get on top of the pain. "Och. I rattled m'skull." I switched on the light and checked my hand, twas a trickle of blood on it. I checked again. The blood wasna much. "Tis good." I switched off the light remembering Kaitlyn stretching the bandage on my forehead at that long ago castle before she jumped by herself tae the future.

I should have made her promise tae do it this time too.

I used the button on my walkytalk tae send her a chirp. That was how we agreed tae contact each other. A sound. It meant: I am alive. I canna speak tae ye though, but I am alive.

We went farther, much farther, creeping along as quiet as we could be until finally I drew us tae a halt. I listened for the noises of the castle above. Twas silent. A place that should be bustlin' with the noise of hundreds of men was silent as a grave. What of Sean's wife and children? The servants? Liam said there would be people there, were they all in hiding?

The openin' tae the tunnels let out on a small storehouse in the back of one of the smallest larders. There was a rickety stair that led tae the kitchen. Still nae people tae meet us. We climbed stealthily up and twas a first that the kitchen was empty.

I glanced at Quentin. He kent this was extraordinary. He gestured we needed tae be cautious. I nodded in agreement.

We checked twas clear, then passed through a small courtyard with a door at the far end that led intae the larger courtyard. I haena seen it since the day it had been blown apart, months before. We clung tae the edges and crept tae the door.

33 - KAITLYN

Every so often all day long there had been drones flying past the house. Every so often there would be the soft knock on the door, the voice of a guard. Lizbeth would answer that we were okay and then we'd hear the guard's footsteps going away.

The whole village was in lockdown, hiding from the drones and waiting for the fighting to end and the men to come home.

Lizbeth and I talked. I told her about Zach and Emma's wedding. I even told her that Lady Mairead had appeared. I didn't tell her that Magnus was going to be a father. I couldn't bear to say it out loud.

I knew that it was not very helpful to lay on your back for the last weeks of your pregnancy, so I talked Lizbeth into getting up and we walked around the room. I turned it into a game of 'follow the leader' and we climbed over a chair, crawled across the bed, twirled in the middle of the room, did a couple of kickboxing moves, and then did it all again. It was silly looking and hilarious until Madame Greer's voice bellowed from downstairs, "What is all the noise up there?" And we collapsed onto the bed laughing.

"Fine," Lizbeth said, "I will just lay here and..." She turned to me, her eyes wide. "Ugh. Either that drink ye made me swallow has turned or I am beginnin' the pains."

"Really? Oh my god, really?" I took to the chair facing the bed. "Now what do we do?"

"I think we best send Madame Greer for the midwife." She clutched her stomach, her brow drawn as she climbed under the covers of the bed.

34 - KAITLYN

My radio squawked.

Lizbeth asked, "What is that sound?"

"It's Magnus." I answered him and we spoke for a moment while Lizbeth watched. She was between contractions. After we said goodbye, I held the radio in my hands and stared down at it wishing he could keep speaking to me for longer.

"Twas Young Magnus's voice? How dost ye do that?"

"It was, it's called a two-way radio. I can hear him, and he can hear me though we are very far apart. It's kind of like how when you cup your hands around your mouth to yell louder? Like that."

"And twas tae say ye love each other?"

I nodded. Then I added, "So he would know."

"I think he kens, ye are his wife."

I smiled. "In the New World, where I'm from, we like to remind each other."

Lizbeth shook her head. "Sounds like a terrible idea tae me, just when ye have some peace and quiet the thing reminds ye tae think on your husband again."

I laughed. "I hadn't thought of it that way. I suppose we're used to it so we don't mind."

"How would ye be used tae it, a voice with nae body ringing around the room? Tellin' ye he loves ye, of course he loves ye, he is your husband!" She huffed and put her hands in her lap, on her rounded tummy. Then the corner of her mouth turned up a bit. "Twas verra sweet though, Young Magnus often speaks tae ye like this?"

I said, "Yes. Always. Whenever he can."

"He is a good boy. I am verra pleased with how he turned out. Sean though..." She sighed and another contraction came on right then.

It had been three hours. The night was fully black. We hadn't heard from the men except for the occasional chirp that meant Magnus was okay but not able to talk right now. I didn't answer it because I didn't want to blow his cover, but I really wished I could just push the button and say hi.

And tell him that I might be in over my head.

To tell him that the midwife hadn't come because the drones scared her away.

That Lizbeth was groaning and the drones were buzzing outside, hovering over our house, and now they had lights shining outside, and scaring the 'ever loving shit,' as my grandma liked to say, out of me.

Madame Greer buzzed in and out of the room. She hadn't had children of her own, choosing instead to overly mother the entire village, and seemed at a loss what to do, possibly for the first time in her life.

My hands shook with fear.

I used a flashlight and reread the passages on first stages of labor. I set up a camping lantern by the bed. Madame Greer wasn't surprised by anything I might have in my possession, there were drones outside after all, so she took it all in stride. Especially when she saw me pray again.

I literally couldn't think of what else to do.

I asked Lizbeth, "Is this how it usually goes?"

She moaned through a contraction. "Aye, Kaitlyn, tis the way of it."

"Okay, I'll keep asking this. I just — I don't know, so I'll keep checking in on it. But don't worry. I know what to do. If it comes to it."

My hands shook. I begged God, the universe, and anyone else who might be listening for help. I really really thought there should be someone else here.

I spread out the first aid kit on a clean towel.

I put my wedding ring in a box for safe keeping and washed my hands in boiled water for the fifteenth time.

35 - MAGNUS

We rushed out into the open courtyard of the dark castle and my eyes adjusted tae see Sean, crouched on top of a pile of rubble, sword in hand, near the broken-down front wall of the castle. He glowed in the headlight of one of the vehicles sitting in the middle of the rubble. I made a quick count, five. Lined up against the wall.

Quentin said, "Before I left I dismantled the ignitions. I guess they haven't figured out how to fix them yet."

I had tae project my voice across the way. "Brother, how have ye been?"

Sean glared. "I have been better, Young Magnus. Before ye came and destroyed our home, our family."

"I haena meant tae."

"Why dinna ye go tae your kingdom, take your throne?"

I took some steps toward his pile of rubble. "I was injured. You ken this. I couldna fight in my condition. I had tae heal, but I am back now tae clean up the mess. Tae see ye. Tae meet Lizbeth's bairn, bein' born tonight in the village."

Sean scowled. "I told her tae stay here under my protection.

She is as impetuous as always." He stepped down the pile of rubble, coming closer.

"She said the same of ye. I think she believed the man, what is his name, Commander Davis? She believed him tae be dangerous." I drew my sword. "And she is right, Sean, he is too dangerous tae ally yourself with him. He works for my Uncle Samuel—"

"They are here, looking for ye. You should have fought them there, now ye have brought their fury on us all. I have tae decide tae side with them and our family will live, or side with you and what...?" He swung his arms out. "We all die at the mercy of their flyin' weapons?"

He continued, "All I have tae do is kill ye or turn ye over, and they will leave."

I shook my head. "You daena want tae go down that road, Sean, tis a dark place."

Quentin and Tyler were circling the courtyard, slowly, moving toward the vehicles.

"What is, killin' brothers? You seem tae think nothin' on it."

"I think on it much. Let us go intae the keep, and sit, and talk tae each other over a mug of ale. We can rid the lands of these men, and then I will go fight for my kingdom. I will, I have spoken of it with Kaitlyn, we have decided. I will have a son, as you have a child, as does Lizbeth. I'll go fight and then we'll all live safe."

He scoffed. "You have done nothin' but bring darkness on us all." He looked down at the ground and shook his head. Then he raised his sword, bellowed, and charged me preparin' tae swing.

36 - KAITLYN

Lizbeth's hand gripped mine. She was moaning and writhing with the contractions, then coming out of them to talk in a floaty, spacey way, a little out of her head. Madame Greer entered and asked, "How is Lizbeth, dear?"

I had just gone through my protocol: First I would ask, "Does this feel like your usual births?" Lizbeth said yes, but she also seemed a little like she didn't hear me. Second, while trying not to panic, I would flip through the pages of the Emergency Childbirth book again, hands trembling, to see what I needed to be watching for.

I answered Madame Greer that it seemed like it was all going well.

Another contraction began. They were very close now.

Madame Greer said, "Well, that sounded like it was a'nearin'."

My stomach dropped for the tenth time that hour. "Can you boil me some more water?"

Madame Greer squeezed my shoulder and left the room.

I listened to the moans of Lizbeth. The sound of the drones as they hovered over our house. A drone fired shots along the street, so terrifyingly loud I slammed my hands over my ears. Lizbeth whimpered.

I tried to console her. "The men are looking for the navigators, as soon as they find them the drones will stop. Soon."

I put my hand on the radio, wishing I could talk to him, to tell him how scary this was.

Lizbeth was drifting in and out of consciousness between the contractions, then reviving to raise up and moan. The contractions were coming faster. She sounded weak and exhausted.

I pulled her up during a contraction to see if that would help. I held her around her shoulders while she stood and moaned and her sounds changed to an active groaning growling sound that surprised me.

She dropped to her knees by the bed.

"Oh, oh, oh!" I scrambled for a stack of towels and shoved them around her knees and all around her legs. I wished I had spent the afternoon washing this floor instead of whiling away the time talking. I could have been useful. It was bacteria that was the biggest issue after all. The thought made the blood rush to my head like I was going to pass out from fear of germs.

Madame Greer came into the room again. I was so relieved to see her that I started to cry. "Can you um, oh God, um, hold her shoulder, help her stay here like this, um, I have to — again." I poured alcohol on my hands and wiggled it into all the cracks and crevices, tears streaming down my cheeks. I was not cut out for this. What was I doing, trying to save someone's life? My new sister that I loved. I was way way way over my head. I should have time-jumped a midwife here instead of stupid Tyler.

I turned back to Lizbeth and held her up under her arm

while Madame Greer held her up by the other arm and Lizbeth's noises turned to a groaning and shrieking sound. "She's pushing," I said to no one but myself. This was where it would get serious. I had to get on top of my fear.

I wanted to read my book again, but we were already here in needing-to-know.

Lizbeth collapsed her head down on the bed with a whimper. I leaned beside her almost nose to nose. "You're doing great. You're going to meet your new baby soon. Does that sound good?"

"Aye I want the bloody bairn out of me now, Kaitlyn."

"That sounds good, let's do that. I'm going to look and see what's happening, okay?" A drone hovered lower outside, buzzing and worrying us with its insistent noisiness.

I reached for my flashlight, pulled up the hem of her shift, and shined the light between her legs. I didn't really know what I was seeing. It was dark and freaking weird looking, but it looked like a solid curve was pressing against her skin, bulging out.

She tensed and raised up again. Madame Greer held her shoulder and made soothing sounds as Lizbeth groaned and whimpered and it was happening — a baby's head was pushing down and out. I dropped the flashlight to the towels, quickly pulled on a pair of latex gloves, and got my hands there in time for the whole head to emerge.

"The head is out, oh my god, it's—" I cradled the head and pushed the towels up to create a pillow for the landing, Lizbeth rested for a moment and pushed again and the baby slid, slippery as fuck, right through my hands to the towels. "Oh my god, it's a baby Lizbeth. A baby!"

She said, "I should hope so, Kaitlyn, I have been birthin' for too many hours for it tae nae be a bairn."

I laughed one of those laughs that was really on the verge of hysteria. I pulled a clean towel from my pile and with my hands still shaking I wrapped it around the baby who started to move a bit. I passed the baby up through Lizbeth's legs to her front and helped her turn around so she was sitting on the towels leaning against the bed. Her baby on her stomach.

I beamed at them. "So that was easy."

Madame Greer batted me with a handkerchief she kept in her apron. Lizbeth laughed. We sat for a moment watching the baby as it pinked up and made some mewling sounds.

37 - MAGNUS

I dodged his blade. "Sean, ye daena want tae kill me. I daena want tae kill ye. Please, let us talk it through."

"If ye are dead and delivered they have said they would leave our family alone. They would let us keep the weapons and I would be favored by the king."

His sword swept down and I met it blade tae blade. I argued, "We can defeat them. You daena need tae take their side. How can ye brother, you have never raised a blade tae me, how can ye take the side of a stranger tae us?"

His eyes looked a deep betrayal.

I said, "You canna trust them. Ye can trust me, Sean. Ye can trust Lizbeth. We are your family. We will—"

"You are only my brother by half." His sword swung from the right, aimed toward my side. I dodged it but twas too close for someone who wasna tryin' tae kill me.

Quentin's voice came from behind me as I stumbled. "You got this, boss?"

"Aye." I dinna take my eyes from Sean.

Sean said, "You daena have this, Young Magnus, I will kill ye tae protect my family."

"Why? Tis nae body left tae protect. They have all left ye. The weapons, these men, they are destroyin' our family, nae me."

"Tis nae your family. Your father is nae a Campbell. He werena even Scottish. Ye haena been raised among us. We will be better off without your side of the family."

My fury was rising. I prowled to his right. "I ken tis hard tae use your brain when ye have been used tae Lizbeth thinkin' for ye, but if ye winna listen tae her on this you will have tae try tae think for yourself — ye are speakin' as Mairead spoke tae me just yesterday. Are ye proud tae be takin' after our dear mother, Sean?"

Sean growled and bore down on me, his sword arcing down, left and right. I blocked and backed up across the courtyard.

"Who dost ye trust more, me or Commander Davis?"

Sean said, "I daena trust ye, you brought them here."

I swung back hard, our blades crashed, then our arms locked together face to face. "If I brought them here, let me take them away. My kingdom is nae lost. I will fight for it. I will remove these men from our lands. I need ye tae fight with me, Sean. We can do it together."

He shoved me off, but then Quentin was right behind him, a moment later Sean was convulsin' and then he crumpled tae the ground.

Quentin said, "Sorry Boss, it's a taser. It drops assholes. I mean, I get that he's your brother, but he has been needing to stop his bullshit for a while. I couldn't watch it anymore."

Sean was a pile of lifeless body on the ground.

I asked, "Will he be okay?"

"Yeah, he'll be fine, grab his sword. He'll come out of it in a moment and he might be cranky. But we'll be long gone anyway."

The sound of the buzzing of vehicles came from the direction of the woods beyond the walls.

38 - KAITLYN

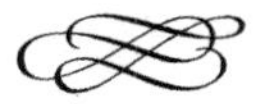

I had been told what to look for, but I hadn't considered what it would be like to do it for the first time in the dark. The placenta was out and in a bowl. I asked Madame Greer to hold the flashlight over it while I picked up the placenta and checked every section of it. I had been told to look for lobes that didn't match and one looked weird. I flipped it over and looked from every angle. One section did have a suspicious looking dip, like a crater on the surface, kind of like a small open wound on something that could only be described as a big open wound.

No.

I took a deep breath. "Lizbeth, I was told that I needed to get all of this out. I'm sorry, that's what I was told. Okay? Can you lay back down?"

The midwife I spoke to had shown me the pages that I would need in this instance. I had a bookmark. I flipped to it and broke the back of the binding so the book would lay flat. Then I changed my gloves and it wasn't easy because my hands were shaking like dry leaves on a tree. In an windstorm. In a freaking earthquake.

"This will be super uncomfortable and it might hurt like hell, Lizbeth, but I have to..." A drone retuned to the window, its searchlight sweeping across the panes with its too-loud buzz filling the air around us.

Madame Greer got down on her knees beside the bed and began to pray.

"Tis okay, Kaitlyn." Lizbeth gritted her teeth and went quiet except for low moans. I placed a hand on her stomach and held while I put my fingers up inside her and swept around with my finger edges for a — there was something. It was stuck but when I brushed along it again it peeled away, holding it in between my two fingers. I pulled it out. Was that it? Enough? I pressed it to the placenta and it looked like the part that had been missing.

Lizbeth looked pale and weak. Madame Greer was praying with a steady murmur.

There was also a jagged tear to deal with. I yanked the midwifery kit closer and pawed through it for the needle. My hands were shaking even more. I changed my gloves for the third time and then got the alcohol bottle and poured alcohol on all the things I had just pawed through. I had pads with numbing stuff and I swabbed it all around and then I cleaned the area, and pulling the two edges closer, jabbed the needle into her skin, oh my god, and pulled it through.

"I'm sorry, I'm so sorry." She was crying, I needed to do at least one more. "Just one more don't worry, please don't worry." I was trying for my most nurse-like voice, but I—

I did it once more then created a knot. I changed the towel under Lizbeth and pulled off the latex gloves and began opening bottles of medicines and pouring them into a small bowl. I passed them to her with filtered water.

"We have to keep that area clean. That's what these towels are for. Clean towels."

The buzzing sound of the drones was getting louder and

louder. I pulled a towel up between her legs and then I pulled the covers up to her chest and wrapped a swaddling blanket around the baby. "We have to make sure you don't run a fever. If you get hot, will you tell—"

There was a loud banging on the front door.

Madame Greer said, "Tis probably the physician." She stood and brushed off her skirts.

My eyes went wide.

Lizbeth asked, "You winna show him any of these contraptions?"

Madame Greer said, "I wouldna dream of it — Madame Kaitlyn, is Lizbeth finished with the whole experience, can we tell the physician he is nae necessary?"

I nodded. "But please don't say anything, you know, that will get me in trouble."

Madame Greer put her hand on my cheek. "Did ye save her life?"

"I hope so."

"And I have watched ye in prayer most of this day, it must have been God working through ye. Tis the only explanation as ye have nae bairns of your own."

Another loud bang on the door.

She huffed. "Please hide all of this verra fast, I will attempt tae keep him down the stairs for a fair while."

She bustled down the steps.

I slammed all the midwifery tools into their case and locked it. I scooped up the towels and shoved them under the bed. The swaddling blanket was a wool-like fleece. I could defend it by saying it was from the West Indies.

I remembered in the last moment to turn off the flashlight and lantern and shove them under the bed, throwing us into pitch blackness as footsteps clomped up the stairs. Fast.

39 - MAGNUS

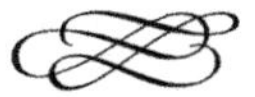

The sound of the vehicles drew closer, their noise growin' louder. Quentin jogged tae the corner where the weapons were chained together ready tae go. "Come on boss, jump with us!"

Sean was groanin' and beginning tae get up. I stood over him, with both of our swords in my hand.

A storm built in the open space above the courtyard, wind gusts blowing dust and debris around in circles.

Tyler gestured for me tae come on. Quentin held the vessel, he called, "Come with us to Florida. Davis is coming, this is a losing battle."

Sean looked up at me. "What did ye do tae me?"

"One of my men grew tired of your stubbornness. Ye are ruttin' and bellowin' like a stag without the sense tae ken ye are wrong. He disarmed ye tae protect me."

Sean held his head in his hands.

I said, "My kingdom is nae lost. I will fight for it. I will remove these men from our lands. I need ye tae fight with me, Sean. We can do it together." The storm was a full blown frenzy.

Through the wind I barely made out Quentin's voice, calling me to come with them.

I yelled, "Go without me!"

Headlights glared around the space as three vehicles crashed through the hole in the wall and climbed up a pile of debris.

I shielded my eyes from the blinding lights and the windswept dust.

I tapped the switch on my radio. "Kaitlyn, I love ye. I fought Sean, I tried tae reason with him, but I am captured. I am goin' tae the future but I will come home. I promise."

There was static and Kaitlyn's voice, "Magnus—" and then nothing.

Sean looked up at me from the ground. "Why arna ye leavin' again?"

"I told ye, I will stand and fight with ye."

"And I told ye that I daena fight on your side. I mean tae kill ye — will be easier."

I shook my head. "Easy? I will make it verra difficult. But you daena want tae kill me. Trust me in this. I am the king. I will stop their attacks—"

The winds whipped faster, a storm built above us, wind and lighnin' and spiraling gusts causin' me tae stumble.

"Fight with me." I yelled against the wind as I tossed his sword tae the ground beside him. He groaned and lumbered tae his feet. The winds shoved him back.

One of the men stepped from the vehicles and trained his gun on me, yellin' across the courtyard. "Are you, Magnus Archibald Caehlin Campbell?"

I answered, "Aye!" As I was buffeted forward.

"I am Commander Davis, I have orders to place you under arrest."

I said, "Commander Davis, I winna fight. I ask that ye daena leave any of your weapons behind."

Commander Davis grunted. "Yeah, we're taking everything."

The winds were still spinning the space but beginning tae dissipate. I kept my eyes on Sean as I tossed my sword tae my feet.

Commander Davis said, "Drop to your knees. Hands behind your head."

Lights were blindin' me. Commander Davis stalked closer.

"Sean, will ye see tae the family, bring them home?"

Sean said, "Aye." He looked away.

Commander Davis yanked my arms down behind my back, shoved me forward onto the rocks covering the courtyard floor. He bound my wrists.

"I said I will go easily, daena hurt anyone else."

I shifted in the gravel to look behind me. The corner where the vehicles had been grouped looked empty. The winds had grown calm. Quentin and Tyler were headed tae Florida with the vehicles.

Commander Davis stepped on my back, forcing my air from my lungs. "Gather your things men, we have what we need."

Three more vehicles drove into the space. The men brought the vehicles in close together. Headlights shone toward me. The men were silhouetted as they landed the drones and packed up equipment, preparing tae leave.

Another captive was yanked from the back of a vehicle and shoved toward me.

"Och, nae," I said intae the dust and gravel of the courtyard ground.

40 - KAITLYN

I was shoved to my knees beside Magnus.

"I'm sorry, they came to the house, they got me—" I struggled against the ties on my wrists but there was no breaking them.

"What of Lizbeth, is she delivered?"

I nodded. "She had a baby boy. I think she'll be okay. I hope so, I — what are we going to do?"

Magnus shifted to raise his head a bit. "Tis lookin' verra bleak, mo reul-iuil. Our only hope is my barbarian brother standin' over there starin' down at his sword and I daena think he is tae be counted on. Next time I see him I will kill him sure as he's standin' there doing nothing."

I bit my lips. "If you see him again."

"Och, aye." He shifted in the dirt, his cheek on the ground. "We are headed tae the future, I wish I was on my feet tae protect ye."

A loud clanking noise sounded behind me, I scrabbled closer to him and collapsed against him. "I wish I could chew through your bindings."

"What have ye got in your pockets?"

"Nothing, the walkie-talkie. I was so hungover when I got up and just thinking about what I needed for the birth, I didn't put on a knife or anything. I am such a—"

Another person, silhouetted against the lights was shoved to the ground beside us. "Tyler?"

"Yep." His arms were bound behind his back. He was twisting himself around on the ground.

Magnus said, "Why didn't you jump with Quentin?"

"I don't know why the fuck I do anything." He shoved his ankle near my hands. There's a knife there. Right there."

I was clasping and wriggling my fingers, straining against the holds to get to it. "Katie, it's right there, get your fingers on—" He yanked his ankle in the opposite direction and a knife slipped through my fingers and thumped to the ground.

He scrambled up to a sitting position. I dove backwards to pick up the knife.

Magnus met my eyes. "You have it?"

I nodded.

A man came over just then, "All of you, get up."

It wasn't easy to stand. It was dark, but we were also illuminated. I couldn't use my hands, stumbled on my skirt, and almost dropped the knife. Also, it was right behind me in my hands. I didn't know how to get it anywhere safe and hidden. There were men on all sides of us. We were forced to move toward the vehicles. Magnus brushed close to my back. He took a step to turn from me, brushing his hand to mine and taking the blade into his hands.

We were by the vehicles. Pushed into a tight circle, men all around us. I pressed to his back. Tyler pressed close to the other side. We blocked Magnus's hands from view as the clouds built above us.

Tyler's said, "Are we going to do this shit again? Fuck."

I said, "Hold on."

Magnus was silent while he tried to get the knife into a manageable position and then the time jump hit me with a brutal slam to the gut and then it began to feel like I was ripping apart into pieces on a cellular level, molecular, so much pain—

PART II

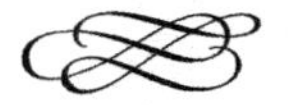

41 - KAITLYN

Darkness, noise, screeching and pain enveloped me, but far away in the distance, Magnus's voice, as if it was miles away. *Kaitlyn.*

Then, *Kaitlyn, get up. We have tae go.*

No no no no no no—

Kaitlyn, get up, we have tae run, now.

I pried open an eye. Magnus's face was close, very close.

He said, "I need ye tae get up so we can run."

I moaned, nodded and pulled myself to a sitting position. We were on a low rooftop, surrounded by grassy lawns.

I turned to look, but Magnus held my cheek, brought my eyes back to his face. "Daena look. Stand up." I stood.

"Look directly at me. Good."

What's happening? I didn't know if the words actually came out of my mouth or stayed rattling around in my head.

Tyler's voice beside us, also standing. "Shit, we've got to get out of here, fast. Get the weapons off them."

Magnus said, "Keep your eyes closed Kaitlyn, stand there." I heard a rustling as he and Tyler rushed around doing something. Then a second later, Magnus had my hand and he was pulling me into a run.

I couldn't help it, as we rushed to the edge of the rooftop and a metal stair going down, I glanced back over my shoulder. The vehicles and weapons were all there and Commander Davis and his men were covered in blood, dead, piled. Left.

Magnus hadn't wanted me to see, but it was as difficult to see as it was to imagine that all that murder and mayhem happened right there beside me while I didn't see.

We made it to the stairs. Tyler first, me, then Magnus. As the door behind us opened and men came out to meet the time jumpers. Guards. From Donnan's kingdom. They —

If I was too slow, if I stumbled, Magnus was dead. I had to descend, fast, though my body wasn't fully working yet.

Tyler made it to the grass. Then me. Magnus right there. We raced behind the building, Magnus yelled "Run!" and we bolted across a long flat grassy lawn toward an orchard.

The men were fast behind us, and then vehicles, a helicopter took to the air — we made it to the trees but there was no protection. A drone flew close and a dark car bore down on us, a cloud of dust billowing behind it.

Tyler was the fastest, he dove between trees, down paths, taking sharp lefts and rights. I was slowing, Magnus had to pull me along.

Tyler took a sharp right and stopped behind a low shed. We pulled up together. "You cool?"

I said, "Yeah, just needed a breath — how're your lungs, Magnus?"

"M'breaths are nae easy, but we must go."

We raced out from behind the shed as the car chasing us screeched to a dirt-billowing stop. A door slid open. Lady Mairead said, "Get in the car, Magnus."

Magnus pushed my lower back up into the car. I climbed into the back. Tyler followed. Magnus sat beside Lady Mairead and the door slammed shut behind us. The car careened us away.

42 - KAITLYN

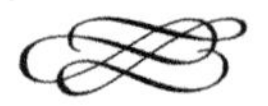

The back windows were blacked out so we couldn't see what was happening outside, but I could tell we were going very very fast. I tried to catch my breath while staring at Magnus's neck and shoulders in front of me, the side of his face. His eyes open. The strength held there in his neck, the corner of his jaw, clenched as we took corners way too fast. I held the seat. Tyler gripped the seat in front of him.

Magnus asked, "Where are ye takin' us?"

Lady Mairead sat stiff and unmoving. "I have an apartment in the city."

I asked, "Will we be safe there?"

Lady Mairead said, "You'll be safe for a time, while Magnus prepares tae battle. Now, if ye can calm your questions, I will speak tae ye on it when we arna drivin' at this speed."

We were going very fast, but it was pretty funny that she couldn't talk through it.

After a very long drive we hit traffic, I could tell because we slowed, stopped, started, slowed and stopped again. Maybe we were in a city? I guessed it meant we were close to where we were going — Lady Mairead's house?

It was odd to be transported without knowing where we were going. Hadn't I been warned to not get into the back of a van with evil diabolical people? Yet here I was. The back of her neck was stiff and straight, thin and weak looking. I could kill her, with my hands, right now. Flashes of Donnan's brutal death slammed into my head again. I took a sharp breath and another. The line between breaths and hyperventilation was a lot thinner than I liked. Panic, panic that I had been swallowing down for hours threatened to pull me under. I looked down at my hand, to spin my wedding ring nervously, but it was gone — I pulled at the bottom of my bodice.

Magnus caught my movements from the corner of his eye. He turned in his seat and reached for my hand. I clutched it in both of mine. There were splatters of blood around his fingernails, I gasped for air. I wasn't close enough. I wrapped around his arm and tucked my face into his shoulder and wished I could go home.

43 - KAITLYN

Our car turned, crept along for a moment, turned again, and finally stopped. Our door slid open. Magnus stepped out then Lady Mairead said, "Follow me," and left before I was all the way out of the car. A total bitch move.

Magnus put his hand on my back to help motivate me to actually want to follow her at all through the parking garage, every space occupied by a similar self-driving car with darkened windows. We went through a fancy door into an elevator and zoomed up to, my guess because it was so fast, the third floor, but my stomach dropped like we were much much higher.

The elevator opened onto a large, luxurious apartment that was full, like every other space in Lady Mairead's life, with a hoard of art and antiquities on every square inch of floor. She said, "I needs be removin' some of this tae my store house, but in the meantime enjoy it. It has been a chore gettin' it here."

The ceilings were very high. There was a wall of glass that probably looked down on the whole mysterious kingdom, or at least a city of it, but the windows were a solid white. I wanted to sit down, but stuff was piled on all the furniture except the small sofa and two chairs meant to be a sitting room in the middle.

She waved an arm and lights went on, blinding me. We all winced. Tyler said, "Fuck, that's bright."

Lady Mairead stopped in mid-walk as if she had only just then noticed he was there. "And you are?"

"I'm Tyler Wilson, I'm a friend."

Lady Mairead's brow went up. She looked directly at me. "Oh? Really?" She humphed and leveled her gaze at Magnus.

He said, "He traveled with us tae the past and was captured and brought here. I intend tae take him home verra soon when we have a vessel tae spare. I consider him a friend and need for his life tae be guarded as Kaitlyn's and my own until then."

Lady Mairead humphed again. "If you say so Magnus, though I daena understand how ye run your household. Things that would send most men intae a fit of rage ye take as acceptable. I canna under—"

"My ability tae control my rage is the only thing keepin' ye alive right now."

She wove her way through paintings and sculptures and cloth-draped furniture to the far end of the room. "Down this hallway you'll find your room, Magnus." She opened the door to a room that was luxuriously decorated: a four-poster bed, Persian rugs, silk sheets, antique furniture with a silver cast, silver covering the windows.

She walked farther down the hallway and gestured toward another room. "This will be your room, Tyler Wilson." She added, "If you would like tae get some rest and freshen up, ye may. We will discuss going forward during dinner in three hours."

"I daena want tae rest! We need tae speak of what has happened — how are ye ensuring our safety here? We have been followed, I am sure of it."

"First, Donnan left me this apartment. Tis mine and Samuel daena ken of it. Second, we were followed, but I have friends high up in the government who will help me hide ye until ye are ready tae fight for your throne. They daena want a spent, wounded prince. Tis crucial that ye be ready tae fight. Third, Samuel is nae smart. He winna find us."

"What is my next move?"

"You are too tired tae discuss it now. Ye have traveled far and must rest. We will talk of it at dinner." She left us standing in the hall.

Tyler asked, "Who the hell is that?"

"Tis my mother," said Magnus. "Daena trust her."

"She hates me," I added.

He chuckled. "I can see. Where did she get those scars on her face? They match yours." He pointed at my cheek.

My hand went to it. It was healing fairly well but was still long pink line down my cheek. I had been rubbing vitamin E oil on it twice a day.

I said, "Her's were given to her by her second husband. Mine was, um—" I shook my head.

"No worries, sorry I mentioned it. I was struck that they looked similar. All right, I definitely need that nap."

Magnus said, "Aye, knock on our door when ye are ready tae go tae dinner, we'll accompany ye. You daena need tae dine with her alone, tis too much tae ask of a guest."

44 - KAITLYN

We turned into our room. The whole left wall should have been panes of glass, but instead was solid, silver metallic.

I located a button on the wall and pressed it. The windows instantly changed to clear and, holy crap, we were on like — I peered over onto the sprawling, chaotic, mostly glass and metal, city. We had to be on the 150th floor. There were other towers all around us, their points vanishing into the sky and the ground so far away it was impossible to see. Vertigo inducing. "What city is this?"

Magnus remained sitting on the bed. "I think tis mine."

My eyes went wide. "Shit, this is huge."

There was a sign on a building opposite. A woman with her arms around a man. The words said, "For when you're ready for anything," the brand name was 'Notwen'. I had no idea what they were selling, but the words were English. Could this be an American city? New York? A drone, similar to the ones that had been terrorizing us in the eighteenth century buzzed up the side of the glass on the floor below. I pressed the button and instantly the glass tint returned to solid silver.

The bed was ornate, antiqued silver. I tried without success to pull at my laces while Magnus took off his now-empty sword belt, sporran, and shoes.

Magnus pulled me over to stand in front of him while he loosened my lacings. I looked down at the bare ring finger on my left hand and tears welled up in my eyes. "I don't have my ring, Magnus, I left it in Lizbeth's bedroom and it's gone..."

Magnus was quiet as he worked on the laces. "Tis nae matter in it, mo reul-iuil, I—"

"There is a matter in it. There is. That was the ring you gave me when we married."

"Twas too small though, ye need a larger stone such as Emma—"

"Magnus, you hush, that is not what the situation calls for. That is my wedding ring and I love it. It's from the 1600s the same as my husband. It has an eternal knot around the band and the garnet might be small but it was a stone passed down through your family — it symbolized everything about us, and now my hand is bare in your mother's house. It seems really really awful that it's gone now." My lower lip trembled and full-blown tears were sure to come next.

"Tis nae gone, Lizbeth has it." He had my laces loose enough and turned me around to face him.

"What if it's lost?"

"Madame Greer will keep it for ye. She kens the worth of jewelry. We will return for it as soon as we can."

I took a deep breath and pouted. "But how will people know we're married? It's the symbol of—"

Magnus gave me a sad smile. "Tis the symbol of my love for ye, but tis nae my love, mo reul-iuil. Tis only a reminder. There is nae magic in it."

"Are you sure?"

"Aye. I am sure. And if ye need a reminder, ye just ask me tae tell ye. I will say it. I mayna be as pretty, but I will say it louder."

I sighed and joked, "You are plenty pretty enough."

He chuckled as he helped me pull the bodice up and off over my arms. My breasts, my ribs, my lungs, my whole self went phew and relaxed downward. It had been days of wearing it. I hung forward. "I may never be straight and perky again."

He joked, "Tis a shame, ye were quite nice when ye were perky."

I stood up straight and released my skirt and pulled my shift off over my head and then started peeling off my long underwear. Until I was naked standing before him. "I want you to know this isn't an invitation. This is me getting comfortable for a nap. My birthday suit is the only pajamas I have."

He grinned. "Your birthday suit — och, I understand the words now."

The bed was covered in fancy pillows. I plowed them off to the fancy rug-covered floor and pulled back the blankets and started to slide in between the sheets, except I was probably completely filthy, having been in the eighteenth — I sighed and climbed off. "I have to take a shower first. I don't want to get out of bed but I have to, and this totally sucks. But you have to too, the thread count on those sheets is too high for us to be this disgusting."

Magnus followed me into the giant bathroom. I used the bathroom, remembering I didn't have any period products with me, because those assholes stole my bag when they kidnapped me away from Lizbeth's bedside. God, she was going to be so worried. Madame Greer would be so worried. I hoped they wouldn't have repercussions for helping me, for hiding my things.

I checked, though, and it looked like my period was basically over, which was good.

While Magnus used the bathroom I turned on the shower, warm, very warm. I climbed in leading him behind me. We stood together under the water, arms around each other, not speaking, just holding each other as the water rained down.

After a while I wondered if we might both be asleep. I pulled away by a step and poured shampoo in my hand. He dutifully leaned forward. I rubbed the citrus scented shampoo around, massaging his scalp, working it through his shoulder-length hair. He moaned happily.

I said, "I saw you had your eyes open in the car when your mother was driving us here... That was new."

He chuckled. "One of them." Then he added, "I kent I had tae watch where we were goin' tae protect ye. I will do anythin' tae protect ye."

"I love you."

"Aye, mo reul-iuil, me as well."

I lathered up my own hair and we stood smiling, looking into each other's eyes with piles of lather on our heads, steam all around, and it was lovely. Like being at home in Florida in my time, that kind of lovely.

I rinsed his hair, bubbles sliding down his muscles, and rinsed my hair, and we both waved the shower wand around our bottoms. I conditioned our hair and rinsed that, too. Toward the end it was getting kind of hot, temperature and sexy-wise, but still — *tired.* Magnus ran his hand down my back and then caught sight of his fingernails, dark with blood. His focus changed to scrubbing his hands.

We just needed to take a nap. This was all to get us to be able to go to bed without mucking up our sheets with blood and dust and dirt and grime from the past.

"Perfect." I declared. I grabbed towels from the pile and Magnus and I wrapped them around our heads and our bodies and finally we crawled onto the bed and slid into the sheets. I climbed in under his arm, across his chest. He adjusted my hair-towel, so it wasn't smothering his face.

His skin was fresh, steaming, warm, faintly smelling of citrus and spice. I hugged my arm across his chest. My body went heavy. I was very close to sleep but right before — before I even knew that I planned to say anything, I said, "Lizbeth had a baby — it was..." I nuzzled into his side. "I don't know..."

Magnus's body stilled with listening.

"It was scary, and overwhelming but happy also, plus crying and..." I wiped the corner of my mouth. Gravity was dragging my lips down and I was drooling on Magnus's chest. "I just..."

I dragged a finger back and forth down his bicep. "I was thinking we should, I don't know... like try again. I mean, I know it's not a good time, that there are a lot of reasons.... but I want that and maybe we could talk about it, soon — trying, I mean."

Magnus asked, "Tae have a bairn, Kaitlyn?"

I nodded up against his chest. "Yeah."

"Aye, I would like that." He tilted my face up and found my lips and kissed me. Sweetly and softly. "Aye," he said again. "Just nae today, I am verra sleepy."

I tucked my head back onto his chest. "Yeah, me too. I just meant we should talk about it. Make a plan. But I would like to."

He said, "Me too," and then we both fell asleep.

45 - KAITLYN

I woke up a bit later totally disoriented. We were in Lady Mairead's apartment, at some strange hour in some unknown century, and we slept in total trust that she wouldn't kill us.

Why was she still alive? Oh right, because even though she wanted to kill me she was also keeping us *alive.* The thread-count on her sheets was quite nice though. Like I could live in this bed.

Magnus rolled onto his side and pulled me close, groggy and not fully awake. He pulled my leg up to his waist, and yes, he was fully awake. I tucked in and wiggled closer and nuzzled into his neck. My lips pressed on the thrum of his heartbeat. His fingers dove between my legs, pulled me forward, drew me closer — he slid inside. It was all so urgent but also sleepy, insistent yet lazy. Wake up sex was awesome like this, familiar, and necessary, but then my excitement was building as he pushed and pulled against me and I held on around his musclebound back, moaning into his neck, breathing this moment, him, into my lungs. This brought clarity — Magnus. Waking in his arms, meeting the future together. He rolled onto his back pulling me up and on him. His hands rubbed down and held my ass, close, tight, firm, I arched back — *ohgodohgod* —

There was a soft knock on our door.

I collapsed down on Magnus's chest. I whispered, "Is the door locked?'

"Aye."

Another soft knock. Magnus's hands tightened against me pulling me closer.

He answered, louder, "Aye?"

Tyler's voice came through the door, "Checking if you guys are awake, I'm starving."

"Aye, we are just awake. Give us a few moments we will come for you in your room."

"Cool."

I giggled, stifling my mouth into his neck as Magnus rolled us over, climbed on and finished, fast, quiet, done. He collapsed onto me. This had become my favorite moment, okay, one of them, him, strong yet weakened. His back taut from holding himself up above me, now spent, on me, his arms collecting me safe, his body holding me down, warm, still inside me, soft and gentle, his breath close to my ear reminding me of him, his heartbeat against my mouth, alive.

All of it. I loved.

He whispered into my ear. "Twas terrible timin'."

I giggled again. "It was. But you still finished strong, my love."

He turned his head to see my face and grinned. "Did I tell ye today that ye are a verra good wife?"

I raised my brow at him. "Isn't that what you were saying with your big manly cock?"

"Och, now ye are definitely the verra best wife."

"By calling your cock big and manly I went up a notch from good to best? Now I feel challenged to see how far I can go."

"Ye can go as far as ye want, I will nae complain." He smirked and rolled off me and disappeared into the bathroom. I heard the familiar sound of him pissing into the toilet. He came back, tossed me another towel. And then we both realized we had to put on our 18th century clothes again. Muck and mire and...

I sighed and pulled the shift over my head and dropped it to the ground.

Magnus put on his kilt while I pulled up my skirt and yanked on my bodice. I stood in front of him so he could tighten my lacings.

He tightened them and tied the knot and then like every time, put his hands on my waist and paused. I gathered that this created big feelings for him, me, from his future, bound up like someone from his present, or past, because he was in both worlds now. He had a tendency to sit there and think on it, possibly enjoy it.

I turned to face him and his expression was less enjoyment and more worry like he wanted to stop time, hold us here forever.

I looked down at him and he met my eyes. His brow creased with worry. I gently rubbed my thumbs along the ridge of his eyebrows, massaging it away. And then I put my hands on his shoulders. "Did you kill those men?"

He nodded. "Aye. While they were collapsed from the pain of travelin'. Tyler helped me on it, but twas my decision." He winced. "I daena like myself much because of it, mo reul-iuil."

I nodded.

"But I couldna let them take us through those doors. Twould have been end of us. I ken tis true, but I am nae the kind of man who wants tae kill like that."

My mouth turned down and I sighed. "You aren't that kind of man." I massaged his forehead and ran my fingers through his hair, pushing it from his face, making it lay down after the damp sleep had riled it up. "You are a gentle man." I pushed up his chin and pressed my lips to his forehead. "The gentlest man I know.

You are also 'Master Magnus' and you handle shit when it needs to be handled. And that shit needed to be handled. So you did. Like this needs to be handled. And guess what? On that rooftop you took step one, get off that rooftop. That's what you had to do." I squeezed his shoulders. "I'm very glad you got me off that rooftop. I'm not sure how glad I am to be here, in Lady Mairead's house. But if there's food involved, I'm willing to deal with just about anything."

Magnus kissed me on the lips and stood. "I am terribly hungry too." As if to punctuate it, his stomach growled. And he and I both laughed.

46 - KAITLYN

I should have recognized trouble ahead when I saw the empty seat, with the place set, but we all sat down without noticing it or forgot to remark on it when we did. Lady Mairead was dressed in a suit dress, a little like something a First Lady might wear, but of that filmy material, and accented with fur and with jewelry that looked gold and sparkly like diamonds. I was of course wrapped in filthy wool. She winced when she saw me.

"Remind me tae have your clothes laundered and suitable clothes brought tae ye, Magnus."

Apparently she wasn't speaking to me. She took her seat at the head of a very long lavishly set table, and her staff, numbering at least eight from what I could see, began buzzing back and forth to the kitchen.

She gestured for Magnus to take the seat to her left and gestured for me and Tyler to sit across from Magnus. Tyler tried to put me close to Lady Mairead, but I dodged for the chair farthest away. I sat down, relieved at my strategy: I would use

Tyler to block my view of Lady Mairead, or better yet, block her view of me.

I swear every time she looked at me her brow raised and her eyes flashed maliciously.

Magnus said, "I need tae take Tyler home as soon as possible, I have a vessel. On the morrow I will deliver him back to Florida." Our glasses were filled with wine.

I asked the woman serving me, "Can I have some water please, I'm very thirsty."

Lady Mairead rolled her eyes in my direction. "Tis always about ye, Kaitlyn? We daena need tae ken your thirst, just ask for water and be done of it."

I hated her so much I wanted to leap across the table and start swinging.

Tyler's expression was 'oh shit, she did not just say that to you,' which was a very small comfort.

I met Magnus's eyes across the table. His expression was 'I love you.' That was enough.

Magnus said, "Explain tae me how we are safe here. Your windows are verra large. I see that they are shielding us from view, but there are drones flyin' around outside. I can hear them."

Lady Mairead waved it away. "You winna be safe here forever, of course, but Minister Donahue at the war ministry is on the other end of the information the drones are gathering. He likes you. He wants ye tae be the next king. More importantly, he likes me verra verra much. I have made it so he feels he canna live without me. He winna tell Samuel where ye are until tis time tae plan your battle."

A basket of warm bread was delivered to the table. I was famished. Tyler and I bumped hands reaching for it. I slathered butter all over a piece and ate hungrily. Magnus ate a piece in two bites and reached for another.

Lady Mairead continued, "Samuel has seized the throne. He is tryin' tae have ye declared dead in absentia'."

Magnus scowled.

She took a demure bite of bread, chewed, and swallowed. "You arrived at the right time, Magnus. We will challenge him tae a battle and—"

A full plate of what looked like pork, potatoes, and vegetables, piled high, was placed in front of me.

But before I could enjoy it a woman I had never seen before entered the living room, swept a long coat with fur accents from her shoulders, and dropped it to the couch. Then she crossed toward the table. To say she walked slowly would be lying, it was more like time stopped around her. She was beautiful: petite, dark, barely dressed — a tight filmy dress that hugged every curve and exposed her very rounded pregnant stomach —

My heart dropped to my feet.

And as she caught sight of Magnus a slow, sexy, very very happy smile spread across her face. She came to the table with her eyes intent only on him.

My face flushed. Warm.

Hot.

Motherfucking sweltering.

Beet red - burning.

Lady Mairead's eyes were settled on my face.

I didn't know what to do. Watch this woman — what was her name?

Or watch Magnus — his elbows were beside his plate, staring straight ahead, alternating between checking my face and looking ahead, then checking my face again.

Here was the thing — I had two courses of action. Freak out. Create a scene. Act like I was losing Magnus.

Or I could — do what? Who was I kidding, I had no idea how

to be a grown up in the current situation — but I could pretend, maybe.

I changed my expression to one that I hoped exuded grace. And competence. I was going for Audrey Hepburn. Wishing I had a cigarette. The ability to exhale smoke rings.

Scratch that.

I wanted to be a dragon. I could catch her chair on fire.

The woman slid into the chair beside my husband. "Hello, Magnus." I hated her fucking face.

"Hello, Bella." He gave her a curt nod. He said, "I'd like tae introduce ye tae my wife, Kaitlyn Campbell. And this is our friend, Tyler Wilson—"

She said, "Oh, really?" With a level of condescension that I might hope some day to aspire to. Bitch.

Her hand went to her stomach and her eyes leveled on me. "It's a pleasure to meet you, Kaitlyn. Magnus has told me so much about you."

I took a deep breath in my 18th century just-been-at-a-birth bodice and muttered, "Jesus-fucking-H-Christ you did not just say that to me." Probably in my head, but how could I tell, the blood was rushing around all up in there, it was likely that I was a step away from eruption.

Lady Mairead said, "I am verra glad ye could join us Bella, we have much tae discuss with Magnus over our plans and his child with you."

Tyler's eyes cut to me, to check on me — no worries, none of this was new information.

I took a sip of my wine. Lady Mairead watched me the whole time with that malicious spark.

She said, "Are you enjoying the wine, Kaitlyn? I had a special one decanted for—"

Poison.

I spit my wine onto my plate.

I scrubbed my tongue with my white cloth napkin. Tears welled up in my eyes.

Either my mother-in-law just killed me. Or I spit on my plate, scrubbed my tongue, and embarrassed myself in front of Magnus's mistress. Plus look how I was dressed in front of her.

Oh god I was not doing this well.

I used my napkin to dab at my eyes, unadorned, because I had no makeup. Bella was, of course, perfectly made up.

Magnus picked up his plate. "Tyler, would ye mind changin' places?"

Tyler said, "Yeah, of course, sheesh, this is — whoa."

Magnus gestured for me to move my plate to the side. He put his plate and his wine in front of me. When the waitress bustled over to take my plate Magnus said to her, "All of Madame Kaitlyn Campbell's dishes and drinks should be placed here, so I may taste of them first."

Lady Mairead said, "I hardly think that is necessary."

Magnus said, "Tis necessary. Ye have threatened her life many times afore and ye have used poison in the past, have ye nae?"

Tyler glanced worried at his food.

"Suit yourself," said Lady Mairead.

Magnus had a new plate brought to him and I was finally able to eat and breathe and deal a bit more with Magnus beside me.

He asked, "So why has Bella been brought intae this?"

"Because her child is now directly in line for the throne."

"I haena married her. I daena intend tae. And when Kaitlyn has a child, our son would take the place."

Lady Mairead made a high pitched 'hmm' sound, a lot like someone who was saying, we shall see. Like she had already seen. And it hit me that she might know my future. And from the expression on her face, she looked like someone who had the foreknowledge to pick a team and the team she was picking was clearly Bella's.

Was I never able to have Magnus's child?

I moved my hand to Magnus's thigh. It was jiggling up and down like he wanted to rush into a fight.

Lady Mairead asked, "Were you able tae get Quentin home from my brother's castle?"

Magnus said, "Barely. Commander Davis was stationed there. Your son, Sean took his side. He turned me over tae him."

She shook her head, "He has the wisdom of his father. If he is nae careful, he will have his early death too." She took a bite of her pork. "What of Lizbeth?"

Magnus said, "Kaitlyn helped her tae deliver safely. You have another grandson."

Lady Mairead nodded and met my eyes. "Well, Kaitlyn, that is excellent of ye, I thank ye for the help ye gave tae her."

"I — you're welcome."

Magnus squeezed my hand.

She picked up a fork and knife. "I regret that while Sean has taken after his father, Lizbeth has taken after me. I fear she haena embraced motherhood as she should have, twould be an easier life for her if she could manage the work of it better." She sighed. "I sent ye away Magnus, because I dinna feel up tae the task, and I think our trouble comes in a great deal from my lack in those capabilities." She chewed a bit while we all sat stunned.

I ate a bit of pork.

She said, "What was your mother like, Kaitlyn. Was she a particularly caring sort of mother?"

I said, "Um, no, um..." it was a little like getting called on by Snape in potions class — it sounded like a benign question, but would probably lead to death by magical spell. "I wouldn't say she was very caring, she wasn't mean or anything, just sort of preoccupied with other things."

"Oh." Lady Mairead chewed and swallowed another bite. "Bella, what was your mother like?"

Bella flipped her hair over her shoulder. "My mother was very loving towards me. She raised me to be an excellent mother someday." She looked at Magnus, "I intend to be a wonderful mother to your child, My... I mean, Magnus."

I threw my napkin to the table.

Lady Mairead cut another slice of meat. "Yes, motherhood is nae easy for some — Kaitlyn, I have been wondering, next time ye go tae see Lizbeth could ye take her some birth control? You have access tae it, I am sure ye use it, and considering she daena have the temperament for motherhood, twould be for the best. Daena ye think?"

"I already left her some, I didn't have a chance to explain it, but there are some instructions. When I go back I will show her how to use them."

"Good good. It's important for women tae ken what they are good at and tae ken when they should give up—"

Magnus said, "Lady Mairead that is enough. I winna have ye lecturin' Kaitlyn on motherin'. Ye thanked her for her help with Lizbeth, let us leave it at that. I want tae ken the details of the plan." He shoved a bite of food in his mouth and chewed furiously.

She glanced at the gold watch on her wrist. "Yes, Minister Donahue will be here in a few minutes to discuss the matter, so luckily we have time for dessert."

A moment later our plates were whisked away and new ones arrived with something like a molded custard, not at all my style of dessert. It was very pretentiously served.

47 - KAITLYN

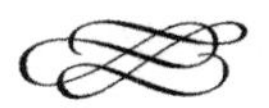

We stood from the table to go to the living room to meet the minister. Bella seemed to wait for Magnus but he was putting his attention on me, so she finally followed Lady Mairead from the room. She looked petulant about it which made me furious.

Tyler asked, "So this is the kind of shit your family does all the time?"

Magnus said, "Och aye, tis a regular dinner for the family of Donnan."

Tyler shook his head. "I want to go to my room, but I also don't want to miss anything, is that wrong? But I really want to go to my room."

Magnus clapped Tyler on the shoulder. "You have been a stalwart friend through this, I thank ye. Go tae your room. Would ye like some ale or wine sent there?"

"Yeah, that would be good."

"I'll arrange it. And I'll arrange your way home first thing."

"Good," he smirked, "Because I wouldn't want to have to

charge you guys with kidnapping." He put his finger and thumb together. "I'm this close."

I said, "That would be great. That's exactly what we need, police involvement."

"You already have people coming at you from all directions." He said, "Okay, as long as you promise to get me back to Florida in time to take my finals. I've been studying, I don't want to miss it." He left for his room.

Magnus wrapped me in his arms. "I am grateful for ye, mo reul-iuil."

"For me? I haven't done anything but spit on my plate. That was embarrassing. Oh and I sat there and got insulted. I look like poop and she's really pretty and I thought of ways to get rid of people with a time machine. I'm thinking I could take Lady Mairead to the Jurassic period and introduce her to a dinosaur. Or get her tickets on the Titanic. Or take her to Europe in the Middle Ages to catch the plague. There's Vesuvius too. That would be cool."

"I haena any notion what ye are speakin' of."

I looked up at him with a half-grin. "History of the world stuff. When this all gets taken care of I'll tell you all about it: dinosaurs, the American revolution, the Titanic, some natural disasters thrown in. The point is, I haven't done anything for you to be proud of me for."

"You just said, 'When all this gets taken care of.' He brought my hand up to his lips and kissed the back of my hand. "You show me in your eyes and in your words that we will get beyond this and back home together. Sometimes I canna believe tis true, but I look at ye beside me and tis in you: your mouth is set, ye are making a list in your head, ye are holdin' my hand. You are leadin' me tae our future."

"God I hope so, it seems kind of bleak today."

"Tis nae bleak, tis simply the next step. And ye are forgetting, I am Master Magnus. I get shit done." He grinned, put his hand on my back, and we walked to the meeting in the other room.

48 - KAITLYN

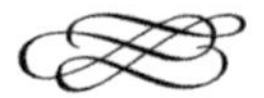

The Bella woman was sitting on the couch with her feet tucked up under her. Lady Mairead was across from her on a chair. The man we were meeting with stood to the side. He was waiting to pick a seat. The space beside Bella was empty, but no one was moving toward it. There were so many artifacts crowded around the space that it was a little like hunkering down in the back room of a crowded antique shop. Lady Mairead's hoarding seemed like the kind that needed professional help.

I glanced at Magnus for cues. I didn't want to sit beside Bella but didn't want him to sit beside her either. The man warmly shook Magnus's hand. Lady Mairead said, "Magnus, ye remember Minister Donahue?"

"Aye. We met at Donnan's Equinox Gala."

Minister Donahue glanced uneasily at me. I tried to meet his eyes while trying not to look like a murderer.

Magnus said, "Minister Donahue I'd like to present my wife, Kaitlyn Campbell."

The Minister shook my hand as if I was distasteful.

After the civilities were over Magnus looked at Lady Mairead. "And…?"

Lady Mairead asked, "What, Magnus? Have a seat."

"There are nae enough seats, ye can see this." He gestured for me to take the chair near Lady Mairead and offered the end of the couch to the Minister. "But tis nae matter, Bella will be unnecessary at this meeting. We will discuss her first and then she can go home. I will stand until then."

"Bella is necessary she is carrying your heir—"

"Will she be fightin' alongside me for the throne? Nae." He turned to Bella. "Bella, when is the bairn due?"

"Your son will be born on June 13th."

"Aye. And are ye safe? Do ye have a place tae live and enough food for ye and the comin' bairn?"

She nodded. "I do. Lady Mairead and Minister Donahue have given me a place in town. It's hidden enough. I have a car and everything I need." Very quietly she said, "Except you."

Her eyes were locked on him and watching it was very very very traumatizing.

So I stared down at my hands, bare, minus my wedding band. And then I closed my eyes because it was all too much to take in.

Magnus's voice. "I am glad ye have what ye need and that ye are safe, Bella. I will protect ye, I have promised that much."

"Thank you for not leaving me to deal with Samuel, that was—"

"You have Kaitlyn tae thank for this. She decided we would protect you and the bairn."

"Oh." She glanced at me. "Thank you, Kaitlyn."

I nodded. "You're welcome." I wanted to add, "I didn't do it for you, I did it for Magnus," but every word I spoke would bring me closer to tears and betray me as 'in over my head,' so I decided to manage my words, keep them close. I looked away.

Magnus asked Minister Donahue, "I think tis all we need

Bella for? She is tae have enough food, whatever she needs. Other than that..."

"Yes, yes, I think that's all we need."

Lady Mairead said, "She needs be there when ye fight Samuel."

Magnus said, "Bella, Lady Mairead needs ye tae accompany her tae the upcoming battle. Minister Donahue will inform ye of the time and place."

Bella said, "Oh."

Magnus said, "You can go home then. I see nae need for ye tae remain."

"You're being so cold to me, My Magnus—"

My head shot up.

Magnus's eyes held a quiet fury.

He watched her for a moment. "I winna argue with ye about the things ye said and did tae me, because I daena care enough tae discuss it. I told ye the truth when we were imprisoned together and I haena changed my mind." He looked down at his hands. But then raised his head and met her eyes. "You kent Kaitlyn was there, Bella, and ye dinna tell me. I understand why ye did it, twas because ye wanted tae survive, but twas her death sentence. So there is nae comin' tae an agreement about it with ye."

She said, "Fine." She stood and smoothed out her dress. She asked the room, "Do you need anything else then?"

Lady Mairead said, "Nae, ye can go home, Bella."

Bella wove her way through the artifacts to the elevator doors.

Magnus slumped down on the newly vacated couch: his elbow on the armrest, his fingers on his mouth, watching me.

I met his eyes.

He nodded and mouthed, "Are ye okay?"

I nodded and mouthed back, "Thank you."

Lady Mairead said, "I suppose ye art proud of yourself, Magnus?"

I interjected, "If he isn't, I am. He managed to get through this whole evening without flying into a rage, I think he's amazing."

He grinned and his eye twinkled. "Why thank ye wife."

Minister Donahue cleared his throat. "Speaking of — to get down to business. There's the matter of a warrant that has been issued for the arrest of Kaitlyn Campbell for the charge of murder against Donnan the Second on the night of the Equinox Gala—"

Magnus said, "Twas self defense."

"Well we are a kingdom of laws. A court will need to decide it. I am bound by the law to turn her over—"

Magnus stayed completely still, relaxed on the couch. "I am the next king, ye winna touch her."

Lady Mairead said, "Magnus, what I think Donahue is trying tae say is that he winna turn her over, but he is bound tae do it. You will need tae move tae take your throne fast if ye want tae keep her from going tae trial. When you are king ye can have her pardoned, isna that right, Donahue?"

"Yes, you could pardon her after her arrest. There would need to be a semblance of propriety, a trial, but yes, you could pardon her."

Magnus leaned forward. "You are sayin' that as the king, my wife would be put on trial for murder? Most of the kings have taken the throne by killin' the man that stood in their way — tis nae fair."

"It's different for the king, Magnus."

"Well that is the first rule I will change then. How do I challenge Samuel?"

"He's taken over the castle, and the running of the kingdom. He's challenged your bloodline through the courts. The case will be heard two days from now. You have a great many people in the government on your side, but the challenge will need to be fought, as you know, in the arena."

Lady Mairead asked, "Does it? A bit of poison perhaps, a tastefully done accident? Or a lowly prostitute could take him tae bed and kill him as Kaitlyn—"

Magnus jumped from his seat, crossed in a step, and yanked the arms of her chair to get her attention. He leaned over her eye to eye and growled, "Watch your tongue. I winna stand for another word of disrespect from ye. I am either a dead man or a king. Kaitlyn is either a widow or a queen. Ye best show us the respect we deserve."

"I was only laying out our options."

"You ken what ye were sayin', daena lie, daena pretend tae be doin' what ye are nae. Tis a deception I am growin' weary of watchin'."

He yanked her chair again and returned to his seat.

Lady Mairead smoothed her hair.

Minister Donahue said, "The only option Magnus has to rule as the legitimate king is to kill Samuel in the arena. Samuel has supporters and they will not accept Magnus's rule without a show of force and power. I will tell you though, he is injured. He hurt his shoulder in a training exercise yesterday."

Magnus met my eyes.

Yes.

Aye.

He said, "Then I challenge him tomorrow."

Minister Donahue said, "You are ready to fight?"

"I am ready enough. Twill be by sword?"

"If you request it."

Magnus nodded.

Minister Donahue said, "It's done then. I'll let Mairead know the details." He straightened his coat. It was adorned with braids and fur and medals of some kind. He seemed pretentiously important, like a cartoon-character general, but I was so glad he was on our side. He seemed convinced he could get things done and that made me feel a little better about all of this.

He shook Magnus's hand again, warmly. "I can't wait to tell my Margaret about meeting you again, she has been all aflutter since you said 'Aye' to her at the Equinox Gala. What a lovely night that was... Until all the drama occurred, of course. But we are setting it to rights now. I will be very glad to see Samuel taken care of. Just between us, he is an evil man."

He clasped Lady Mairead's hand in both of his. "Always good to see you, Mairead. Thank you for bringing the king home."

Then he left.

Magnus returned to his seat and gestured for me to come sit beside him. I did gratefully.

Lady Mairead sat back down across from us.

He squinted his eyes causing her to squirm under his gaze.

She asked, "You are sure ye are ready tae fight on the morrow?"

"Aye." He watched her a moment more. "Answer me this, Lady Mairead, how many chairs do ye have in this apartment?"

She looked around at the furniture and artifacts. "Quite a few."

"Next time ye invite me and Kaitlyn tae your home I would like a seat. Also, in all of this — what is this?"

"I think of it as my collection."

"In all your collectin' ye dinna have the forethought tae make sure Kaitlyn would have some clean clothes tae wear? Before ye invited Bella tae dinner?"

"I daena just have her size—"

"I am askin' ye, as your son, tae show me and my wife respect. I apologize for losin' my temper in front of Minister Donahue, but I canna continue tae allow ye tae treat her this way. You must do better and twill be easier tae practice doin' it now than when I am king and I demand it."

She said, "I meant nothing by it, I—"

"You have been schemin' for so long ye have lost track of doin' it. You should apply yourself tae rememberin' that I deserve better treatment after all that ye have put me through." He stood. "Kaitlyn and I are going tae our room tae rest for the morrow."

She said, "Let Tyler ken that I will arrange tae have someone accompany him tae Florida tomorrow afternoon."

"See, ye can be helpful, thank ye."

Magnus and I swept from the room. It was fun to be the one doing it for once. Leaving Lady Mairead alone to think about what we just said. Mostly Magnus, but it was all for me.

49 - KAITLYN

We took a bottle of wine into Tyler's room to tell him about the plan for tomorrow. He sat on his bed with a glass in his hand. Magnus sat in a chair. I slumped on the floor, bottle in my lap. I kind of thought I should drink a lot, I also didn't really want to, but holding it felt good. Like maybe in a safer time I could drink the anguish away.

Tyler asked a lot of questions.

The biggest one was, "What the hell are you thinking? You're going to fight to the death tomorrow?"

Magnus answered, "Och, aye."

"Why would you fight someone for a throne you don't want?"

"I will let Kaitlyn tell ye on it."

I said, "My thinking is that any king that isn't Magnus is going to chase us through time. And our children through time. Forever. But if Magnus is king, he keeps his children safe."

"Even if they're from another woman?"

"Even then. I can't ask Magnus to choose between me and one of his children, so yeah, we'll protect his son. Even if his mom is a total bitch and I want to smack her stupid bitch face with her stupid fucking bitch smile."

He joked, "You seem pretty chill Katie."

"Considering I just met the woman who is having Magnus's child, yeah, I was surprisingly chill. I may have had a small stroke." I took a swig of wine. Then decided I didn't want to drink anymore and pushed the bottle away.

"That was like a reality tv show, I was expecting chairs to fly."

Magnus joked, "I wanted tae throw a chair but Lady Mairead daena have enough tae use as weapons."

I said, "God when you called her out about it, and when you shook her chair and growled at her — I was so impressed."

"Tis all it takes tae impress ye?" He shook his head. "She has been playing games with us for so long, she daena ken she is doin' it."

"I almost feel sorry for her. I mean, beyond the whole she has been trying to kill me part of it. She's been surviving here, thriving actually, and the one thing she wants is to be a—"

"Mother of a king."

"And she keeps getting so close." I dropped my head back to the wall, with a moan. "Bella is so beautiful. I can't believe I'm going to have to live with that knowledge now."

Magnus started to speak, but Tyler said, "I don't know about that, I mean she's pretty, but I don't think she is prettier than you."

I blushed and glanced at Magnus.

He was leaned back in the arm chair, his mouth leaned on his fingers, his brow drawn down, squinting at Tyler.

Tyler raised his glass to Magnus, "I mean no offense, I assume you tell Kaitlyn that she's beautiful all the time, I just thought hearing it from someone else might help."

Magnus nodded then said, low and slow. "She deserves tae hear it." Then he said, "I think I need tae head tae bed."

Tyler said, "I have one more question about tomorrow. When you go to battle in the arena what will happen to Katie? What if you don't survive it?"

Magnus and I both looked at him without speaking.

"It is possible. I know you've won every fight you've ever fought, but it might happen. Why doesn't Katie come back to Florida with me?"

I shook my head. "Nah, I wouldn't know what's happening." Then I glanced at Magnus's face — he was nodding. "Wait, Magnus, I won't know if you survive it or not."

Magnus said, "Och, I ken it, Kaitlyn, but he may be right in this. While I fight ye would be unprotected. Twould be far safer if ye traveled with Tyler, tomorrow, first thing—"

I glared at Tyler for bringing it up. I said to Magnus, "I disagree. I won't know anything, I'll just be waiting for you again without—"

"I will come the verra next day, ye winna have tae wait."

"Unless you don't, and I won't ever know what—"

Magnus said, "I have spoken on it. Tis decided."

"What? Great, you guys are ganging up on me! Since when does Tyler have any say at all in anything, especially me? Thanks Tyler for sticking your nose in where it's not wanted."

He held his hands up. "I didn't mean to start a whole thing, but seriously, what's to keep Lady Mairead from having you 'taken care of' while Magnus is fighting? She was looking at you at dinner like she was making a list of the ways she would end you."

"Magnus—"

He took a deep breath, his face clouded over. "I want tae spend our last few hours together without argument, Kaitlyn, and I have decided what ye will do on the morrow. You have decided our entire future, would ye nae let me decide something this simple, tae take ye from certain danger?"

I started to speak, but he interrupted, "—and tis nae Tyler decidin' it, tis me, but ye are arguin' against me in front of him. Tis how ye want tae carry on?"

I clamped my mouth shut, opened it again, then clamped it shut again. "No I guess not."

"Good, and so when Tyler jumps tomorrow ye will accompany him. We can leave Lady Mairead from the task."

I didn't mean to say anything more, but I did because I was uncontrollable, apparently. "Will Bella get to be there to congratulate you when you win?"

Magnus's jaw was set. He stood. "Tyler excuse us, we should head tae our room and leave ye from the rest of our discussion." He opened the door. "Kaitlyn, come."

"Fine."

As I left I heard Tyler say, "Sorry m—"

My tempter flared. "Sorry! What are you sorry to him for? I'm the one that deserves an apology because you're messing around in my life with all your asinine opinions!"

"I was going to say, to you, 'Sorry, my bad for involving myself, Katie."

"Oh."

Magnus gestured with his arm, 'after you.'

I did my best impression of a flounce but my heart wasn't in it. It was probably a lot more like a drag.

50 - KAITLYN

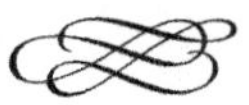

In our room Magnus spoke first. "What are you thinkin', Kaitlyn, with disagreeing with me in front of Tyler? And then bringin' Bella intae it? Ye ken we wouldna have tae deal with her if—"

"If what? Because of me? Because I chose to protect her baby? Well great, I'm seriously regretting that now — and what are you thinking about commanding me in front of him? Why does he bother you so much? He gets you all crazy, and you've never spoken to me like that before."

"I canna explain it, I daena trust him, tis hard tae ken what tae do."

"Well, you shouldn't do this. You think you're keeping me safe but I don't want to be safe if it means I'm not here while you're fighting to the death. God, what if something happens to you and I'm not here to know about it?"

"Nothin' will happen tae me." He sat down on the bed.

"But—"

"And if somethin' did happen tae me, twould be nothin' ye could do on it. Tis only me that can fight."

"You know what? Listen. You don't get to do this. You promised. You promised me that we would be together and that we weren't going to keep doing this, separating from each other. Now, first thing, you're sending me away."

"When Minister Donahue was talking about it, he said there has tae be a trial. Even if I am king, I canna keep ye from it because there are rules — I realized I winna be able tae protect ye. The government wants ye tae stand trial. I daena think I can stop them from acting on it. And while I am in the arena would be when they would take ye."

"I don't care. Let them arrest me. I killed the king. You'll fight in the arena and you'll be the next king and then you'll pardon me. And if you die in the arena, I'll know. And it will be bleak and awful and possibly the end for me, but I would know, Magnus."

"I want tae protect ye—"

"See, that's your big burly man-muscles talking. I killed a man—"

"It very nearly destroyed ye."

"But it didn't. I put on my bodice, too tight by the way, and I went to the 18th century and I freaking stitched up my sister-in-law's hooha after watching a baby come through it and guess what? I want to have a baby now. I'm the bravest fucking girl in the world. Maybe in all time. I have shared a meal with Lady Mairead and just now I said I felt sorry for her. You are not giving me enough credit for how fucking awesome I am. I'm a terrible terrible terrible arse." I grinned. "And I'm not leaving. You'll have to change your mind and you'll have to tell Tyler that you changed your mind on it. You two can commiserate with each other about how hard it is to manage me."

Magnus shook his head and sort of smiled. "Och, tis hard tae be married tae a terrible arse."

"Well you married me. Of your own volition without any

input from anyone else. That's what you'll have to live with forever." I folded my arms across my chest. "There are worse things."

"Okay, I winna send ye away."

"Good. Thank you."

"And I daena ken if Bella will be in the arena or watching on a screen. I canna worry about it. I have tae fight."

"You know what, I said that in anger. I don't give a shit where she is. I'm ten-to-one a better woman. And you know it." I chuckled. "I can see it in your eyes."

"Aye, mo reul-iuil, ye are." He shook his head. "But ye will be arrested."

"Yep, and when you win, you'll rescue me. You better win."

"Ye ken I will win Kaitlyn, this is nae the end of us."

I plopped down on the bed beside him.

He put his hand on my thigh. "And when I win I will be crowned king and I will pardon ye and ye will live here as my queen."

"We will vacation in Florida. Do you think Zach would come here to cook for us?"

"He would have tae or the whole plan is awful."

"Agreed."

Magnus and I both laid back on the bed. Shoulder to shoulder heads turned toward each other. "And we will make many princes—"

I half-smiled. "Or princesses."

"Or princesses, tae carry on my bloodline."

"I don't really care about that part. Bella's baby can have the throne after you. I want our baby to have a normal life with Mommy and Me playgroups and riding a bike through the neighborhood and friends..."

"Aye, me as well, Kaitlyn. Tis wondrous that our bairn could live his whole life without drawin' a sword. Or fightin' a battle at the castle walls. I wish that for my son, the chance tae ken peace."

We turned toward each other. I wriggled up to him chest to chest and wrapped around him.

He added, "I like tae think on a future with ye."

"Me too." I kissed his collarbone. "I'm sorry I created a scene in front of Tyler."

"Aye. I shouldna have been so forceful on it with ye, but I daena ken his purpose, what he is about bein' here. He has become involved and I have tae trust him because of it, but he may still be an adversary. We daena ken the truth of him. Tyler Wilson has caused me a great deal of worry and I am sorry I spoke tae ye so harshly."

I hiked my skirt covered leg up to his waist and pressed against him. "Thank you for apologizing. I'm sorry that I argued in front of him, it was bad form."

His hands hiked up my bunches of skirts in the back and squeezed my ass and growled happily into my shoulder. "You, mo reul-iuil are the best of forms. From your perfect arse tae your little flower garden..." His pinky finger slid between my legs and wiggled there.

I giggled into his neck. "My flower garden?"

"Och aye, the garden planted round your castle, I have discussed this afore." He chuckled into my ear as his fingers played around inside me. "Do you want me tae tell ye all about it again?"

"No, I remember the whole thing, castle walls, your big cannon..." I nibbled his ear. "Just keep doing what you're doing."

"Aye, ye have watered your garden for me, tis like a dew covered morn—"

A fist pounded on our door. Lady Mairead's voice, "Magnus! Something's happened. Oh no. Something — hurry!"

My eyes wide I asked, "What do you—?

But Magnus was already up headed for the door.

51 - KAITLYN

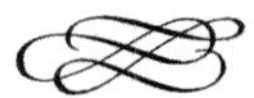

The room was blaring, tear-inducing white. The news story was projected large on the far wall of the living room. A live-video: a dead body in the grass with the police milling around. There were smaller projections down the side: One a desolate parking garage. One a door. One a stairwell. A voice was explaining that this was Minister Donahue shot dead on the steps of his home. But I didn't need to be told, I recognized his uniform, the coat with the medals and the fur trim. He hadn't made it home from our meeting.

Then another smaller feed started in the bottom left corner, his wife, dead in the hallway of their home.

I clutched Magnus's arm.

Then another live stream, a dead man slumped over in a car.

Lady Mairead was frantic. "I have a vessel. We could leave, but then we would never be able tae come back... what tae do?" She wasn't talking to anyone in particular, just herself. "We need tae go tae the roof."

He asked, "How long do you think we have?"

Lady Mairead's eyes looked terrified. "I'd say minutes—"

A terrifying roar blasted from outside the windows. Then for the briefest of seconds the wall of windows switched from solid white, fully screened, to clear, see-through, oh my god there were machines, like ten, hovering right outside the windows, facing us, weapons trained on us, and then before we could duck an explosive pulse, quivering the air, vibrating the sound. In the amount of time it would take me to clap my hands, a sonic boom exploded the glass, and shoved me toward the back wall and stole my air, my thoughts, my consciousness with a slam.

52 - KAITLYN

Coming to was odd. All around me was super bright, but also slo-mo, sound waves vibrating the air around me. I couldn't focus, my ears rang, I had to keep shaking my head to clear it and then try again to understand. My arms were bound behind me. I was jerked to standing. I tried to look for Magnus but my head was wobbly, my balance off. Like I was seriously drunk and maybe on some weird sixties acid trip, like in movies, where the colors spin.

I was shoved through a door and against a wall, my stomach dropped as I rose, or rose as I dropped, the doors of the elevator opened on a rooftop, vertiginous edges, swirling wind, dark gray night sky above, so many men in uniforms — my focus returned, "Where are you taking me?"

I was shoved forward to a waiting helicopter. I tried to brake, to brace my feet against the rooftop, to pull back and not go in.

Where was Magnus?

I struggled against the men, trying to keep them from putting me on one of the helicopters. Who knew where we were going, but also, no. I was too scared of heights for that bullshit. I fought harder but the two men holding me gripped me tighter.

Magnus's voice interrupted my struggle. "Kaitlyn!"

I craned my head to see him, across the rooftop, being led toward us. "Magnus!"

The men practically picked me up and threw me into the side of the helicopter, banging my thigh — "Ow, fuck. That hurt!"

Magnus yelled over the sound of the propellers and engines, "Kaitlyn—" The engines went louder cutting off the end of his sentence. I was crammed onto the floor of the helicopter, my arms jerked to the side, the cuff around my wrists was attached to a bolt on the floor. I was bent over sideways and very uncomfortable. Men took seats all around me, knees pressed close to my nose and cheek. Pressing me up against the bulkhead.

Magnus was shoved into the helicopter behind the seats, his bound arms chained to a bar on the floor. Magnus would be terrified, he had never flown before. Under the seats I could see his fingers curled into fists, his wrists bound, the veins of his arms straining in his struggle against the binding. Our helicopter lifted into the air.

After that it was just trying to keep my panic under control. I faced a gaping hole in the side of the helicopter. It was night, tiny lights below us, the sound of the propellers so loud it was breaking my ears. We flew over a sprawling, endless, overcrowded city, through air that was full of drones and copters and other unrecognizable machines zipping and buzzing and careening around. I curled forward and concentrated on Magnus's hand.

53 - KAITLYN

The helicopter landed on the same rooftop where we had raced from — when was that, yesterday? There had been a pile of bodies, but it was all cleaned up now.

Magnus was yanked from the helicopter first, then the rest of the men climbed out, the last one unbolted me from the floor and pushed me from the helicopter. I was shoved into Magnus, but though our shoulders met, we couldn't touch or even hear each other over the roar of the rotors.

We were forced across the rooftop and through a door to an interior hallway.

"Tis much more dangerous than we suspected, I daena ken if they are plannin' a—"

"Shut up," said one of the guards pushing Magnus to walk faster.

The hallway was tightly packed with artifacts, much like Mairead's coffers, and I vaguely recognized being here before. Our shoulders jostled together. Three more steps and he tried again.

"Tyler isna here."

I glanced around. "Or Mairead." A guard shoved me so hard I stumbled into the wall, banging my cheek. Tears sprang into my eyes.

Magnus swung his elbow back, hard, right into the guard's face and then three men descended on him, punching and kicking him to the ground.

I pressed to the wall to get away from the fists and boots. "Stop! Stop please. Don't hurt him."

A guard said, "Shut your mouth or you'll be next."

I clamped my eyes shut and cowered against the wall.

They finished beating Magnus and jerked him to standing. His face was swollen. Blood streamed from his nose. "Kaitlyn, daena provoke them."

One of the guards said, "I didn't say you could speak to her."

"I will speak tae her, she is my wife. And I am your king. You best nae harm her."

The man sneered. "Your wife, huh? Well she's a murderer. And you're no king of mine. Samuel is my king."

"You will live tae regret—"

'What — this?" He pressed me up against the wall. Men were laughing. Hands were on me.

Magnus roared and charged. He shouldered the guard off me before he was wrestled to the ground. Men kicked and punched him again and I couldn't bear it, the sound was gruesome and—

Behind us, down the hallway, a door slammed and someone was running, charging, footsteps clomping, echoing through the halls. Tyler with guns drawn. He charged into the space, red in the face. "Give me the girl!"

His guns, one in each hand were aimed at all the men.

"Get behind me."

I tried, but a guard held fast to my skirts. Tyler said, "Let go of her, don't make me shoot you man, let go." He was pointing at each man there. "Toss your weapons, then hands up." He looked at the next man. "Your weapon on the ground, your hands up too, do it, now."

Two men tossed their guns to the ground and put their hands up, one tried to aim it. Tyler fired.

I shrieked.

The man was set off balance, a bloom of blood on his shoulder.

The fourth man pulled Magnus up by the hair and held a gun to his head.

I begged, "No, please!"

Tyler said, "You don't want to do that man. That's your king."

"Not if I kill him first. Give us back the girl."

"Keep your hands up. Everyone, let me see them." His guns were moving back and forth. His focus intense. "Let Magnus go."

"Give us the girl. You won't make it out here alive."

"Oh I will, I'll kill all of you. Give me Magnus."

Magnus's face was intense, red, bloodied, his eyes wild. His neck taut, prepared to fight. Footsteps were clomping down the tunnel from the other direction.

"Give me Magnus!"

A guard dove for his gun and fired it toward us. I ducked, shrieked, and begged, "Please, no, don't."

Tyler fired and that guy lay still on the ground.

Magnus said, "Tis okay, Kaitlyn, daena be afeared, we—"

The guard holding him pressed his gun harder into Magnus's temple. "More guards are coming, you don't stand a chance."

"Give me Magnus and we'll see if I do."

"Nah, Samuel only really wanted this guy anyway." The two men started pulling Magnus down the hall. He struggled against them, they were reaching the corner.

Men behind them were closing in.

Tyler said, "Kaitlyn, count of three you run."

I was fully crying. "I don't want to, please get him, get Magnus, please."

Magnus, struggling, said, "Go! Kaitlyn, go!"

"No, please," I reached my hands out toward him, "I can't leave without you."

"Kaitlyn, ye have tae, go with Tyler."

"Katie you better run, I have to hold the guns. I can't carry you but I fucking will if I have to, one, two—"

"Please don't make me – Magnus!"

He was dragged around the corner.

His voice came to me from further down the tunnel. "Run, Kaitlyn!"

Tyler said, "Three."

I turned and ran.

54 - KAITLYN

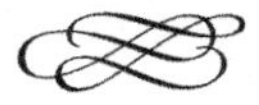

Tyler slammed into me at the door. "Through, go through!"

"I don't want to, we have to go get Magnus, please."

"Go through the fucking door Katie, now. Right now!" He holstered one of his guns and slammed against the door and shoved me out to the rooftop.

The sky was the cool grey of almost-dawn. The helicopter was parked, spotlights were shining around the perimeter. I stumbled toward the middle.

"Get behind it!"

"I don't want to, I don't want to leave him!" I tried to race back for the door and Tyler blocked me, grabbed me around the waist, and carried me to the helicopter. He flung me onto my ass on the hard cold roof. "Don't move Katie, I swear to god, I'll shoot you, I've shot every fucking other person so far."

From the waistband of his pants he pulled a vessel.

"I won't go! No! No! I don't want to go."

He dropped onto me, his knee on my stomach, pinning me down. I flailed against him trying to rip the vessel from his hands.

"What are you going to do? Storm the castle by yourself? I already did that, he's captured, now stop struggling and—" He twisted the ends of the vessel and started reciting numbers.

I gave up fighting and tried for pleading. "Please don't," I begged. "You have to save him, we can't — no, please."

Tyler reached the end of his litany of numbers and the pain of the jump-through-time smacked into me, clenched around every single particle of my body, and ripped me away.

55 - MAGNUS

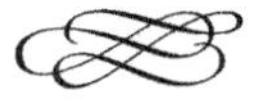

Putting on my shirt was painful. I had tae stretch out my shoulder tae prepare. I winced when it pulled down over my arms and had to take deep breaths as I pulled up the kilt and buckled it around my waist. It was slow and methodical. I placed the clothes out, put them on slowly. I hadn't much to do except this and the battle beyond.

I was nervous about the battle. My form had been good until the guards roughed me up, now I was in terrible condition. I wasn't ready and Samuel kent it. He was plannin' on it. He wanted a big battle, lots of attention, and he wanted me tae die.

I couldna blame him.

My door slammed open early, I turned to meet it and Lady Mairead was shoved in with an irritated huff. "Daena push me!"

She smoothed her dress and stood spine straight in the middle of my room while the guards slammed the door behind her.

"Samuel has allowed me tae see ye before your battle."

"How did ye persuade him?"

"I promised him something if ye lose. Tis nae matter, I daena expect tae have tae make good on it."

I took in a breath. "I haena lost one yet."

"Exactly. Though ye look terrible."

"The guards beat me with their boots, there arna many places on my body that daena feel broken. But I plan tae win. Kaitlyn wanted me tae, so I will."

"The guards told me she escaped arrest?"

"Tyler rescued her. He has taken her tae Florida."

She peered at me with an inquisitive look. "I assume ye ken what happens next?"

I ran a hand through my hair. "I have seen it." I shook my head. "I ken they have a bairn together. I ken she will be happy. I learned it a while ago, but when I asked again last night, twas the same. A bit of the story was different, the timin', but the bit about Kaitlyn becomin' a mother tae Tyler's bairn — tis still true. I am learnin' there is nae changin' it. It has been written."

Lady Mairead pursed her lips. "Hmmm, well... I ken tis small comfort but she has always been difficult tae manage. When I picked her—"

"You dinna pick her, I did."

"When you picked her I saw nae difficulties in the alliance because she was so spirited. But it dinna take long before I learned of the great many demerits of her character, not the least of which is her desire tae take every man tae bed—"

I clenched my jaw. "Daena say another word."

"Fine, but I am sure ye see she has been a complication tae your rise in power. If ye would forget her tae her history, allow her tae live out her days, happily, I might add, as a mother and a wife tae Tyler Wilson, I think ye would be doin' your best by her."

She smoothed the top of my shirt across my chest. "Finally. Because tae be truthful, Magnus, being married tae ye canna have been easy. You owe her the kindness of allowin' her tae be free of this danger and tae have a normal life. She was verra brave when she chose that ye would fight for your throne. I was impressed with her decision. I think in many ways twas her decidin' tae let ye be, tae live in your own future, with your kingdom, tae take care of your son. I think she was ready tae let go and finally live a normal life."

I nodded starin' at the wall, tryin' tae stay on top of my grief. "Have ye gone tae our future, seen what is comin'?"

"Nae. I only visit the past, tis commonplace tae visit what has already happened. I like dropping intae a story, as it has been told, and changing it in small parts, but going tae my own future is verra like playing God. I did it only once. I couldna sleep or eat for wanting tae change what would happen."

"How did ye get over it? Were ye able tae change it?"

"I daena ken. It haena happened yet." She sighed. "It is something I will never be able tae get from my mind." She patted me on both shoulders and looked me in the eyes. "Tis our glory that we are heirs of these vessels and our privilege tae live outside of time, Magnus, and tis our burden that we canna fully love someone who lives inside of time. But ye must steel yourself tae your life. When the doors of the arena open ye must meet Samuel and take your throne."

She continued, "Samuel has told me I may watch the battle. He has also told me that when ye die he will be merciful towards me. I want ye tae ken he has never been merciful tae anyone and so ye must win today. Your son is countin' on ye as am I."

I nodded again, quietly.

The door opened and the guards barged in.

We left Lady Mairead with a guard leadin' her tae her rooms.

They forced me intae step alongside them down the halls, through the tunnel, and left me outside the familiar arena doors.

I did try tae steel myself tae the battle ahead. And when the arena doors opened with a burst of bright sunlight, I tapped my chest, over my heart, the place where the walkytalk had been, as if twas as easy as that tae speak tae her hundreds of years in the past, and said, "I love ye," as I crossed the threshold tae meet my future.

56 - KAITLYN

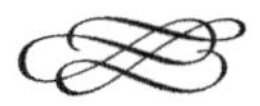

I was in grass. On mud. It was all pretty gosh darn wet, but not as bad as the time I woke up in the swamp. I opened my eyes and tried to lift my head. It was dark, forested, but I was in a clearing, a slope, my head lower than my body. I twisted to look down. The dock, the spring. A few boxes and bags lying around. A couple of swords strewn in the grass. A flashlight, faint but still burning, laying in the grass.

I turned my head and looked up the slope. Tyler's truck, parked, door open. And then beside me, Tyler's foot.

I dragged a hand up and jiggled his foot. He groaned.

I smacked his foot. Then grumbling, pulled myself to sitting over him. He was laying sprawled, his eyes opened but I could tell he wasn't really seeing me. "I hate you. I hate you so much. I can't believe you did that."

I collapsed back on the grass and stared up the pine trees to the sky above, light gray, on the verge of turning a tint of blue. "I hate you so much."

Tyler pulled himself up to sitting. "You know what. I'm not that happy with you either. What the fuck, Katie. You know how hard it is to deal with you?" He ran his hand over his now scruffy hair. He banged his hand flat on the ground beside him. "Fuck. I had one job to do for him. All this other shit was just extra. I mean what the fuck, you have a freaking death wish?"

I stared up at him dumbfounded.

He pulled himself up to standing. "God, you are such a pain in the ass. If someone tells you to run, you run. Why do you have to argue about every fucking thing?" He brushed off his jeans and straightened up with yet another groan. "And you know what? I could have gotten killed, killed myself, and for what, so you could hate me? Well fine, I didn't do it for you, so yeah, fuck you." He started limping to his truck. "And you know what the worst part is? He doesn't even know me now. Thanks for that. It's just great."

He made it to his truck, climbed in and tried to start it. The ignition went 'click'. He stepped out and yelled down the slope at me, "And now my battery is dead. Fucking great. I saved your life for him and I can't even get a break."

"What are you even talking about?"

He popped his hood, lifted it and peered in, jiggling the battery cables. "Nothing. Don't worry about it. My wife freaking warned me, too. Now she's right."

I stood, tried to brush the top layer of grime from my skirts, but I was seriously filthy, like a destitute wench from the 18th century grimy. "Okay, you just now said a bunch of shit that makes no sense. Either you have a concussion or you are talking about someone and only you know what the hell you're talking about. You have a wife? And who is 'him'?"

He leaned on the front of his truck. "Do you have the keys to your Mustang?"

"Seriously?"

"Yeah, I want to go home and I need to jump my battery."

"Fine." I schlepped myself up the slope to the far edge of the clearing where the Mustang was parked. The trunk was still open. I looked in the driver's side window. The keys were in the ignition. "I've got keys!"

I checked the trunk. "I've got jumper cables too."

"I've got my own, thank you."

I stood half in and out of my car and yelled at him. "You know, you don't just win because you're angrier than me. That is such a man thing. You freaking dragged me away and left Magnus to die."

"I saved your life. For like the third time, actually. You're welcome." He dragged a box from under his seat, clicked it open and dragged out some jumper cables.

I started my Mustang and drove it down the slope toward his truck, stopping short, nose to nose. I popped the hood and jumped out of the car. "And another thing, if Magnus dies I will never forgive you."

"You won't need to worry about it, you've got no reason to ever see me again anyway." He clamped one of the cables to his battery and then fed the cable across to my car's battery.

I squinted my eyes. "We run in the same circles. Of course I'll see you. I'm asking again, what are you even talking about? What do you mean you're married, you had one job? Who's 'he'?"

Tyler leaned wearily on his truck. "Can you start your car?"

"Who's he, Tyler?"

He took a deep breath. And another.

"Tell me."

"Magnus. Magnus is 'he.' Now start your car. Please."

"What?" I was so confused that instead of standing there until I got answers I sort of short-circuited and just went in and started the Mustang and revved it a few times and then he started his truck and then he got out of the truck and started removing the cables from his battery all the while I sat in the driver's seat staring at the steering wheel. Wondering what the hell he was talking about. He was talking about Magnus? Like, what was with Magnus? Like he had something going on with Magnus that I didn't know about? He was married?

Tyler dropped my hood and I turned off my car.

I stepped out, confused, shaking my head. "What is happening Tyler? You can't leave me like this, I don't understand. Please tell me what's happening. I might never see him again and this is — I need to know everything."

His truck was running, recharging itself.

"I've got to sit down."

"Of course." I sank down into the driver's seat of the Mustang and Tyler walked around and dropped down into the passenger seat.

I couldn't wait for him to get comfortable. "So what, you're married?"

"Yeah, my wife, her name is Samantha. We're newlyweds."

I squinted at him, because now I was wondering if he was joking, bullshitting me. "Why haven't I met your wife?"

He sighed. "Because she lives in the future, Katie."

"Okay, what the hell are you talking about? You're from the future? You've been bullshitting me this whole time? Who are you? Oh my god, are you one of Magnus's brothers? Were you planning to kill him?" I clapped my hand over my mouth horrified. "Oh my god, you left him to die—"

"Katie, I swear to god, stop saying that shit. I am in no mood." He drew out another long breath. "I don't know if I'm supposed to tell you this. I don't know the rules and I can't even imagine what might happen — Magnus is my father."

"What — your... what? Magnus is your..." I leaned my forehead on the steering wheel. "Tyler, can you say this very plainly so that I can understand?"

"Magnus is my father. Bella is my mother. I am next in line for the throne. I was born in the year 2382."

I shook my head on the steering wheel. "Why in the world? What?"

"I came back in time to 2019, to help him with you."

"With me?" I turned my head to see his face.

"Yes, because those men killed you, here, on the night you guys tried to go back in time for Quentin. You died right there on that dock."

"Really? I died?"

"Yep. Apparently Magnus tried to loop back and fix it, again and again, but the fight kept getting worse and still you died. He looped back and fought the men a third time but you died again and—"

"Oh no, that's horrible."

"He had to stop trying to fix it. He was still distraught telling me about it after twenty-five years."

"Oh."

"And watching Da cry is not easy."

"That's what you call him?" My voice was small, full of wonder.

He nodded.

"I've been there. If he's crying I want to do anything to help him."

"Yeah, me too."

I watched his face for a few moments. "So you're his son? You kind of look like him too. Now I see it, not in your coloring, you're darker and smaller, but in your facial expressions. I don't know why I didn't notice it before."

"I'm glad you didn't, it would have complicated things a great deal."

I ran my palms down the leather-wrapped steering wheel. "When did he tell you this?"

"A few nights after my wedding. I knew you died before I was born but he never told me the full story. I think my wedding made him relive it. He talked about it for a long time, told me everything."

"Did he tell you how it worked?"

"He said he was watching you guys and helping you guys fight. But the fight kept changing: more men, more brutal, bigger storms, and your death came faster."

"So he was an extra — *himself*?"

"Yeah, that's as good a reason as any to not jump into your own past, huh?"

"Totally."

"He watched you die and he saw himself die. And to call him broken-hearted would be an understatement. He called Zach, said goodbye, and left for good."

"So I died and he never got to go back to Florida?"

"And my whole life he seemed very broken and I never understood why."

"For twenty-some years?"

"Yep. I mean, kind of. I don't think it was a straight twenty years for him. He took his throne from Samuel, but after a few years he left grandmother in charge and he—"

"Grandmother?"

"You know her as Lady Mairead."

"Oh Jesus Christ."

"Yeah, she was very different from how I know her."

"I bring out the worst in her. Go on, I'm sorry I interrupted."

"He began traveling, looking for the men who killed you, and fighting anyone that might want to claim our throne. He fought to protect me mostly. I worried about him a lot." He flicked the air vent on the dash, up and down and back up again.

"For twenty years he just fought people?"

"Well, he and Lady Mairead have a way of jumping in and out of years, checking in, so they don't age as fast."

"So Magnus just checked in with you?"

"Yes, for a couple of months every year. The rest of the time I lived with my mom."

"Oh. And he didn't live with, um, your mother?"

Tyler shook his head. "No, he never did. He was alone my whole life."

I chewed my lip. "I'm so sad for him, but I don't really understand, not really."

"He told me all about the night you died and how it proved we couldn't use the vessels to go back and fix our own lives. He was so depressed. He wondered if he should have kept trying, if he quit too soon, but if there was nothing to do about saving you he didn't want to go back and erase any of your time together. He had been torturing himself about it. Wanting to go to the past to see you again, but believing you would die anyway."

Tyler shook his head slowly. "Imagine being faced with that, someone you love dies and you know you can see them again. You can change the past, but you don't know if you can change it for the better?"

"That would suck."

"Yeah it would. My wife, Samantha, and I got him talking about your life together on Amelia Island." Tyler put his head back on the headrest. "He told me about the night grandmother told you Bella was pregnant and how you chose to protect me. He said you never faltered. Da said he was grateful to you for saving my life, because even though you were gone, he had a son, and I had been the only person that made his life worth living."

Tears welled up in my eyes.

"And that's why I'm here. I figured if he couldn't fix what happened maybe I, a new actor in it, could."

I fished around the backseat for a box of Kleenex and pulled out a tissue. “You were around for a long time.”

“I jumped in and out. I couldn’t really figure out when it was going to happen. At the wedding I knew.”

"You were the one who told me about the storms, you were involved in everything. He knew you before the day on the dock – wouldn’t he recognize you? Know that you were his son, or know that his son was Tyler, or *something*?"

"I have no idea. The Magnus I met here in Florida hasn’t had a son yet. The night I met Magnus at your housewarming party, I wondered if he would recognize me. I had a whole plan where I would act like I was there as a joke and then I would run away. But he didn’t recognize me at all. And when I was growing up Da never said, ‘Hey, son, ye look just like a bloke from Florida named Tyler.’ It’s like I looped back but only in the current time-line."

I sighed. “We know so little about these vessels we’re insane to use them at all.”

“That is true.”

“So you saved my life on that dock right there?”

“Yes. And now I’ve created a whole second trajectory of Magnus’s life. One where he’s my dad, but he doesn’t recognize me.”

“Oh no, Tyler, I’m so sorry, that’s awful.”

“Yeah. An unintended consequence.” He clenched and straightened his hands. “I’m a little worried my whole life might be ruined now.” He ran his hands down his face. “Who am I kidding, not a little worried, a lot worried.”

“Probably not though, right? I mean, no matter what we’ve done to history we haven’t messed up the big historical—”

“I’m a prince. Or I was.”

“Oh yeah, right.” I paused and thought it through. “So you don’t know if Magnus survives this, because this is a totally new timeline.”

"Exactly."

"Okay." I leaned back in my seat and we both stared out the front window.

Finally I said, "I owe you a huge apology. I had no idea you were there at such a cost and I didn't know what your ulterior motives were but that doesn't excuse it. I behaved like an ass. I'm sorry. Thank you for saving my life. If there's anything I can do for you, ever, just ask. I owe you. Because of you I was able to go back and be there for Lizbeth's birth and you know — that means something. If nothing else — if Magnus doesn't — I did that."

He gulped. "And I wouldn't be here if it wasn't for you. If Da hadn't fought for his throne, Samuel would have killed my mom. I wouldn't be here right now. So," he half-smiled, "you do still owe me, but I'll give you a break on some of it..."

I joked, "Although, you did tell me about the storms in Scotland. If I hadn't gone, I wouldn't have had all that terrible stuff happen to me at the hands of your evil grandfather..."

"Maybe, maybe not. I can't tell what I changed, what happened before." He rubbed his palms on his thighs and stretched his back. "Time travel, it's the greatest thing and the absolute worst in one small machine."

"And it hurts like hell."

"True that."

"So I'm kind of like your step-mom? I'm so embarrassed, I totally thought you were hot for me."

"Nope. I actually think you're very exasperating and totally self-absorbed. And did I mention how reckless you are?"

"Ugh." I blew out a gust of air.

"But that being said, you're perfect for Da. It's really good to see him happy."

I fiddled with the car keys, it felt good to have them in my hand after days and days of not driving. I was so glad we left them in the ignition. If I had had them in my pocket, they would have been lost and I'd be screwed. I asked, "What do you think will happen to him?"

"I don't know." Another sigh. "But I'm still here. I didn't disappear into a cloud of black dust like in the Avenger's Infinity War."

"How do you know all that stuff? I swear you seem like you're from this time period."

"When I dropped in and out I spent a lot of time with Michael. I especially like Marvel movies. Thor reminds me of Da." He grinned.

"Yeah, me too." We smiled at each other for a moment. "Was he a good father?"

"He was really great. I mean, he wasn't around as much as I wanted. It caused me some grief that he was away fighting, but when he visited, I knew he really wanted to be there." He nodded. "It was good."

"It's good you have those memories. Even if he doesn't. And I'm really sorry he doesn't." I sighed. "One more question, and this is... weird, but would you say your mom was a good mother? I mean, I'm asking for a friend."

He gave me a small smile. "I'm not really comfortable talking about that with you, but I get why you're asking, she and grandmother were not nice to you, and so I'll just say when she was telling Da what a great mother she would be I was really, really, really surprised."

"Oh."

"Yeah. But hey, it's a new timeline, maybe she'll do better." Then he chuckled. "It was so hard being around Magnus all week without blowing my cover. I almost called him Da at least ten times."

"That would have been so weird."

"Here's another thing. I got the deputy minister to get me a fake name and the credentials. My name is actually Magnus

Archibald Caehlin Campbell the second, everyone calls me Archie."

"Really?"

"Yeah."

"Humph. I guess I should have thought about getting Magnus credentials. I could have taken him on an airplane."

"Here." He shifted in his seat and patted his pocket. "Wait, I left it under my seat." He got out of the car and stalked up to his truck and returned a moment later. He sat back down and unzipped a messenger bag. "There's this." He opened a Manila folder and pulled out a birth certificate. The baby name was Tyler Garrison Wilson. He dug through the bag and found a passport and opened it to the name page. He got out his wallet and pulled out the driver's license. "You can have these. When Magnus comes back, he can use them." He passed me the rest of the pile. "There's a high school transcript, a credit card, even a Jamba Juice club card." He grinned.

"You aren't going to need these?"

"Nah. I think I'm going to be busy for a bit. Princely duties of the realm. Da fights so I don't have to, but that means I have to run the business of the kingdom, and if I've screwed it up and ruined it all — I'll have to woo my wife back to me. Man, I hope she's still there."

"I hope so too."

"Wait, and just in case..." He pulled a piece of paper and a pen from the messenger bag and leaned forward to write on the dashboard. He wrote about ten lines of script, then added a list. He considered for a moment and then wrote a little bit more. He got down to the bottom of the page, folded it and handed it to me. "This is for Da if you see him before I do. This is what he knows about General Reyes after years of fighting him. Maybe it will help him get the upper hand."

I put the folded paper with the rest of the credentials in the glove compartment.

He put his hand on the door. "It dawns on me I don't actually need my truck after all. I should just head home. Do you have some way to get it to your place?"

"Sure. I'll send Quentin for it, I'm assuming he's back."

"Cool. Tell him I'm really glad he got home. And say goodbye to the gang, maybe I'll see them around some day."

"Definitely."

He put his hand on the door handle. "Help me pick up all this stuff?"

We both stepped out of the car.

The vessel was laying where we dropped it in the grass. "You want it?" He asked.

"Don't you need it?"

"Nah, when the shit got real there, grandmother gave me one to get away. I didn't have the heart to tell her I already had one because I was her grandson, the heir to the throne. I might have given her a heart attack."

"Okay then, I think so, yeah. I would like it. Just in case."

We picked up the weapons and the boxes of things that had been forgotten in the rush and put them all into the back of my Mustang.

Lastly, we hugged each other good bye.

"Here are the truck keys. Just come get it whenever."

"I'll do that. And thanks again Tyler, I mean, Archie."

"If you see Da, tell him I liked fighting alongside him, that was cool. He should let me do that more often."

I nodded and smiled. "I will, and if you see my husband tell him I miss him and to please come home."

Archie walked away.

I got into the Mustang and drove it to the beginning of the woods, the edge of the trees and then I watched where he stood on the dock, looking down at the vessel as the storm built around him, dark and wind and flashes of light — his hand went up, goodbye, and though I tried to watch to see how it went, visibility went to zero. It was impossible to see — then without a doubt he was gone.

57 - KAITLYN

I barely remembered the drive to Amelia Island. My mind was alternately spinning and fuzzing over with sleep. I stopped for drive-thru twice. Once for breakfast and coffee and once for a Coke and while I was at it some French fries. Both times I thought about curling up in the seat and sleeping in the parking lot, but I really wanted to get home. I had to sleep. I had to figure out what just happened and how to fix it. I had to—

The vessel was on the seat beside me. I was terrified it would hum to life and rip me away somewhere or that men on horseback would jump onto my car and sword me to death. It was like having something that was both lifesaving and very very deadly in my care. I had no idea what to do with it or how it would behave.

I had told Zach to move our house, but that was only yesterday afternoon. It was only the next morning. He was probably still at the hotel on their honeymoon. I really wanted to go home and curl up on my bed.

I needed to be able to smell Magnus on the sheets.

To see his toothbrush in his cup.

God, where was he? How would I get to him?

My grandmother always told me to stay in one place if I was lost. Was I lost? Or Magnus?

I took a big swig of coffee.

So much had happened since we left. Days and days of drama and intrigue, from Lizbeth's birth to Magnus's capture, enough awful for a lifetime.

I wondered where Quentin was — he wouldn't know how to find our new house. And if Zach and Emma were still on their honeymoon....

I pulled the car onto the highway and called Zach.

"I'm back."

"Awesome," He spoke off phone, "Hey Em, Katie is back." He returned to me. "Quentin just called, we're in the car taking me to rent a truck. He's apparently got a bunch of ATVs to load up? Then I'm headed to pick him up on the beach near Peter's Point. You with Magnus?"

"No, he didn't make it back, he's in the future and there's so much to tell you about, but mostly I need to sleep and I don't know where to go."

"Let me see..." I heard his hand tapping on the dash, a sure sign he was thinking.

"We've been at the hotel, I could book you an extra room?"

"Could you call Hayley? Tell her we all need a spot to rest? I need it to be near the beach though, just in case..."

"I'm on it. I'll call you in a minute."

A few minutes later my phone rang — Zach.

"Hayley said to meet us at the light house."

"The actual light house?"

"No, that one on the beach, the rental. The octagonal shaped house, the one that's been there since forever."

"Okay, remind me the address, I can get there but don't want to think. And when did Hayley become a property manager, just whipping rentals out of her ass every time we call her?"

"Probably when her best friend started running from evil men and needed safe houses."

"What I really need more than anything is clean clothes. I don't know if it's safe to go to the house, and I can't think straight."

Emma's voice came over the phone. "Sweatpants, t-shirt, that kind of thing?"

"Yes, god yes. Clean underwear?"

"Plus toothbrush, when will you get there?"

"Two hours."

"Coolio, it will just be me and Ben at first, maybe Hayley, you want clean clothes and — you really don't have Magnus?"

"No, but... now that we're so good at our timing and locations, maybe he'll be here by the end of the day."

"That would be great."

"Yeah. That really would."

58 - KAITLYN

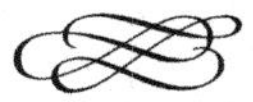

Though I had been using this beach house as a landmark since I was really young, because it was a round house, the only one of its kind on the beach, I had never actually been inside it before.

The house was dark, cozy, parts of it felt almost like a cave, wood paneling, old-school-style. Instead of Beach House Modern, this was Beach House Grandma. There weren't big sweeping windows, but there was a nice deck with plenty of chairs. The perfect place to have a coffee and watch the waves.

Inside it was a little like a fabric store explosion: stripes, checkers, dots, sometimes a golf pattern, sometimes wicker. It wasn't my style at all, but it was not on the north end or the south end of the island. It was in the middle. And it looked out over the beautiful dunes, had a view up and down the beach, and today was a clear crisp day. Its television carried the weather channel and it had a bed and nobody could find me here, yet. It would be a haven, comfortable and completely necessary.

Except there was nothing here that was part of Magnus. Except me.

~

Emma and I hugged with Ben between us. Hayley hugged me too. They knew I had been through a lot, but they couldn't really grasp how much. The wedding had been just a couple of days ago. Whereas I had experienced hundreds of years of danger since.

Emma handed me a Target bag full of clean clothes and some basic toiletries and they made me go take a shower before there was any kind of discussion. In the bathroom I gave myself a pep talk: tell them just enough. I couldn't bear to tell them about Magnus having a child with another woman. I loved him too much. I understood too much to let his reputation be harmed like that. I couldn't bear to have him judged in that way. I understood all that he went through, and what it had cost him.

It would be our family secret.

59 - KAITLYN

I showered, wiping the grime of a birth, a few time travels, and a couple of kidnappings off my body. I begged the universe, God, and anyone else listening that Lizbeth remained clean enough and free from the effects of ravaging bacteria.

I scrubbed my hands for a fourth time. My bare hand. What if I didn't have my wedding ring ever? Ever ever? And I kept thinking about Magnus's face when I was behind Tyler, his sounds when they were beating him, the look of despair in his eyes — the last thing I saw as he was pulled away from me.

"Please, please, please be okay. I love you. Come home. Please."

I toweled myself off and realized it had been too long without checking the weather. While I dressed I called to Hayley, "Turn on the weather channel!"

She called back, "Are we doing that again?"

"Still! Maybe forever!"

~

Zach pulled up outside with Quentin in the passenger seat. He was still wearing his kilt and a sporran, looking like he lived in the Scottish Highlands. Quentin slammed his door open and climbed out with a groan. "I've got a truck full of future-weapons hidden in the parking lot of the storage units on 8th street. We'll have fun figuring out what to do with them."

"I'm just so happy you're home!"

"Aye, but tis nae our home, tis a rental again, ye keep gettin' intae trouble lassie." We both laughed and hugged for a really long time. That rocking back and forth, thank-god-we're-alive kind of hugging.

He added, "I'll be gettin' all the girls with m'new Scottish accent. Though in Scotland I was gettin' all the girls with my New World accent."

"Did ye now?"

"When did you get back?"

"Just now."

"And Magnus isn't with you?"

"Nope, but hey, maybe any moment?"

"Let's go upstairs, get me out of my Scottish garb and we can discuss what comes next."

"Good because you smell like an eighteenth century pigsty."

He joked, "They had, as you know, stupid ideas about baths, plus the soap smelled worse than the body odor. And I'll have you know I just traveled three hundred years."

"Oh yeah, I just traveled 350 years, I totally win."

We all convened in the living room. Quentin said, "First, I have to ask, how worried are we that someone is coming?"

"Worried-worried. We need to hide the vessels we have and all the weapons."

"I need some weapons, I'm not a very capable guard right now."

"I have weapons in the trunk of the Mustang."

Zach said, "Is Emma safe here, Ben?"

"I think so, but, Quentin, will you step up security, like a lot, just to be sure?"

"Definitely."

Zach asked, "Okay tell us, where's Magnus?"

"We were captured, in the eighteenth century—"

Quentin asked, "With Tyler right?"

Zach said, "Whoa, how did Tyler — what?"

I said quickly. "Tyler, come to find out, came from the future to help us. So he showed up when Magnus and I were jumping to the past. He helped us rescue Quentin and then when we got Quentin out of there he traveled with us, me and Magnus, to the future. Then we were captured there and Tyler rescued me but he couldn't get to Magnus." Zach passed me a glass of ice water. I took a big drink and added, "He got me to the land in Gainesville and then left to go back to the future. He's gone now."

Zach said, "Tyler? My brother's friend?"

"Yeah, he was at your wedding, remember?"

"Yeah, and my bachelor party. I just can't believe he'd be from the future. He didn't seem weird at all. Just kind of a know-it-all."

Hayley said, "I always thought he reminded me of Magnus, I mean, smaller, not as handsome, the same kind of facial expressions, like they could be distant cousins or something."

I said vaguely, "I guess, we didn't really talk about that. We need to go to Gainesville sometime and get his truck." I jokingly waved my hand. "Add that to a list." I lay back on the couch and acted overwhelmed, although I actually *was* pretty overwhelmed. I just knew that I had people around me now to help. "My really long list of things that are left undone. Right under the list of people who are probably trying to kill me."

"Speaking of, where's Lady Mairead?"

"She's in the future. I think she was captured at the same time as me and Magnus. She's probably negotiated her way out of it by now. Which is fine by me, as long as she also negotiates Magnus's freedom too."

Zach leaned forward. "So what do you think is happening?"

"Magnus was going to fight for his throne. There are a lot of rules apparently about how that works, but then it all went kablooie and he was captured and — I don't know. I hope he survives."

Hayley asked, "Are you going to spiral again?"

"Not really. At least not yet. The thing is he can come back, now, to Florida. If he lives through what he's doing, then I should see him by tonight. So ask me tomorrow if he's not here." I looked around at all their faces. "He'll be here if they let him fight. I know it. Because I told him to. And to get home he has to win and that's his goal."

Zach said, "So that's Katie's story, how about you Quentin, how was your time in the 18th century?"

"Every day was just a bit of warm mush to eat, a bunch of disgusting men, so disgusting, the smell, ugh, we just played with our weapons. And I'm not kidding about that. I learned to ride a horse. That was cool. The food, when it happened, was awful. It was kind of like being a part of an army, but without any kind of logical leader or purpose beyond maybe we should go fight those people. Or like being in a gang without any danger of being thrown in jail. But literally anyone could kill you at any time and barely anyone would blink about it and I was at the bottom of the pack. No one would have noticed if I just disappeared."

Zach said, "How the hell did you survive?"

Quentin joked, "I slept like this," He leaned back in the chair and mimed sleeping with one eye open looking around terrified. "And when I was awake. I was like this..." He stood and with his hand on a pretend sword he startled and did a 360, "What are you doin'? What do you want? Why are you sneaking up on me?" He laughed. "I'll probably be a better security guard now because I'm jumpy and I can't sleep longer than 15-minute intervals." He grinned. "That being said, it was also awesome. I'd go back in a second if there were showers. And better food. Magnus's family was mostly pretty great. They treated me well. Plus I've got a girl there, Beaty. I'd like to see her again."

I joked, "Oh, that's really great. Two of us with someone we love stuck in another time."

There was a long pause. My eyes flitted to the screen, I watched the radar, Florida. The entire state looked clear.

"I've got one thing. Can we look up the website for Lizbeth's history?"

Zach said, "Sure. Wait, crap, my laptop is dead. I'll charge it and since it's past lunch, I'll run for food since I haven't shopped. Then we can look it up after and finish the day with naps and waiting for Magnus. Everyone hungry?"

60 - KAITLYN

Zach had bookmarked the website. He turned the laptop around on the dining room table and I sat beside him, Hayley sat beside me. Emma stood rocking Ben in her arms watching over our shoulders. Quentin, freshly showered, stood right behind me.

Zach cracked his knuckles. "Here goes — something." He clicked the link and we all watched the slowest page in the world load on the screen. Using his cursor he scrolled down and to the side on a very long family tree. Down some more, down even more. Back up. "There it is, oh my god!"

Elizabeth Campbell
1676 - 1723

Tears welled up. "Oh my god, she lived for twenty more years. Oh my god." My friends were patting me on the shoulders and hugging each other and squealing and congratulating me and us and…

I just stared at the screen with tears streaming down my cheeks.

It had said 1703 and now it was different. As sure as I was sitting here. I had freaking changed time.

I had saved her life and oh my god — Lizbeth lived. Her son, too, Ainsley Campbell, he lived to be — I counted on my fingers — thirty-two years old. He had children, grandchildren, there was a whole branch of a family tree that I saved.

I cried so many tears, streaming down my face, occasionally laughing because this kind of happiness was fraught with emotion.

Zach said, "You did good." He put an arm around me. "Wish Magnus was here to share it, but he will be, soon."

I nodded into his shoulder.

"Yeah, any minute now."

The day was almost done.

And Magnus wasn't here.

He knew the date.

At any moment in his future he could come home, he'd come to that date.

If he was alive.

But he didn't come home.

Maybe he wanted to give himself a day, for ease of transition.

Maybe he wanted me to get some rest before he showed up.

Maybe he was already here, in Florida, it would just take him a moment to get out of the swamp he accidentally landed in.

It was really cold outside so I tried not to think about all the little awful things that could happen.

That might have happened.

~

He didn't come the next day.

~

Or the next.

61 - KAITLYN

On the night of the third day I lay in bed with a notebook on my knees and drew a spiraling time line. If Magnus had gone in a circle from the past to the future and then had come back to the past again and had looped around my death on the banks of the spring two or three times — I wrote in caps, with an underline, 'we can change time!' — and if Tyler had existed to help us change time, was the fact that Tyler still existed proof that Magnus was still alive?

I couldn't come to a conclusion on it.

I needed Magnus to come home. Now.

Because I couldn't go get him. I wouldn't know how. I didn't even know what the date was.

I was a dumbass that I didn't know the date.

From now on my time-traveling ass was always going to know the date.

Not that it mattered anymore.

Unless Magnus came home where would I even —

. . .

And that's when it hit me. With an intake of air that threatened to make me hyperventilate. In and in and in and in. Oh my god—

Old Magnus.

I stared at the low geometric wood paneled ceiling that made the room seem like a cave. There was an old Magnus in the past. What timeline was that even? Mine? The new one, the fresh one?

What if...?

I threw my covers off my legs and jumped from bed. I ran down the steps to the living room yelling, "Zach! Emma! Oh my god, Quentin!"

Quentin slid open the deck door. He whispered, "What is it, a storm?"

Zach came out of their room. "Everything cool?"

"I just figured something out!" I slammed the notebook on the counter. "Look!"

They stared at the timeline, spirals, circles, the words 'We can change time!' And the scrawled dates of a possible lunatic.

Quentin said, "What are we looking at?"

"Oh, nothing there, actually." I placed my palm on it. "It just reminded me of Old Magnus." I spiraled my hand around. "Old Magnus, remember, Zach? Have you heard about him, Quentin?"

Quentin shook his head but Zach said, "I remember you asking me to look him up that day we looked up the history of Magnus."

"Exactly!" I was exuberant. "And he wasn't in the listings of family members, but Lizbeth told me he existed, when she was young — *Magnus*."

Zach went to the refrigerator and started making us drinks.

"So what are you saying? Pretend like I was just sleeping and you woke me up and so far you aren't making sense."

"Magnus is in the past. He's old and he's in the past. That means he lived."

"He's old? Weird."

"I literally don't care. He can be seventy for all I care. It's Magnus."

They made me sit down at the dining room table.

Zach said, "What if you've changed the timeline so much he isn't there?"

I shrugged. "What if? I'll time travel back to the castle and I'll look for him. He might not be there. That's true. But what if he is?"

Quentin said, "But why? Why not come here?"

I shook my head, thinking, shaking my head more and thinking more. "I don't know. But I know he looped around. He was old and he went to the past before he was born. I don't know why. But he did it. And since I've been with him he's never been old and he's never looped to before he was born, so if he did it, it was in the future and phew! I sound high—"

"You sound like I'm high."

"But I have to go see if he's there."

Quentin said, "I don't want to go again, I just got—"

"You don't have to go, as a matter of fact, you shouldn't go. You would be a liability."

He feigned disbelief, "A liability?"

"I don't know if you know this, but you're blacker than everyone in Scotland in the eighteenth century, the seventeenth century I imagine would be even worse. And Magnus might not be there to vouch for you."

"As your security guard though, Magnus might be pissed."

"Magnus is forever grateful to you. He won't hold anything

against you. I promise. And this is of course if he's there. I'm going. Alone."

Emma shuffled into the room. "What's happening?"

"Katie's going to the 17th century to find Old Magnus and find out—"

Her eyes went wide. She whispered. "Is it Magnus?"

"I don't know. Maybe. I'm going to go see."

"After a good night's sleep though, right? We need to help you pack again."

~

It was very hard to sleep that night.

62 - KAITLYN

First thing when I woke up I checked the weather. I really hoped that I was wrong and Magnus was coming to the present now.

Because the alternative: What if he was old?

What if Tyler telling me the story had changed us so that our time loop went weird and loopy?

What if the old Magnus in the castle was a Magnus from my future and by seeing him I was removing a whole chunk out of the middle of our lives?

The more I thought about it the more confused I got, the more uncertain and weirded out.

He promised me he was always coming home.

So why wasn't he here?

Emma helped me get dressed. My shift was washed, the woolen outer layers had been spot-cleaned and seriously Febreezed.

Zach and I spent the morning with the computer out, the

ancestry website open while we figured out what year I should travel to. Lizbeth had told me she remembered Old Magnus from when she was little. Like maybe the age of three?

She was two years younger than Sean, five years older than Magnus. He was born in 1681. So if I went to Scotland two years before Magnus was born...

I chose the summer. Lammas Day, because that was his favorite holiday. If he was in the past-past for some reason, it would make sense that he would want to be there for his favorite day.

Lastly the question was where? The castle at Balloch? At one point Magnus mentioned that when he was very young he lived at a castle in the Argyll region, but how would I know how to find him there? And why would Old Magnus go to a castle I had never been to before? Unless he was trying to hide from me and that didn't make sense.

The only thing that made sense was that Magnus for some reason was stuck in 1679. Lost. And if he wanted me to come, if he wanted there to be a possibility of me finding him, he would go to Balloch. Definitely.

We strapped another handbag to my waist with leather strips and filled it: beeswax candles, matches, a basic first aid kit, and a few protein bars unwrapped and folded in waxed cloth. I had knives strapped to my body in three different places. Last minute, I realized, there might be a chance, a slim possibility, that the timeline might have made it so Magnus wouldn't recognize me. That he might not remember me.

I printed out a small photo of us together, cut it down smaller, and placed it in my bag, too.

Like if I had proof I could solve anything.

Quentin drove me to the south end of the island again.

When he let me out to walk across the sand he said, "You

know, you don't have to do this. I can go. I will. I'll go get him and bring him home—"

"Nope this is for me to do." I straightened my skirts and pushed the hair from my face. "I'm the one, I'm going to go get Magnus."

"You might be one of the bravest people I know."

I took a deep breath. "Yeah, well I'm the one that needs to take care of shit." I put my hand on his cheek. "Speaking of which, fellow person who takes care of shit, take care of Zach and Emma and especially Ben, okay? Don't let anything happen to them." I clicked open the handbag wrapped around my waist and checked inside, it was all there. I had checked already eight times. "And Hayley needs someone to take her to a meeting. She quit drinking, but she can't seem to totally quit it, maybe you can, I don't know, be her buddy system or something. Would you do that for me?"

"Aye," he joked, "but I never took her for a quitter."

"Well this she ought to quit. And she can do anything she sets her mind too, she just needs a little help."

He smiled.

I asked, "What?"

"You. Going three hundred years in the past to rescue a warrior. It's pretty bad ass of you."

"A whole different century too. Technically it's four hundred years. By myself. Magnus called me a terrible arse. He got the words all wrong."

"Go get him. And don't get in any dark back rooms with any of the other Campbell men, trust me. They are not the modern men you're used to."

"Yeah, I figured that out pretty early on."

He said, "See ya." And turned to walk back to the car.

I wiggled out all my arms and legs and rolled my head around on my shoulders.

I was doing this. I was going to time-jump by myself to a forest in the 17th century.

I had been doing the 18th century, but this was — the 1600s sounded really really far back there. I pulled the vessel from my pocket and twisted the ends. I took a deep breath and shook out my right hand passed the vessel to my other hand and shook that out too.

Quentin was leaned on the car, watching.

I had to do it. He told me I was brave, I couldn't chicken out now.

Magnus was there. Waiting for me. He hadn't come home, though I one-hundred percent knew he meant to.

And I wasn't going to wait anymore.

Three days? Long enough.

Old Magnus, I was on my way.

I began to recite the numbers but then stopped. Deep breaths.

I jogged. And then did sort of a jig, jiggling from one foot to the other. I got this. I totally got this. I was the motherfucking matriarch. I recited two of the numbers. I wasn't scared. Two more. I knew the forest, I knew the castle. I had done this before. Three numbers. This shit was totally handled. One last number and the screaming, awful, horrible ripping began.

63 - KAITLYN

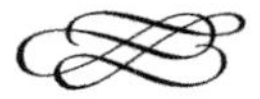

I peeled my eyes open. I was face down on a forest floor. I flipped to my back and stared up at the careening primordial trees pointing up to the sky. I would have given anything to have Magnus's hand on my hip, guarding over me while I floundered.

A rustling. What the...? I lifted my head—a red squirrel was about a foot away from my fingers, sifting through the leaves. I dragged my hand, stealthily, to my side. It scurried away. I probably should have forced myself up, but I could barely move. I sank back down into unconsciousness.

This time when my eyes opened I forced myself up. Still dazed I opened my backpack took out a protein bar, ate it, and washed it down with water. I sat for a few moments with my head on my knees listening to the soft rustling noises in the surrounding woods.

Then it crossed my mind that soft rustling noises meant that shit was in here with me and why would they not want to eat me? I would be delicious, full of vitamins and yoga and McDonald's French fries. I would be the greatest feast a varmint in the year sixteen-something ever had.

I climbed to my feet, stretched out my legs, slung the backpack across my back and trudged in the direction, I hoped, of the castle.

64 - KAITLYN

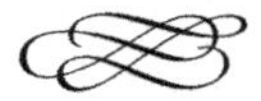

Balloch loomed large. I slowed down and didn't really want to keep going. I really needed Lizbeth to be there to greet me. It was evening, by the looks of the sky, but summer, so I couldn't really tell.

It smelled of baking grains and horse shit. The stable was right there, same place. Actually not much had changed which was a major relief. I would walk right up to the guards at the gate and ask to see Magnus.

If they didn't know who I was talking about, I would run.

Easy.

One, two, three, go.

65 - KAITLYN

The men were smelly, dirty, and terrifying.

I channeled a sort-of impression of Lizbeth. “Good day sirs, um, I be needin’ tae speak tae Master Magnus, might I partake of the inside of the...” I wasn’t sure what I was saying. You would think that on a trip of four hundred years I might have taken a moment to practice.

One of the men grunted.

The other spoke in Gaelic to the first and then swigged from a mug close by. Great, just my luck they were drunken guards.

I was trying not to look nervous. Trying for imperious. Also trying to watch their faces. Did they know who I was talking about?

“Master Magnus?” I interrupted their discussion, they laughed. But they were looking at each other not at me, maybe it was an inside joke. “I am here tae see Master Magnus—”

The other man spit on the ground and gestured with his head for me to head through the gate — holy shit.

My heart soared. I stopped myself from asking, “Master Magnus? He’s inside right?” No questions, just walk in, get past the Campbell guards, find Magnus. He was inside or else why would they tell me to go in?

I straightened my spine, rolled my shoulders back, and walked straight across the courtyard toward the main doors. A group of men leered at me as I walked. I picked up my pace and I wished for Lizbeth's arm to loop through mine.

How many times had she wiped my tears and helped me get my act together?

I didn't need help though.

This was me being a hero.

66 - KAITLYN

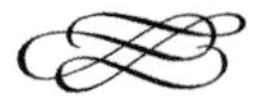

The longest walk of my life: through the doors, across the foyer, down the halls, past the ornate and lavish walls, the sweeping high ceilings. The only difference between this time and twenty years after was less furniture. I headed toward the Great Hall. Groups of men and women were bustling around, traveling in and out of doors and stairwells. The entire place smelled of baking bread. And everyone seemed busy and as if they had been celebrating, which was perfect. They weren't inclined to notice me much. It was evening and yet, so bright. Another thing I had counted on. Happy residents, in case I was cornered and questioned, and plenty of light in case I needed to flee.

At the last wall, missing the tapestry that I usually admired just before going in to eat, I took a deep breath — a group of rowdy men and women bustled out of the room. I stepped back and shielded my face until they passed. I took another deep breath and entered.

There were easily a hundred people in the room. Sitting and eating. Bagpipes played at the far end and it was loud as hell, though quietly loud, because I was in that thing again: darkness clouding around my sight, my breath echoing in my ears. I scanned the room, but all I could see were indiscernible faces looming in and out of the darkness, forward and back as I focused. I checked a group of men, not him. I scanned toward one of the tables. It was less lavish than the one I was used to, the chairs were blockier, less comfortable. There was a group of men and women who were holding onto each other and I remembered the time I saw the girl — what had been her name — touching Magnus's shoulder.

He wasn't there, I scanned and wove through the crowd. I saw a back that looked close, but not tall enough, and when I drew near I saw he was mostly toothless and — I kept walking because I thought if I stopped someone might want to talk to me. But now here I was at the end of the hall near the bagpipes and I hadn't found him yet.

I turned and took in the room behind me and then —

Magnus.

Unmistakable except almost unrecognizable. He had a beard, not a scruffy bit of beard like he hadn't shaved for a while, this was a long beard, a full beard, like a—

He was in conversation with a group of men and suddenly his eyes swept the room and landed on. Me.

I smiled.

Yes.

Aye.

. . .

He pushed through the crowd to me. His linen shirt stretched across his wide shoulders, his kilt draped around his legs in a deep blue and green plaid. He wore a dirk at his hip, and a sporran. It had been a long time since he looked like he truly belonged here in Scotland, but he looked at home, rough and ancient, a little barbaric. Except in his eyes — leveled on me. Wanting me. Those eyes were the eyes of my husband, carrying the whole history of us—

It felt like it might take forever but then he was right there and I threw my arms around him and he lifted me from the floor. His face pressed against my neck, his first word, simply my name, spoken into my skin. I wrapped around the back of his head and held on. And I didn't think he would ever let me down — he rocked me back and forth.

"How?"

I turned to speak into his ear. "You didn't come home. So I came to find you. You aren't old, you don't look that much older at all."

"I feel a lifetime has passed, mo reul-iuil." He nudged my cheek with his and met my lips with a kiss and we kissed long and delicious my lips and tongue exploring his mouth. He carried that familiar smell the one of dust and incense and—

"I love you, where have you been?"

"I daena ken, I dinna think it at the time, but now I see ye, I think I must have been lost."

I ran my fingers down his long hair and brushed it behind his ear and gave him a sad smile, "Well, you did just what you're supposed to do, sit tight and wait for someone to come find you."

He dropped my feet to the floor. Then led me through the crowds to the edge of the hall, to a small table, and leaned against it. I stood between his legs. His arms around. "How long was I gone?"

"Three days."

His eyes looked deep into mine.

I ran my hand down his beard, long and bushy and a bit tangled. Growing up toward his cheekbones, accentuating the crinkle under his eyes — the one that came from smiling. "How long have you been gone, Magnus?"

"Och." He winced as if the words were painful. He shook his head. "It has been some verra long years."

"Years, my love?" He nodded, his eyes full of sadness. I kissed the ridge of his nose and pulled his head down to my shoulder and held him huddled, mouth to ear, my eyes closed. I didn't need to see, just hear... "But you beat Samuel?"

"Aye, Kaitlyn, and I have been tryin' tae come home. Every few days I travelled tae see ye but there is a man — remember the men who fought us on the banks of the spring? I have learned they are led by a General Reyes, I have been in a personal war with him, and it haena ended... He kens how tae track m'movements over Florida, and is always waitin' for me when I arrive. He has threatened your life; he kens ye are there." He shook his head and winced. "I have been wantin' tae send ye a message, but I couldna figure out how tae. I dinna want tae go tae our past again; Chef Zach said I shouldna and I dinna ken what else tae do. I had just decided tae change the date I would come home. I kent ye would be worried, but twas the only thing I hadna tried yet."

"Oh. And so what have you been doing since?" I stroked a hand down his shoulder and pulled him closer.

"I have been fighting. The first year there were so many battles, but then there was a war, on the eastern ridges, I..." He shook his head again.

I lifted his chin and looked in his eyes. "Tell me honestly, Magnus, is there something you need to tell me about?" I found his two hands and clasped them in mine. His wedding band was on his left hand, just like it had always been. "Did anything happen while you were gone?"

"Nae." He shook his head. "Nae, Kaitlyn, I have nothing tae tell ye of. I haena strayed from my path as your husband, but, I ken something about what you..."

He put his hands on my face and kissed me long and slow and deep and — he tucked my head to his chest and held me.

After that hug I raised up and held his face in my hands and looked into his eyes.

"Tell me."

"I lied tae ye, mo reul-iuil. I am sorry that I did. I said I had nae discovered the history of ye, but I had, and it hasna changed —" He shook his head. "When I am in the kingdom I check it every day. I canna stop checkin' it. Tis close tae driving me mad. I daena like bein' there because of it and it hasna changed."

I stroked down his cheek, soothing and smoothing. "Tell me."

"If I tell ye, it may hurt ye tae ken what is happenin'—"

"I'm a big girl. I just stormed a medieval castle with nothing but a protein bar and a vague idea that you might be here. Tell me."

He searched my face and then said, "You will have a bairn with Tyler Wilson."

"Oh." My sad smile grew. "This is not what you think it is, my love — you have been torturing yourself about this for how long?"

"For a little over four years."

"Oh my poor Magnus, poor wonderful Magnus, you are mistaken about it — it isn't true—"

"But tis true, tis in the history of ye." His brow drew down. "Just because it haena happened yet — daena mean—"

"So you were thinking it might be better to just let another man have me, Magnus? I truly expected you to fight harder for me."

"I canna fight the men of your time, ye winna let me."

"Well, yeah, with swords, but my love, in the future, I expect you to fight for me, whatever time period. And by the way, Tyler isn't from my time period. He's from the future. He's your son."

He continued to search my face.

"He came to the dock that night to help you fight those men because the first time it happened they killed me."

"General Reyes's men killed ye?"

There was a dawning realization on his face, but before he confused it further I added, "His name is Archie, right? That's your son's name?"

"Aye, but—"

"To help us he used a fake name. He had a fake birth certificate, and when he left, he gave them to me, for you. So I could take you on an airplane someday. I don't know what or how or why, but I think you might be the Tyler Wilson you're worried about. Maybe because we need to hide you in the future. Or maybe we need to hide our baby. But that's the truth of it Magnus, you've been mistaken about it and by not telling me you've suffered about it for four years. So yeah," I stroked his cheek and kissed his lips. "My future is with you and you should always tell me everything."

"Och," he shook his head. "Och." He ran his hands through his hair. Then put them back around my ass, pulling me forward and close. "Tyler is my son, Archie?"

"Pretty amazing, huh? The whole thing is a lot of crazy-looping around through time. I have a diagram in my backpack that I can show you, but right now I really just want your arms around me. I don't want to let go." I put my arms around his head and he held me around my back. "I was so worried about you when you didn't come home."

"I tried mo reul-iuil... I dinna want tae worry ye."

"Yeah, well... I was. But now you're in my arms. Tell me about Archie."

"He is a wee braw lad, ye would like him verra much."

"How old is he now?"

"Just four years auld. He is verra smart." He asked a passing servant for a mug of ale. Then his brow furrowed. "I raised my hand tae him when he came with us through time. I canna believe I did it."

I stroked his hair from his forehead. "He understands. He does. I don't think he regrets it, not really. He told me to tell you he liked fighting alongside you. And that you should let him do that more. I guess, in the future. When he's not four-years-old." I smiled.

He shook his head and returned my smile. "I daena want him tae have tae fight. He is a wee lad, tis verra hard tae imagine it."

"He'll grow up some day, and we know he turns out pretty great."

"Aye, he does." We kissed and when our ale arrived, we drank thirstily. He gestured for another.

"So what are you doing here?"

"I have been jumpin' through time lookin' for General Reyes, he is searchin' for me. And I needed a place tae rest. I have been comin' here every few months tae live. Tis familiar, protected, but winna involve Archie or Sean or Lizbeth or..."

I swigged from his new ale. "When you get in your head, my love, you really do a number on yourself. I literally can't believe you thought I might be better off with Tyler—"

"I dinna want tae tell ye of it, that ye were goin' tae do it. I dinna want tae blame ye for it, or make ye feel ashamed of it. I brought such grief tae ye, I thought ye might want tae have a normal life..."

I huffed out some air. "Well, those are not decisions for you to make."

I shook my head. "I should be furious, but you have been trying to get home while feeling this for years, and it was only three days for me, so I'm going to forgive you for it. It would be like being angry at someone for getting lost at Disney World, unfair and a waste of time. I'm glad I found you and I'm not planning to waste another minute. Plus you're pretty hot now with this little wrinkle here," I pressed my lips to the spot just below his eye and above his cheek bone. "It's even more pronounced now that you're what — seventy?"

"Probably a score and eight."

"Twenty eight, and you have this beard all the way to your chest, which is pretty damn hot and I'm just glad to see you. Did you go see Lizbeth? I saved her life."

"I dinna go, but I looked up the history of it. I was verra proud of ye. Sean and Lizbeth are here ye ken, they are verra young bairns. I like tae watch them though I try tae keep them from seein' me too much." He pulled me closer between his legs up against his front.

"What about Lady Mairead?"

"She has left them and is off searching for her next husband. I think she will meet Donnan verra soon and I will come soon after. I won't come back then, I am mindful nae tae loop on myself."

I took his mug and slugged back a long drink.

He grinned and gestured for another one. "And where is Quentin? I could use his help. He dinna come with ye?"

"No, I thought it would be too dangerous for him."

"Och, Kaitlyn, ye have such a big heart ye mean tae keep the security guard safe? Tis nae the way it works."

I shrugged. "But it's one of the things you love about me."

"Aye, tis true."

We sat looking into each other's eyes grinning.

"I was so scared when you were ripped away from me by the guards, and now look, you're unharmed, alive, covered in hair. Like a big bear done hibernating."

"It has been a verra long time since that battle, I have had many a wound since. I daena scare ye, look too much an animal?" He stroked the end of his long beard.

"No, it's kinda sexy actually."

His eyes crinkled and he grinned. "I am randy like a just-woke bear too. I have been arguin' with the walls. My cousins were close tae sendin' me alone tae live in the forest."

He raised his mug at a group of men and they all raised their glasses to him with a laugh.

"They're probably wondering who this is rubbing up against you."

"Aye, they have been questioning my commitment tae m'manhood. I have had tae take a fight or two tae prove my steel."

I pressed against him. "Och, aye," I joked, "I can feel your steel."

He chuckled with his head on my shoulder, collapsed on me. "Ah, mo reul-iuil, ye have a fine wit and a scandalous tongue."

I stepped back from him and brushed the hair off my face. I raised my brow and smiled. "My tongue is not so full of scandal, sir, it's full of sweetness and longing."

He moaned and reached for my skirts to try to pull me closer again.

I stepped back further, and teased, "And if you would like to reacquaint yourself with it, my tongue, Master Magnus, I think you best be getting onto your back. By my accounts you have suffered some long years without me, and I believe you must be parched."

He groaned happily. "Ye hae used my words."

"And this has been entirely too much talking."

He hung his head. "I canna take ye home tae Florida, tis unsafe, and here I daena have a room with a bed. I haena the status of married Young Magnus, nephew of the Earl of Breadalbane. Now I am only Magnus, I have nae connection and nae comfort. Plus on the eve of Lammas there are many guests sleeping here. There winna be privacy."

I put my hands on my hips. "So where do you sleep?" I grabbed the mug, drained at least half, and wiped my mouth with my arm. I was beginning to have a nice buzz.

"In a room with hay spread upon the floor, some bundles pretendin' tae be mattresses. About ten men. Quentin wasna jokin' when he said twas a frightful stench."

"And we can't go home?"

"I canna. I have tae deal with this first."

I sighed. Then I smiled and raised my brow mischievously. "Remember on our wedding night, you told me that when you were with women before it was always—"

"Och, ye would?"

I nodded.

He looked left and right up and down the hall and stood and took my hand. "I ken just the place."

67 - KAITLYN

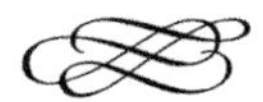

He led me out of the Great Hall and through the corridors, our footsteps rushing, echoing through the rooms to a circular stair. It was dark, but not pitch black because of the ambient light from a small rectangular window that was not more than a sliver. It had a protruding brick below it, a bit like a windowsill. Magnus stood with one foot on a lower step the other on the higher step and lifted me to the window sill, his arms around, my back to the stone. The smell of baking bread wafted through the tiny window on the wisps of a summer breeze.

My husband's hands on my bodice, his mouth on my neck, his beard against my face — he smelled like himself, yet everything about him was older, even more a man —

You're scratchy. I whispered it into the shared air between us.

Aye. I daena ken ye were comin'.

I chuckled into his ear and his wet lips found mine and we kissed, breaths and heat and words only for each other... *I love you. I missed ye. I want you.* He grabbed my ass through my skirts and hiked the whole bundle of me to his front. He breathed into my ear and kissed along my neck, nibbling and licking while his hands pulled up handfuls of skirts until my legs were exposed. My bare thighs against the wool of his kilt, scratching and soft and pressing and hard and rough and — his fingers explored between my legs, the sensations overwhelming. Cold brick pressed against the back of my neck, hot breath on the edge of my throat. My middle bound and constricted, hand rubbing up and down, friction and heat, yet bare and open from my hips down, cool in the stairwell drafts, scandalously bare.

He wanted me so much I could feel it in the tremble of his lips.

The sweat on the back of his neck.

With a moan of helplessness he pulled the front of his kilt to his waist and entered me, a sigh on his breath like relief. His forehead against the wall, cheek to cheek I arched toward him, weightless, he pulled and pushed with me. My hands up under his shirt, pressed to the ridges of the scars criss-crossing the landscape of his shoulders. Just underneath his skin, his muscles taut and rippling as he held me up and pressed me close. I rocked against him finding a rhythm and — *ohgodogodogod* — I drew in. My breath, my strength, I gathered him in. close. more. held. Waves rolled down through me—

I flung my hands out to the stone walls and used them for counterforce — *I canna wait* — *I know* — *it's okay* — escaped on my breath as he rode me hard and fast and deep and finally he ended with a near total collapse. My body reacted with a shiver. I wrapped around him, holding tight, in case his knees buckled and gravity took him down the stairs.

His voice emerged with the familiar rumble from deep in his chest. "Ye are a'quiver."

"Yes."

It was all I could think of to say.

He held me longer, breathing into my shoulder. Kissing the

edge of my ear. Then he slid from between my legs and helped me slide down from the sill. And we put our skirts to rights as voices came from above, two or three men descending the stair. I looked at him with my eyes wide.

"Tuck in, mo reul-iuil," he whispered. I tucked my head to his chest. His arms around me protectively we clung to the wall, his shoulders guarding me from view, as the group passed us, loud exclaiming, pushing, some jovial and not so jovial words, a couple of grabs around Magnus to try to touch me.

Magnus said something sharp and loud and the men laughed and continued down the steps.

He held me a moment more and then led me by the hand down the steps, back through the stately rooms to the Great Hall. Fewer people were there now, the blasted bagpipes weren't playing, no one was dancing, a fire roared at the end of the room and there were a few people curled up near it.

As we headed down the room toward the blaze a fight broke out between some drunken men in the corner, Magnus pulled me close to his side and led me to a free spot near the flames.

I pulled my tartan from my shoulders and untucked it from my waist.

Magnus untucked his long kilt from his belt and pulled the loose ends to his shoulders and sat down, leaned against the wall with his legs spread, his arms out. I sat between them leaned on his chest, curled between his legs, his arms and the woolen tartan around me and us. Cocooned beside the fire.

It had grown dark and there were whispered voices nearby, people close, there for sleep, warmth, all of us guests without the favor of the Earl, taking our sleep where we could find it.

I snuggled into Magnus's chest.

"You are a king now?"

"Aye, though our current quarters belie it, I am the king. Tis a dangerous status. I have left four men tae administer the kingdom while I wage war." His arm tightened its hold on me.

"And we can't go back to Florida?"

"General Reyes would follow us there, tis too dangerous. I canna go back until I have finished him. But ye could go back tae 2019. Ye could go somewhere else other than Florida and I will come tae ye when this is done."

I nodded. "True, but I won't. My place is with you in your kingdom, here in the past, or wherever you are. Even here on the hard ground of a 18th century castle."

Then he took his warm, strong, rough hand and lifted my chin and sweetly kissed my lips. He tucked my hair behind my ear. "Then it looks like I am home, mo reul-iuil."

I nestled into his chest, pulled the tartan closer around and said, "Me too, my love."

THANK YOU

This is still not the true end of Magnus and Kaitlyn. There are more chapters in their story. If you need help getting through the pause before the next book, there is a FB group here: Kaitlyn and the Highlander Group

Thank you for sticking with this tale. I wanted to write about a grand love, a marriage, that lasts for a long long time. I also wanted to write an adventure. And I wanted to make it fun. The world is full of entertainment and I appreciate that you chose to spend even more time with Magnus and Kaitlyn. I just love them and wish them the best life, I will do my best to write it well.

As you know, reviews are the best social proof a book can have, and I would greatly appreciate your review on these books.

Kaitlyn and the Highlander (Book 1)
Time and Space Between Us (Book 2)
Warrior of My Own (Book 3)
Begin Where We Are (Book 4)
Entangled with You (Book 5)

Magnus and a Love Beyond Words (Book 6)
Under the Same Sky (Book 7)
Nothing but Dust (Book 8)
Again, My Love (Book 9)

SOME THOUGHTS AND RESEARCH...

Some **Scottish and Gaelic words** that appear within the books:

Chan eil an t-sìde cho math an-diugh 's a bha e an-dé - The weather's not as good today as it was yesterday.

Tha droch shìde ann - The weather is bad.

Dreich - dull and miserable weather

Turadh - a break in the clouds between showers

Solasta - luminous shining (possible nickname)

Splang - flash, spark, sparkle

Mo reul-iuil - my North Star (nickname)

Tha thu a 'fàileadh mar ghaoith - you have the scent of a breeze.

Osna - a sigh

Rionnag - star

Sollier - bright

Ghrian - the sun

Mo ghradh - my own love

Tha thu breagha - you are beautiful

Mo chroi - my heart

Corrachag-cagail - dancing and flickering ember flames

Mo reul-iuil, is ann leatsa abhios mo chridhe gubrath - My North Star, my heart belongs to you forever

Dinna ken - didn't know

A h-uile là sona dhuibh 's gun là idir dona dhuib - May all your days be happy ones

May the best ye've ever seen
Be the warst ye'll ever see.
May the moose ne'er lea' yer aumrie
Wi' a tear-drap in his e'e.
May ye aye keep hail an' hertie
Till ye're auld eneuch tae dee.
May ye aye be jist as happy
As we wiss ye noo tae be.

~

Characters:

Kaitlyn Maude Sheffield - born 1994
Magnus Archibald Caelhin Campbell - born 1681
Lady Mairead (Campbell) Delapointe
Hayley Sherman
Quentin Peters
Zach Greene
Emma Garcia
Baby Ben Greene
Sean Campbell -Magnus's half-brother
Lizbeth Campbell - Magnus's half-sister
The Earl of Breadalbane
Uncle Archibald (Baldie) Campbell
Tyler Garrison Wilson

Archie
John Sheffield (Kaitlyn's father)
Paige Sheffield (Kaitlyn's Mother)
James Cook
Michael Greene

~

Locations:

Fernandina Beach on Amelia Island, Florida, 2017-2019

The Dock by a spring on a piece of unoccupied land near Gainesville, Florida. Owned by Zach and Michael's uncle. Used by Magnus and Kaitlyn to hide the vessels.

Magnus's home in Scotland - Balloch. Built in 1552. In early 1800s it was rebuilt as Taymouth Castle. (Maybe because of the breach in the walls caused by our siege from the future?) Situated on the south bank of the River Tay, in the heart of the Grampian Mountains

The kingdom of King Donnan the Second. We don't know anything more... yet. But I suspect Magnus knows now that he rules the place.

The octagonal house on Amelia Island is called Katie's light. It's for rent if you'd like to go stay there...

ACKNOWLEDGMENTS

Thank you to David Sutton for reading and advising on story threads. From looking out for Kaitlyn's reputation to telling me "You know a taser would solve this whole Sean issue quick fast and in a hurry," and mentioning that Magnus can maybe keep his eyes open in a car starting now — your suggestions and thoughts help make the stories better and better. I appreciate it so much.

Thank you to Heather Hawkes for beta reading, championing, being a long time friend and supporter, and for saying, "I struggle with the amount of stuff they are bringing! What if they leave stuff behind?? Someone in our time would look around and find a 300-year-old cliff bar wrapper?? Or flashlight?? I feel like the first time made sense, but they should be more cautious now. Keep stuff time period..." I agree and did my best to make their packing more thoughtful.

Thank you to Kristen Schoenmann De Haan for reading and loving the progression of the story and for saying, "The Thanksgiving with Grandma Barb was so poignant and true. Just thinking about it again makes me teary." Thank you for saying so.

Thank you to Jessica Fox for reading and advising on the

Doctor Who terminology and telling me that I 'got you' with my reveal. I count that as a win. I appreciate that you've been reading for me for so long.

And thank you to Cynthia Tyler for excitedly reading, and telling me this one was in much better shape than the last by the time it hit your desk. From your advice on scabbards, to your grasp of how Magnus should sound, to your long list of typos, I'm thinking of calling you 'the Sweeper' because you find so much that other eyes have missed. I'm so very glad I found you (or you found me)!

~

My Facebook page was kicking it for a while there. My friends and family weighed in on how to apprehend people on the top floor of a skyrise. The deciding tactic went to my husband, Kevin, though: a sonic wave exploding the glass was just what I needed.

I also asked about birth in the 1700s and received so many wonderful, helpful responses from mothers, doulas and midwives alike that it made me kind of weepy to read through them. Birth has always been a tough slog and I was looking forward to making Lizbeth and Kaitlyn heroic through it. Thank you to Sara Homan, Aimee Stephens, Amanda Gauthier-Parker, Carrie Benitez, Kari Carlin Aist, Amanda Kenworthy, Lynsey K McCarthy-Calvert, Lisa Parsons, Morgan Gallagher, Kristen Vaught Cavuto, Meegan McNelly, Rebekah Costello, Jill D'agnenica, Genevieve Thomas Colvin, Amie Rashe Conrad, Bianca Kamnitzer, and Jen Holland for your thoughts, help, research, and expertise. I'm so proud of Kaitlyn that she was able to save Lizbeth's life.

~

The conversation continued over in the FB group, Kaitlyn and the Highlander. Where I asked, What do you think Magnus should notice, wonder, be amazed about, ask about in book 5? There were so many great ideas, but these were the ones I used:

Spray cheese - Cynthia Tyler

Solar Panels - My family

Razor - Tonya Morgan

Shaving cream - Debbie Hall

Zipper - Rachael Anne

YouTube - David Sutton

Becky Hendren Harbin - Adult toy store and sex toys - Shauna Willoghby (The opening scene was already written, but glad someone else wanted to know what Magnus would think about it.)

Infomercials - Lauren Nichols and Stephanie Stevens Tarr.

Speaking of Infomercials, these were the suggestions:

Drunk guy peddling knives (apparently this is true) - Joshua Waier and Isobel Dowdee. Also the upside down tomato plant thingy.

Flex Seal - Lauren Nichols

These are just a few of the suggestions for Emma's bachelorette party:

Waffle breakfast - LiZa (Zach makes them for her on the morning of the wedding...)

Grandma takes Ben - Tonya Morgan

Spa and massages and going out on the town - Amanda Bodfield

Spa Day - Hilary Baran, Kayla Swallow, Barbara Anne, Natasha Howard, Kim Stevens, Beverly Leonard.

Night club to stretch her wings - Pam Furze

~

I asked for a name for the woman who Lizbeth is staying with in Scotland. From the hundreds of suggestions I chose Greer. Thank you Tori Bourne, Michelle Maroni, Shauna Conner Pelfrey, Wendy ElDin, and Karen Clark.

I chose McClelland for the surname, suggested by April Graham. (Her mother's maiden name.)

And Ailbeart for the husband, suggested by Donna Blickenstaff.

~

And I also asked, in fun, if you could get rid of someone evil with a time machine where would you take them? I received some wonderful suggestions. They weren't going to make it into the book, that's not where the story is headed, but then they appeared in Kaitlyn's imagination. Thank you.

Land of the Dinosaurs - Alison Howard

Titanic - Diana Toles

Plague - LiZa

Vesuvius - Patty Wayne and Heather Story

~

And I finally got around to describing Kaitlyn's ring and it's a beauty. Thank you to Isobel Dowdee, Joshua Waier, Gloria Michaels-Brown, Christy Baxter, Heather Hawkes, Kristen Schoenmann De Haan, Dayle Brunson, Leisha Gosling, Molly

Lyons, Jennifer Babcock, and Heather Story for sharing ideas with me. This is Kaitlyn's ring. The one below it is Magnus's.

And thank you to the artist, Volodymyr Tverdokhlib, for the photos of this amazing model through shuttterstock.com. He is a perfect Magnus and I'm grateful for him...

Thank you to Kevin Dowdee for being my support, my guidance, and my inspiration for these stories. I appreciate you so much. And thank you for listening to me as I flesh out my theory of time travel. That was a big help.

Thank you to my kids, Ean, Gwynnie, Fiona, and Isobel, for listening to me go on and on about these characters, advising me whenever you can, and accepting them as real parts of our lives. I love you.

ALSO BY DIANA KNIGHTLEY

Can he see to the depths of her mystery before it's too late?

The oceans cover everything, the apocalypse is behind them. Before them is just water, leveling. And in the middle — they find each other.

On a desolate, military-run Outpost, Beckett is waiting.

Then Luna bumps her paddleboard up to the glass windows and disrupts his everything.

And soon Beckett has something and someone to live for. Finally. But their survival depends on discovering what she's hiding, what she won't tell him.

Because some things are too painful to speak out loud.

With the clock ticking, the water rising, and the storms growing, hang on while Beckett and Luna desperately try to rescue each other in Leveling, the epic, steamy, and suspenseful first book of the trilogy, Luna's Story:

Leveling: Book One of Luna's Story

Under: Book Two of Luna's Story

Deep: Book Three of Luna's Story

ABOUT ME, DIANA KNIGHTLEY

I live in Los Angeles where we have a lot of apocalyptic tendencies that we overcome by wishful thinking. Also great beaches. I maintain a lot of people in a small house, too many pets, and a to-do list that is longer than it should be, because my main rule is: Art, play, fun, before housework. My kids say I am a cool mom because I try to be kind. I'm married to a guy who is like a water god: he surfs, he paddle boards, he built a boat. I'm a huge fan.

I write about heroes and tragedies and magical whisperings and always forever happily ever afters. I love that scene where the two are desperate to be together but can't because of war or apocalyptic-stuff or (scientifically sound!) time-jumping and he is begging the universe with a plead in his heart and she is distraught (yet still strong) and somehow, through kisses and steamy more and hope and heaps and piles of true love, they manage to come out on the other side.

I like a man in a kilt, especially if he looks like a Hemsworth, doesn't matter, Liam or Chris.

My couples so far include Beckett and Luna (from the trilogy, Luna's Story) who battle their fear to find each other during an apocalypse of rising waters. And Magnus and Kaitlyn (from the series Kaitlyn and the Highlander). Who find themselves traveling through time to be together.

I write under two pen names, this one here, Diana Knightley, and another one, H. D. Knightley, where I write books for Young

Adults (They are still romantic and fun and sometimes steamy though, because love is grand at any age.)

DianaKnightley.com
Diana@dianaknightley.com

ALSO BY H. D. KNIGHTLEY (MY YA PEN NAME)

Bright (Book One of The Estelle Series)

Beyond (Book Two of The Estelle Series)

Belief (Book Three of The Estelle Series)

Fly; The Light Princess Retold

Violet's Mountain

Sid and Teddy